THE HANDOVER

David M. Barnett

ORION

First published in Great Britain in 2021 by Trapeze
This paperback edition published in 2021 by Orion Fiction
an imprint of The Orion Publishing Group Ltd
Carmelite House, 50 Victoria Embankment
London EC4Y 0DZ

An Hachette UK Company

1 3 5 7 9 10 8 6 4 2

A CIP catalogue record for this book is
available from the British Library.

ISBN (Mass Market Paperback) 978 1 4091 8524 6
ISBN (eBook) 978 1 4091 8525 3

Typeset by Born Group
Printed and bound in Great Britain by Clays Ltd, Elcograf S.p.A.

MIX
Paper from
responsible sources
FSC® C104740

www.orionbooks.co.uk

THE HANDOVER

To Charlie and Alice, as they stand on the threshold of the future. And for everyone who needs to get their Tigger on.

I have stayed in Athens, and Athens is a marvellous city; I know my Paris, and Paris is not without fascination; I have been to Cairo, and bazaars of Cairo seemed to me so wonderful that I held my breath as I passed through them. But these places are not Manchester. They are not so glorious as Manchester, not so vital, not so romantic, and not so adventurous...

Gerald Cumberland
Set Down In Malice, 1919

I

Daisy

Before he even speaks, I know what he's going to say. He just looks the type. He's got a beard, but one of those trendy, hipsterish things that you can buy wax and oil and all kinds of things for in Boots; not a wild, fluffy, bird's nest of a beard like Uncle Alan used to have. He wears little, round, horn-rimmed glasses and his face is shiny with moisturiser. I swear down, there's more things for men than women in Boots these days. His forehead doesn't move when his eyebrows rise up over his glasses. I wonder if he's had that Botox? They do that as well, these days, the men, don't they? And look at her, the one he's with. Hair done every month, probably costs more than I get paid in a week. Long camel coat. Shiny black boots.

I wonder if I can sidle away from them but he's already fixed me with his piercing blue eyes, his waggling eyebrows not making a dent in the smooth tundra of his forehead. Here it comes.

'What,' he says loudly, glancing sidelong at her so she knows there's a good one on its way, 'what on *earth* is a dinosaur doing in a museum of social history?'

I look up at the collection of bones assembled on a podium at the centre of the Horridge Wing, seven and a half metres from the tip of its tail to the end of its crocodile-like snout. To be honest, it's not an unreasonable question. It's just that I hear it about three times a week. And always from people like him.

'Because,' he says and, I swear, he nudges her in the arm, 'because the ones I saw on *Jurassic Park* weren't what you'd exactly call *sociable*.'

'We're the Manchester Museum of Social History,' I mutter. 'Not Sociable History.'

They share a glance. They obviously thought I was going to collapse into a helpless heap of sobbing laughter. He looks back at me and we stare at each other for a bit. Then he says, 'No, not sociable at all.'

I start to tell them that I'm a security guard, not a museum guide, when I feel a presence at my shoulder and their gazes shift up and over my head, just before a booming voice says, 'Ah! You've found Barry, I see!'

'Barry?' say the man and the woman together, as though almost fainting with relief that they don't have to talk to me any more. Nate steps in and points up at the skeleton. 'Lived in the Early Cretaceous period, about a hundred and thirty million years ago. They found this one in a quarry up in Cumbria. *Baryonyx*, which means "heavy claw". But we just call him Barry.'

No, we don't. Only Nate calls the pile of old fossilised bones Barry. But their attention on Nate means I can wander away and stand by one of the glass cases filled with bits of Roman pottery, and check my watch. Five past five. Nate is holding forth about Baryonyx but I've heard it all before, a million times. He should have done the handover by now and clocked off. Nate's a security guard, like me. He does nine in the morning until five in the afternoon, and I do five in the afternoon until one. Janice on reception seems to think this is hilarious, for some reason. If I had a pound for every time she's said, 'Daisy does nights and Nate does days . . . that's the wrong way around, isn't it? It should be Daisy on days and Nate on nights!' followed by her silly, trilling laughter, then . . . I look up at the window, streaked with spring rain. Well, if I had a pound for every time Janice said that, then I could probably afford a holiday.

Besides, it's not actually true, is it? Yes, Nate does days, but I do more what you'd call evenings. Into the night, I suppose. The guard who does the shift after me, from one until nine in the morning, Harold, I suppose he does nights. Though, strictly speaking, you could say he does mornings as well. Until Nate clocks on.

Nate, who is a security guard, not a museum guide, I note furiously once again as I check my watch. Ten past five. If he wants to be a museum guide, he should apply to be one. If he wants to be a security guard, he should stop banging on about dinosaurs and come and do the handover properly. You'd think he didn't have a home to go to.

I decide it's worth risking being talked to by Mr Hipster Beard again to go over and hurry Nate along. He's just finishing up as I stand by him, and the man says, 'Well, thank you, you've been very helpful.' He peers at Nate's name badge. 'Nate Garvey. Very helpful. Five stars on TripAdvisor, I think!'

Then he looks at my badge, and I realise I should have just left them to it. 'And you,' he says, then pauses for long enough for the woman to wonder why he's gone quiet, and to look at my badge too. He does a strange thing with his mouth, sucking in his lips, and his eyebrows dance. 'And you, Daisy Dukes.'

The woman tugs his arm, and if they think that just because they're walking away with their backs to me I can't hear them laughing, then they're sorely mistaken.

I'm not stupid. I know what Daisy Dukes are. They're those tiny little cut-off denim shorts that I would be the absolute last person on the entire planet who would look anything remotely approaching 'good' in. Named after that girl with the long hair and the long legs on that ancient American TV show, with the car and the sheriff. Ha ha, good joke. Dumpy little Daisy. Imagine her in a pair of teeny-weeny shorts?

I glare daggers at the backs of the couple. If only they knew. If only they knew what I was really like. They would think twice about saying things like that.

'Pay them no mind,' says Nate in his rumbly voice. It doesn't help that he's so tall, six and a half foot, I bet. It makes me look even smaller and dumpier next to him. Though I cross-referenced my height and weight on one of those Body Mass Index charts and I'm of very healthy proportions. All that fruit and vegetables that Mother made us eat when we were kids. Never let us have fizzy pop, only had chocolate at Easter and Christmas. Almost makes up for her calling me Daisy when our surname was Dukes. Almost.

'We need to do the handover,' I say crossly. 'Your shift ended fifteen minutes ago.'

Which means there's just forty-five minutes of opening time left, and then the museum will close, and everyone will leave, and I will be alone.

I am very particular about the handover. It's why I come into the museum precisely five minutes before my shift starts, so I can do it and not eat into Nate's free time. I imagine he's got a wife, and children, and will take the tram, or a bus, or maybe the train away from the Northern Quarter to his neat little home in the suburbs. At least, I assume it's neat. I haven't ever seen it, of course, nor asked him about it. I don't come to work to chat.

'Item one,' I say. 'The Report.'

4

Nate nods dutifully and scratches his chin. I mentally note that he could do with a shave, salt-and-pepper bristles making an audible *skkkrtch* sound under his fingernails. In fact, he could do with taking a little bit more care about his appearance all round, now I take a look at him. There's a spot of dried gravy or bean juice on the front of his shirt, right at my eye-level, and his tie is a little crooked. His top button unfastened. We both wear the same uniform, black trousers, white shirt, black tie, and a black jacket if we need to go outside. If I can keep my shirts clean and ironed, with everything I've got going on in my life, I don't see why Nate can't do the same. I'm not talking beard wax and Botox, obviously; just a bit of self-respect. But it isn't for me to say anything; I'm his colleague, not his boss.

'Well?' I say, dragging my eyes from the spot on his shirt and up to his face, which is all scrunched up as though he's a schoolboy trying to think of the right answer to a particularly perplexing maths question.

'There's nothing really to report,' says Nate eventually.

This obviously isn't good enough. I instituted the handover so that the security team could share relevant intelligence from their shift that might impact on their colleagues. There's *always* something to report.

I have a small notepad, the sort that the police use, in my breast pocket, and I take it out and tap it with the end of my ballpoint pen. Nate watches it for a while, then seems to brighten up.

'Oh! There were three kids hanging around the Malone Room this afternoon,' he says. 'I had to tick 'em off for pressing their faces against the glass cabinet. The one with the naked lady in it.'

Nate means the statuette of Aphrodite, circa 1865, from the collection of Theodore Malone, the museum's founder and major benefactor in the nineteenth century.

'Aphrodite,' says Nate, helpfully, as though I don't know what he means, though I'm rather surprised that he knows, 'springing full blown from the brow of Zeus.'

'Yes, I am aware of that,' I say, making a note. 'What time?'

Nate shrugs. 'Three-ish.'

'Can't you be more precise?'

His wide shoulders rise and fall again. 'Okay. Three-oh-seven.'

I write it down. 'Ages?'

'Thirteen, I'd say,' Nate says with more certainty. I wonder if that's the age of his children. 'And they were wearing St Mary's badges on their blazers. Which were green.'

Nate smiles hopefully down at me, putting me in mind of a dog waiting for a pat and a treat. Instead I give him a curt nod and say, 'They shouldn't have been out of school at that time. I'll phone the head tomorrow.'

'Well, you know, they weren't causing trouble. Not really.'

I put my notepad back in my breast pocket and glance at my watch. 'I might see if I can print off some images from the CCTV as well, to email to the school. It's almost twenty-five past; give me the torch and you can get off.'

There's an amused look in Nate's eye which makes me cross, then he gives me a little salute and clicks the heels of his big size twelve black shoes – which could do with a bit of a polish – together, which makes me even crosser. 'I'll just get it from the den,' he says.

By 'den' he means the security office. I don't know why he has to make up stupid names for things, when they've got perfectly good names already, such as 'security office' and 'Baryonyx'. While he's gone downstairs to get the torch I clear my throat and loudly tell the half a dozen people still loitering in the Horridge Wing that the museum is closing in half an hour.

The torch is a big old rubber one with a bright beam and a satisfying weight to it. Mr Meyer, the museum manager, once presented me with some hi-tech flashlight – 'new-fangled', Mother would call it – that had white LED bulbs and didn't use batteries, but charged itself just by you walking around with it. I never took it out of the packaging. It's still in a drawer in the security office. When a thing works perfectly fine as it is, why try to improve on it?

When Nate comes back waving the torch, he's wearing his black jacket with a thin green anorak over it. The Horridge Wing is empty now, and when he's gone I'll go and round up the stragglers in the other five halls, and the cafe, and then I can get the museum closed up for the day.

'Is it still nasty out there?' says Nate, zipping up his anorak.

'It's raining. Average for the time of year, I think.'

'Well, I'll be off, then.'

He's standing there as though he's waiting for something from me. I shrug and say, 'Fine.' I'm never really sure what else is expected of me in these situations.

Nate smiles and says, 'Well, see you, then.'

I watch him walk across the parquet floor and out of the double doors to the staircase, then I look up at the skeleton of Daryonyx. 'Barry'. I shake my head and head in the opposite direction that Nate took, to the Malone Room, to check just how much of a mess these kids have made of the Aphrodite cabinet, so I can give the cleaners a proper report.

On the way through I pass Mr Hipster Beard and his partner. They both smile at me as we cross over. I don't smile back. For reasons I can't quite put my finger on, I'm bothered by them. It's not the laughing behind their hands; I'm used to that, and worse. It's not that they obviously earn more money than me, and have more expensive clothes, and better skincare products (even *him*). It's . . . well, I think it's because they look *happy*. And I can't help wondering how that feels.

2

Daisy

By six o'clock I have ushered the few people still wandering the museum out to the double doors at the ground-floor entrance hall, where I wait patiently for the staff to leave so I can lock up and begin my rigorously planned itinerary of patrols for the evening.

First out of the door, as ever, is Janice off reception. Today is one of her three full days; she also works some mornings, often on Saturdays and Sundays, when the museum opens until 1 p.m. There used to be a weekend security guard but he left due to ill health just before I started here, and now there's a private security firm that does sweeps of the museum every few hours. Mr Meyer says he's still looking for a weekend replacement, but it's been six months at least now and there's no sign of anyone starting.

Janice has poker-straight brown hair and wears glasses with huge frames. She's older than me, maybe forty or so. She pauses by the door and drops her carrier bags on the marble floor. Janice always seems to have three or four carrier bags with her, filled with I don't know what. She winds a long, leopard print scarf around her neck and says to me, 'Did Nate tell you about the party?'

'No,' I say, frowning. 'Why would he?'

'Because I told him to.' Janice rolls her eyes. 'Men. What are they like?'

'I don't know,' I answer truthfully.

Janice does her little laugh as though I've said something really funny. Her laugh reminds me of the phone we used to have when I was small, the olive green one that made a high-pitched *brrr-brrr* sound when it rang. Or maybe more like *blll-blll*. You'd have to vibrate your tongue very quickly at the roof of your mouth to make the sound, I think.

That phone had the receiver longwise, top to bottom, on it, instead of across the cradle on the top, like other phones. That was the one Mother took the call on when Father phoned to say he was never coming to see us ever again. Leaving all of us forever.

'Anyway,' says Janice, 'it's in about four weeks. We're going to meet in the Three Tuns around the corner from here and then go on to the Taste of Rajasthan for a meal.'

I stare at her wordlessly. I'm not sure why she would tell Nate to pass on this information. Janice looks at me curiously. 'You are coming, aren't you, Daisy? It's a Saturday night, so you won't be working.'

'Oh,' I say. 'You want me to come to the do?'

Janice laughs again. 'You are daft. Let me have a fiver by Friday so I can pay the deposit on the meal.' Then she picks up her carrier bags and heads out into the drizzle of the Northern Quarter.

Sue and Sue, the two women who run the cafe on the top floor, leave next, swaddled in big coats and pulling woolly bobble hats down over their ears. One is sparrow-thin and the other one is what Mother would call 'bonny'. Sparrow Sue smiles at me as she passes through the door and Bonny Sue leans in to me and says, 'Put a nice bit of carrot cake in the den for you. It's wrapped in tinfoil. Have a good night.'

So I see Nate's got the others calling the security office 'the den', then. Before long it'll just be me calling it the security office, and what happens then? If the majority decide a thing is true, does that make it so? Even if it's wrong? Speaking of Nate, I wonder why he didn't tell me about the office do, like he was supposed to? What reason would he have for not wanting me there?

'Good evening, Daisy,' says Dorothy, leading the day's trio of museum guides out through the doors. Dorothy is what I'd call a 'power dresser' in that she wears very neat skirt suits and very shiny shoes and looks businesslike and yet very well turned out at the same time. I'd say she is almost as old as Mother, but looks about ten years younger. Dorothy is the only full-time employed museum guide, and working for her she has a small army of volunteers from the Friends of the Manchester Museum of Social History, almost always women of pensionable age who Dorothy tutors in the ways of the museum's exhibits and stories. To be honest, the guides apart from Dorothy all tend to blur into three or four faces; I'm not sure how many of them there actually are and I certainly don't know their names; I'm only in the same space as them for an hour a day, anyway.

Finally, the museum manager, Mr Meyer, and his secretary, Seema, emerge from the offices located behind the wide, mahogany reception desk. Seema doesn't like being called Mr Meyer's secretary; she says she is his PA. I know this means Personal Assistant but I always think of a Public Address system, because that's exactly what Seema is like: Mr Meyer's town crier, or a herald like olden-time kings used to have. She always walks in front of him and announces things, and speaks more than he does at staff meetings. If Dorothy is a power dresser then Seema is . . . what would be better than a power dresser? A super dresser? Well, everybody's heard of Superman and if there is a Powerman then he's not as famous, so it stands to reason that super is better than power. So Seema is a super dresser. Her heels are never less than six inches and her skirts are so tight that you can see what she's had for breakfast, as Mother would say. She must spend a lot of time in the gym, going off the shape of her under that skirt and the crisp white blouses she wears. I bet Seema would look good in a pair of Daisy Dukes.

'Evening, Daisy,' says Seema. Her lipstick is the colour of blood, as if she's a vampire who's just feasted. Mr Meyer, by comparison, is pale and what I think is known as 'wan'. Perhaps Seema *is* a vampire, and she's draining Mr Meyer of his blood every day. I frown. I don't usually think silly things like that. It'll be the influence of Nate, who can be very silly, and his habit of doing things like calling a pile of old dinosaur bones Barry.

'Mr Meyer,' I say, looking at my watch, 'it's almost ten past six and the cleaners haven't arrived yet.' There are usually two cleaners, from a cleaning company in the city, and it takes them an hour to do the whole place. There being six halls and the staircase, plus the cafe, it's a fairly cursory clean.

'That's because we've rationalised the contract,' says Seema. 'They're now coming in three mornings a week before we open, rather than every evening. It's much more cost-effective.'

I think about the smears on the Aphrodite cabinet upstairs, where those three boys were pressing their faces. 'But what about spillages and rubbish that accumulates in the day, Mr Meyer?'

Seema answers for him again. 'Sue and Sue keep the cafe clean anyway. I think we'll all have to do just a little bit more ourselves, muck in throughout our shifts, for the general good of the museum.'

I glance at Seema's long, red-lacquered nails, and can't imagine her doing much mucking in. Mr Meyer smiles distractedly at me. 'Good evening, Daisy.'

I watch Mr Meyer and Seema walk out together, her putting up an umbrella for them both to shelter under, then I close, lock and bolt the big double doors behind them.

I like to keep the security office well stocked with items to anticipate any eventuality, so of course I have some soft cloths and a bottle of Windolene. I have polished the cabinet in the Malone Room to a flawless shine; you would never guess that three scruffy little St Mary's oiks had been pressing – from what I could gather by the evidence left behind – their lips and tongues against the glass. I briefly wonder if it's the same gang who did this who give me trouble pretty much every day on my way into work. But no. Those boys at the bus stop are thugs. The ones who did this are just oiks. 'Oiks' is a good word; it's one Mother uses a lot. I can almost see my own reflection – no make-up, dark hair scraped back into a ponytail – in the cabinet. Once I've switched off all the main lights, and the halls are illuminated only by the tracks of dim security night-lights in the ceiling, I will be able to see my reflection properly; if I feel like doing that, which I probably won't. I've worn make-up, obviously. Never as much as Seema, or even as much as Mother used to wear when we were younger, but like so many things in life, I never felt as though I was doing it *right*. Perhaps I should get some lessons from Rosie before this staff night out.

After that it's time to do my first patrol, turning off the main lights as I go. I always start in the entrance lobby, double-checking the main doors even though I know they're secure because I locked them myself. But you have to do everything in order, don't you? You have to have a system, procedures.

The minute you start cutting corners, that's when you make mistakes, you miss things. That's when things start to go wrong.

I check that the doors into the offices where Mr Meyer, Seema and Dorothy work are locked, which they are. I have keys if I need to go in there, but it's usually enough to shine my torch through the glass walls and check everything is in order. On the ground floor there's one exhibition space, the Standish Hall. This is where the museum hosts its temporary exhibitions and shows. Currently it's a display of photographs by a man who used to work for the *New Musical Express* in the seventies and eighties: black and white pictures of sulky young men smoking cigarettes on bridges or standing awkwardly on patches of wasteland, all singers or guitar players in bands with nihilistic names. Nihilistic is a good word. Not one Mother would use. I think it means believing that life is meaningless. Mother would probably relate to that. Most of the young men in the photographs are dead now. I don't think the pictures are all that good, to be honest. Most of them are very grainy and blurry. You could take better photos on your phone. There is one, though, that keeps drawing me in. A young man with dark hair, lifting a cigarette to his lips, a look on his face like he's been caught doing something naughty. He's not what you'd necessarily call handsome, but there's something about him. Something vulnerable. The caption on the picture says he killed himself forty years ago. Hanged himself in his own kitchen. And him a pop star and everything. How could life be so bad that you'd go and do yourself in? Right in your own kitchen? When you've got everything handed to you on a plate? It's just selfish, that. Some people don't know they're born.

I turn all the lights off and create a pool of yellow light with the torch to step in as I climb the wide staircase that leads to the first floor, and the three main halls – the Horridge Wing with the fossilised bones of Baryonyx on the left, the Malone Room with its newly cleaned Aphrodite case in the centre, and the Lever Wing beyond that. In the Lever Wing the walls are covered with thick tapestries; they're actually trade union banners, from all over Greater Manchester. Bury and Wigan and Salford, all with Biblical or Masonic scenes picked out in cotton, invariably against a red backdrop. I point my torch beam at each one in turn; someone could hide behind one of the big banners, if they were of a mind to. No one ever has, though. The banners have slogans such as *United We Stand, Divided We Fall* or *Unity Is Strength,* and a very elaborate one that says *The Great Appear Great Because We Are On Our Knees – Let Us Rise*! I've never been a member of a trade union. I've never been what you'd call a joiner. Not like Rosie.

Up the stairs is the cafe, a fairly modest affair that sells hot drinks, pop, cakes and toasties or paninis, sometimes jacket potatoes done in the microwave, all served up by Sue and Sue. There are two smaller rooms up here, one with desks and chairs where local schools sometimes come for educational sessions, and the other where the personal effects of Theodore Malone and his family are on display, including the skull of Theodore himself. That's probably the room I like the least. I think it's something about the skull, sitting there on a velvet cushion in its glass cabinet. It's what Theodore wanted, apparently; it was in his will that his skull was to be boiled and put on display in the museum he founded. Why would you want that? Why would you want to remind people of death? I stare at the skull for a moment, its bleached white bone dome, its hollow, dark eyeholes, then turn off the lights. All the way down the stairs to the ground floor, and the security office nestled between the entrance lobby and the Standish Hall. My first patrol is over.

In the security office I write my report, which I will update after each patrol – I will do them every hour. The handwritten reports I will hand over to Harold when he comes on duty at one o'clock. He won't read them. The wastepaper bin in the security office is overflowing with my reports from the previous evenings. He should at least put them in the recycling bin in Seema's office. It irks me that I am never there to see Harold hand over to Nate at nine. I shudder to think how lackadaisical their hand over will be. I bet Harold doesn't even do a verbal report, like I had to reluctantly allow Nate to do once it became evident that he was never going to give me a written one.

When I've written the report I watch the CCTV feeds from each room, split over two computer monitors on the desk. Nothing stirs. I do two more patrols and then take my break, eating the chicken sandwiches I've brought from home and then the piece of carrot cake that Bonny Sue left on the security-office desk.

And then I go to get the book.

3

Daisy

The book is a huge volume bound in green leather, the pages mottled and brittle, that's kept in a locked cabinet in the room displaying Theodore Malone's effects, along with all his other books. It's a Victorian retelling of the Greek myths, and for weeks I've been working my way through it on my break. I lug the book back down the stairs to the security office because I don't like reading with old Theodore's empty eye sockets staring at me. I tried that for a couple of nights but it just gave me the heebie-jeebies (another Mother word).

I'm up to the story of Prometheus, but annoyingly someone has moved the postcard that I've been using as a bookmark and stuck it further back in the book. Although the books are locked away, they are available to view under the watchful eye of the museum guides, who have keys to the cabinet. Sometimes students or academics ask to see them. My postcard has been left in a page about a goddess called Oizys. I don't know how to say that. Oozies? Oizies? Wazzies? I try them all out loud but none of them seem to be an appropriate name for a goddess. I read a little of the page; Oizys is the goddess of misery and anxiety. Cheery. I'll look forward to getting to that chapter, then. That's a joke. Sarcasm, really.

Sarcasm is the lowest form of wit, says Mother, but Rosie is sarcastic all the time.

The postcard is of the harbour at Mykonos, which is a Greek island. Rosie brought it back from a holiday she had a lot of years ago. There's no writing on the back; she said she couldn't be bothered to find a post office and work out how to buy a stamp so she just brought the postcard home and gave it to me. I take it out of the page about Oizys and flick carefully back through the book until I find the chapter about Prometheus.

Prometheus was a Titan, who were the beings that came before the gods of Olympus. He created humans from clay and stole fire from the gods, which he gave to the people to allow them to have light, and cook, and be warm. Zeus, the ruler of Olympus, punished him by chaining him to a rock and sending an eagle to rip out his liver and eat it. The liver grew back overnight and the eagle would come back the next day, and the next day, and the next day, forever. It seems a bit harsh, perhaps, but if you've done something wrong then I suppose you have to be punished.

That sets me off, thinking about the thing that happened when I was nine. I try not to think about it too much. Rosie says it's all best left in the past, which is a kind thing for her to say, considering. But I can always tell when she talks about it – which isn't very often, only when I bring it up – that it makes her nervous. Her eyes flit to one side and she licks her lips. I'm not surprised, really, given what happened. I've often thought about having therapy or something, but it's always been an unwritten rule that we don't talk about it. It's our business, nobody else's. And Rosie's right: it's best left in the past.

When my break is over I take the book back upstairs, carefully lock it away in the cabinet again, and do a patrol in reverse, from the Theodore room all the way back down to the security office. I write a report, and do two more patrols. Then I take the CD-ROM from the computer and label it up with today's date and file it on a shelf with the other recordings from the CCTV cameras placed in every hall in the museum. Apart from me doing my patrols, cleaning the Aphrodite cabinet, and reading the book, there's nothing on any of the footage.

At five minutes to one I put the kettle on in the security office, and two minutes later the main door buzzer goes. I let in Harold, who's wrapped in a scarf and woolly hat, his long nose red from the cold, the shoulders of his overcoat wet with rain.

'Morning,' grunts Harold, and though he's technically right it always feels odd when he says it, because it's really the middle of the night. While he unwraps his scarf and hangs up his coat I make him a cup of coffee, two sugars, one spoonful of Coffee Mate.

'Mmmf,' he says by grumpy way of saying thank you, I presume, cupping his hands around the brew. 'Filthy out there.' I'd say Harold is old; I've no idea how old, but he must be in his seventies, all bony and angular, a slight stoop to his shoulders. He puts the cup down and takes a comb from his pocket, tidying his snow-white hair in the small round mirror hanging from a hook on the wall.

I do wonder what drives an old man like Harold to work such an unsociable shift. But I never ask him. It's none of my business. I give him my handwritten reports and brief him on the day's news, which basically amounts to what Nate told me about the three kids pressing their faces against the glass cabinet. Harold nods distractedly, stifles a yawn, and puts the reports down on the desk. They'll be in the bin tomorrow, but I don't say anything. Instead I just give him the torch.

The handover done, Harold lets me out into the wind and rain, and I put my head down and hurry towards the stop for the night bus which will take me home. 'Gnnnf,' he grunts, which I think might be goodbye.

I let myself into the house as quietly as possible, but the faintest smell of cigarettes tells me that Rosie is still up. The terraced house is small, a hall with a staircase up to the three bedrooms and bathroom, a lounge off to the left and the kitchen at the back, which is where I find my sister, standing at the open door to the yard, smoking.

Rosie is thirty-two, so two years younger than me. She's taller and slimmer, and has long, strawberry-blonde hair. She's wearing a green roll-neck jumper and jeans, and she turns from the doorway to give me a nod. She looks tired. She has bags under her eyes.

'How's Mother been?' I ask, taking off my coat and putting it over the back of one of the chairs at the small kitchen table.

'Difficult,' Rosie answers, sighing. She isn't really supposed to smoke standing in the house like that, but given that it's pouring down and she's obviously not had a good day, I don't say anything.

'Has she taken a turn for the worse?'

'Only in her mood,' says Rosie, bending down and stubbing out her cigarette in a saucer on the doorstep. She closes the door and sits at the table while I make myself a sandwich and a cup of tea. I don't ask Rosie if she wants a brew because she's got a big glass of red wine. I don't really like her drinking when she's on duty with Mother but, again, I don't say anything.

Rosie is younger than me but seems older. She's more what you'd call worldly-wise. Mother says that I take after her while Rosie takes after our father, but neither of us really remember him. He left when we were very small. He's just a vague presence that was there, and then wasn't.

'It's gone one-thirty,' I say, sitting down at the table with my sandwich and my tea. 'You're up at seven.'

'Don't remind me,' says Rosie with a groan. She puts her forehead on her arm on the table, then looks up at me. 'I'm not sure how long I can go on doing this, Daisy.'

'Don't say that,' I murmur. Us *not doing this* would mean that . . . well, that Mother didn't need us any more. And I can't really face that.

'It's going to happen,' says Rosie softly. 'Some time. The cancer . . .'

'The doctors said there's no reason she can't enjoy many years of life, with the right care,' I say firmly.

I know what Rosie's thinking, because she's said it so many times before, but this time she doesn't. Maybe she's too tired, or fed up of saying the same thing. She's thinking that Mother isn't actually getting the right care, not really. Rosie works from eight until four in the office of an engineering works and looks after Mother when I'm at work at the museum. I usually go to bed at two and get up at seven before Rosie leaves for work, then I look after Mother in the day. We both do what's needed at weekends – mucking in, as Seema would say – and Mother's usually quite good at sleeping through the night. It works, I think. As well as can be expected.

Rosie is studying her phone and holds it out to me. There's a picture on there of a man, sitting astride a mountain bike in the sunshine. She says, 'What do you think of him?'

I study the photo. 'He seems like he's got a nice face,' I say. I peer at the paragraph of writing underneath the picture. 'And it says he's got two children, so he's probably a kind man.'

Rosie takes the phone back and pulls a face. 'Ugh. Two kids. No thanks. Swipe left.'

'What's wrong with having kids?' I say.

'It's not that he's *got* them, it's that he's obviously *left* them. Mum might say I look like Dad, but that doesn't mean I want a man like him.' She taps a cigarette out of her packet, which has a picture on it of someone hooked up to drips and machines in a bed, dying of cancer. I don't know how she can smoke those things, with Mother lying upstairs in bed. When she's lit it she sits there for a moment, looking at me. With her left hand she absent-mindedly rubs her right forearm. Where the scar is. She does this sometimes, when she's tired or thoughtful or annoyed with me. It makes me feel uncomfortable. So I'm relieved when she says, 'So, how was work?'

I tell her about the three kids and the glass cabinet, and Bonny Sue leaving me a piece of carrot cake, and the contract with the cleaning company changing. Rosie listens and goes to the door to smoke. I tell her about Mr Hipster Beard. 'A tidy beard, though, with wax and oil in it. Not bushy like Uncle Alan's.'

Rosie looks at me curiously for a moment. 'You do realise Uncle Alan wasn't actually our real uncle?'

I frown. 'Wasn't he?'

She laughs, but not with much warmth or humour. 'He was Mum's *boyfriend*. Did you actually think he was her brother? Or Dad's? Haven't you wondered why you haven't seen him for twenty years?'

It makes me feel embarrassed and annoyed when I find things out that mean I've been stupid, so I change the subject. 'I've been invited to a staff do. It's on a Saturday in about four weeks. Do you think I should go?'

'Of course you should,' says Rosie. 'We'll have to get you something to wear.'

'Janice off reception invited me. Nate was supposed to tell me about it but he didn't.'

Rosie's interest seems piqued. 'Who's Nate?'

'The day security guard. I'm sure I've mentioned him before.'

'What's he like?'

I shrug. 'Tall. Older than me, a bit. Bit of a joker.'

'My type?'

I imagine Nate's picture on that dating app on Rosie's phone. I try to think whether she would swipe her finger to the right or to the left. 'I don't know.'

'*Your* type?'

'I don't have a type.'

'Maybe you should,' says Rosie, bending down to stub out her cigarette in the saucer. She waves her hand in the general direction of upstairs. 'This won't last forever, Daisy, whatever you might think and however upsetting you find that. At some point we're going to have our lives back.'

But this *is* my life. I'm not quite sure what I'd do if there wasn't Mother to look after. And I only took the museum job so that either Rosie or me could be in the house at any given time. If Mother was gone I wouldn't really need to work the night shift. Not if I didn't want to.

'I'm going to bed,' says Rosie. 'I'm going to be knackered in the morning. Though after the evening I've had with her, work'll feel like a rest.'

'Mrs Thatcher only used to have five hours' sleep, and she had to run a country,' I say. That's another one of Mother's. Then Rosie's gone, and I hear her creaking up the stairs, flushing the toilet and running the bathroom taps, then quietly closing the door into her bedroom.

I rinse my mug and plate and put them on the side to drain, then lock all the doors and turn off all the lights and head upstairs myself. Mother's door is slightly ajar and I push it open a little more, letting the landing light illuminate her in bed. She looks so slight and shrunken and old, even though she's only sixty. If I close my eyes I can picture her as she was before, always bustling around, slim but not thin. I can remember what she used to smell like, Elnett hairspray and Silk Cut cigarettes and Forever Spring, a perfume she used to get from the Avon lady and which Rosie and I used to spray on ourselves in secret when Mother was out. It's a year since she found out about the cancer in her bones, and six months since she got so weak and sick that she spends most of her time in bed. It's hard to remember her as she was, but not impossible. She had such fire in her.

I close the door and go into the bathroom, running the taps softly so as not to wake her. In my small room, where I only have a single bed, I hang up my jacket and trousers and put my white shirt in my linen basket, and change into my brushed cotton pyjamas.

I read for half an hour, like I always do. I have a book on the go all the time. Sometimes I get them from the library, sometimes from charity shops. I even buy them brand new, sometimes, but when I bring home a Waterstones bag Rosie always tuts at me, as though she thinks I'm being frivolous with my money. Rosie never reads.

After thirty minutes of reading I turn off my light. In the darkness, with Rosie's room on one side of me and Mother's on the other, I mentally review the day. I linger on the book, the old book at the museum, and reading about Prometheus, the Titan who stole fire from the gods and gave it to mankind. It's as though Prometheus has done the reverse here, crept into our house and for reasons I can't quite fathom, stolen the fire away from us all.

4

Nate

I'm fancying chicken, I decide, as the bus delivers me home. Not a moment too soon. These seats are too small and my legs are going numb. And the bus is packed, too busy for me to even get my paperback out of my pocket. The lady next to me must have a dozen carrier bags, three rolls of children's birthday wrapping paper poking out of the one she squeezes between us on the seat and which keep hitting me in the ear. They say the High Street is dying and everybody is doing their shopping online, but this woman is keeping Manchester's retail economy going single-handedly, by the looks of her.

She tuts and glares at me when I ring the bell and she just swivels her legs sideways into the aisle so I have to practically stride over her, then push and elbow my way to the doors at the front.

'Sorry . . . sorry . . . excuse me . . . my stop . . . sorry . . .'

It's still raining when I get off on to the main road but I don't care. Anything's better than being stuffed on that bus with all those people. I'd probably come down with something if I didn't have an iron constitution. I take a deep breath of damp air, laced with diesel fumes and fast-food aromas, and pull up the hood on my anorak, waiting for the bus to pull away so I can cross the busy road and get to Derek's.

She's a funny one, that Daisy. Serious little thing. You're not supposed to tell women to cheer up or smile any more, but that's what I feel like doing with her all the time. I saw her smile, once. That time we'd had an old drunk man come in just when we were doing the handover and throw up in the Horridge Wing. Real delight it was, that she could do some proper security guarding. Not in a nasty way, though. She was genuinely *happy*. Made her face all light up. Pretty little thing, really. Though I know that's not the most important thing in life.

The takeaway's called Derek's Dominoes, except the Dominoes bit, in white, is huge while the Derek's bit is tiny, so it's more like Derek's Dominoes. The windows are steamed up and when I push in through the door the place is empty apart from Derek, standing behind the counter with his little white paper hat on and his white apron, beaming at me from a face ridged with deep lines. Behind him are his son, Desmond, and his grandson, Dwayne, one shovelling pizzas into a big oven and the other shaving a wedge of doner kebab meat on a spike.

'Nathaniel!' shouts Derek, grinning broadly. 'What can we do for you this terrible evening?'

'Chicken,' I say, pretending to peruse the backlit menu above Derek's head, though I know what I want. 'Family Box, I think, Derek.'

'Family Box!' yells Derek happily. He never says anything at normal volume. 'Four pieces of chicken breast in our secret blend of twelve herbs and spices! KFC only has *eleven*, Nathaniel! We go the extra mile! One portion of wings . . . hot or regular?'

I screw up my face. 'Hot.'

'Hot wings!' bellows Derek. 'Four portions of chips, one tub of home-made coleslaw, and one two-litre bottle of . . .?'

He waits with a smile plastered on his face while I think. '7Up, Derek. No, wait, Fanta.'

'Fanta!' says Derek, as though announcing from the balcony of Buckingham Palace the birth of a new royal baby. He writes it all down and turns and sticks the ticket to a rack between him and the kitchen, calling at his son and grandson, 'One Family Box!' The bell above the door tinkles and a short, stout lady with thick glasses and her hair wrapped up in a tropically coloured turban covered with a transparent plastic rain-hood walks in and glares at the menu.

'Marina!' cries Derek joyfully. She grunts at him and continues to peruse the offerings.

'How's the legal action going, Derek?' I say, counting out my money on to the brushed-steel counter.

'Quiet at the moment,' he shouts. 'All these lawyers, they're all getting ready to be off for spring holidays, innit? Going off on their yachts or to their villas in Tuscany, all on the back of the poor working man like me and you.'

'Are they still saying they're going to close you down?'

'If I don't change the name,' says Derek. 'Which I won't. This is my Waterloo, Nathaniel. My Thermopylae. This is my Rorke's Drift.' I don't point out that he would have been on the 'wrong' side at Rorke's Drift. He takes a deep breath. 'This is my Agincourt!' Then Derek holds up two wizened fingers in the direction of the distant, massed ranks of the lawyers who have been piling their ever-more threatening letters on to his welcome mat.

Marina tuts and bangs the handle of her brolly on the counter. 'I'll chop them off for you,' she says.

'That's the point!' beams Derek. 'The English archers, when they were captured by the French, would get their fingers cut off so they couldn't raise a bow against their enemies ever again. Before a big battle the English would give the Frenchies the old reverse Churchill.' Derek waves two fingers on both sets of hands maniacally towards the misted windows. 'To show them that they were still in business. Isn't that right, Nathaniel?'

Marina squints up at me. 'How would he know?'

Derek leans over the counter to pat me on the arm. 'My friend Nathaniel works in the museum! In Manchester! He is very well up on these sorts of things. History, and what have you.'

'I'm a security guard. But, yes, I do like to take an interest.'

Derek nods vigorously. 'So up yours, Agincourt Frenchies, and up yours, Domino's lawyers.' He throws some more Vs towards the windows, just as a wide-eyed man in cycling gear pushes in through the door, takes one look at Derek's contorted face, and hurries back out again.

Marina turns her attention back to the menu. 'Well, it's your own fault, if you ask me, you silly old fool. I mean, you can't open a pizza shop and call it Dominoes, and not expect to get into trouble.'

'Ah, and indeed HA!' shouts Derek triumphantly, slapping the counter. 'And that is exactly my point! Because I am not running a pizza shop, am I? My primary business is selling dominoes! Hence the name!'

Derek points to the far end of the counter where there are indeed half a dozen long, thin wooden boxes and a faded sign taped to the tiled wall that says, *Dominoes, £5*. 'I have them bang to rights,' he says. 'The pizzas and chicken and such is just a sideline.'

'There is the signage,' I point out as tactfully as possible. 'It's the same colours . . . with a picture of a domino . . .'

'What else am I going to use to advertise my business *selling dominoes*?' Derek gives me a theatrical wink. 'And my livery is red, white and blue because I am a very patriotic local entrepreneur! God save the Queen!'

Marina shakes her head and turns her attention to me. 'Do I know you?'

'This is Nathaniel Garvey,' says Derek before I can speak. 'I bet you knew his father.'

'Marcus?' says the old lady, looking impressed.

Derek waves her away. 'No, no, no. Terrence. Terry Garvey.' He adopts a boxing stance and waves his fists in front of his face. 'The Black Bomber they used to call him. Heavyweight. Saw him fight Chris Coady at Rotters, ooh, must have been eighty-one.' Derek begins to dance on his feet, aiming punches at thin air. 'Never seen a man with a reach like Terry Garvey.'

'Dad,' says Desmond from the kitchen.

'Yes, yes, I know, I am not to over-exert myself, doctor's orders,' says Derek, aiming one more punch at his invisible opponent.

'No, Dad, the Family Box.'

Derek breaks into a wide smile and turns to take my tea from Desmond. 'Mr Nathaniel Garvey, your chicken Family Box! Now hurry home with it and enjoy the best feast that Derek's Dominoes can offer! Before they shut us down! Now, beautiful Marina, what can I offer you from our extensive menu of wholly original and non-trademark-infringing dishes?'

'I'll try one of those Big Mac's,' says Marina as I head for the door, the Family Box under the flap of my anorak.

'A great choice!' yells Derek. 'Named after my beloved grandfather Mac. The apostrophe is all-important! Goodbye, Nathaniel! I will see you again soon! Remember Agincourt!'

★

Nobody had seen a man with a reach like Terry Garvey. His fist would come out of nowhere and before you'd even registered a blur in the corner of your eye, your ears would be ringing and you'd be seeing stars. Sometimes the force of the punch would be so hard that your head would spin round and you'd crack your skull on a corner of a kitchen cabinet or a door, or the wall. Sometimes there'd be blood. I remember coming in from school to find my mum slumped against the kitchen door, a streak of red from her cheek all down the painted wood. I ran to get the phone to call an ambulance but before I'd even realised that Dad was in the room I was flat on my back myself, staring at the ceiling, listening to the dialling tone of the phone, its components scattered across the carpet.

I don't know what Mum had done to deserve it. Nobody ever knew what they'd done to deserve it, half the time. Nobody could remember what they'd said or done wrong, they could only remember what happened afterwards. When Dad started to cry and sob and hug everyone and say sorry and promise that it would never happen again. Then he'd clean us up, talking to us as though we were silly things for going and hurting ourselves like that, and he'd take us out for fish and chips or sometimes to a pub or even a restaurant if things were going well for him, money-wise. And we'd see someone he knew and they'd laugh and say, what's with the wife and kid, Terry? Look like you've all got in the ring and done twelve rounds together, and Dad would smile and tell them that the electricity meter had run out and me and Mum had bumped heads in the dark while we were looking for a pound coin, and everybody would laugh, me and Mum included. Then we'd go home and Mum and Dad would go to bed and shut their door and I would put my pillow over my head so I couldn't hear the creaking of the bed-springs coming from their room. And the next day it would be all right again, and the next, and probably the next, and then it would start off all over and nobody, as usual, would know what they'd done to deserve it.

I let myself into the house and the warmth and the lights and the gentle sound of the teatime news on the telly, and lay down the Family Box on the table in the living room while I take off my coat. It's the same house I used to live in with my mum and dad. Both of them gone, now. No more shouting, no more sobbing, no more making up. No more hitting.

The lights and the TV are on those timer switches that you plug in to the wall. The central heating's set to come on when my shift finishes. I don't like to come home to a dark, cold house. It's bad enough living on your own without letting yourself into a place that's empty and unwelcoming. It makes you feel like you're a ghost, haunting your own home.

I wonder what's worse, sitting here alone or working the shift that Daisy does, everybody gone by six and all on your own until old Harold comes on duty at one in the morning. At least I can go out if I feel like it, go down to the pub. Suddenly I remember that I was supposed to tell Daisy about the office do. Damn. Janice'll tear a strip off me when she finds out. Still, I can tell her tomorrow. It's a while off, yet. If only Daisy wasn't so particular about the handover, as she calls it. All this nonsense about reports and things. Nothing ever happens at the museum; certainly nothing worth writing a report about.

I take off my boots and put them by the door, and sit down in the chair nearest the radiator, the Family Box on a tray on my lap. I start with the chicken first, then some hot wings, then some chips. I won't get through it all tonight, but I do have a big appetite. I'll take what's left for my lunch tomorrow. When I've had enough I wrap it in foil and put it on the stove until it's cool and can go in the fridge, and make myself a cup of tea. Splash of milk, two sugars. I really should cut out the sugar. I pat my stomach. It feels hard and solid and thick. I watch a bit of a show about someone wanting to move house to Greece, and they show shots of old ruins, and that makes me think of the museum. It's a good place to work. I like it. Just enough people coming through that you can talk to them and spend a bit of time with them, but not so busy that you're rushed off your feet. Some people, they can't wait to get home from work. I suppose they have families to go to and things to do, people to see.

I try to read my book, which is short stories by Daphne du Maurier. One of them is the story they based that old film *The Birds* off, but this is a bit more depressing. I'm a bit too tired to read, so I have a little doze and wake up about ten o'clock, just as the news is starting again. It's like déjà vu. All the same reports. Nothing new has happened.

Nothing new *ever* happens.

5

Nate

'I want to be called busy,' says Ben when he lets me into the house. It's just gone seven in the morning and there was the merest hint of a frost this morning, hopefully the last of them. There's definitely been a promise of spring in the air the last couple of days. Ben is still in his Pokémon pyjamas and the face of the yellow rabbit thing – Peekaboo? I should take more care to remember these things – is obscured with a big slop of Weetabix.

'Have you had your breakfast already?' I say. I always get Ben his breakfast.

'You're late and I didn't know if you were coming or not,' says Lucia, poking her head from around the kitchen door at the end of the small hall.

'I'm only a few minutes late,' I say, frowning. 'I always come.'

Which I do. Lucia has to start work at seven-thirty and Ben isn't in school until eight-thirty, so I always come round for seven, give him his breakfast, get him dressed and walk him to school, then get my bus into town and be at work for nine. It's our arrangement, just like me having Ben over every other weekend. It's our arrangement and I always stick to it, without fail. I never don't come.

Ben tugs at the sleeve of my anorak. 'I want to be called busy, Dad.'

'I've given him his breakfast, anyway,' says Lucia, emerging into the hall and smoothing down her skirt. She checks her reflection in the round mirror at the bottom of the stairs and gets her coat from where it's hanging on the edge of the bannister. She looks fine. Mighty fine. I think about telling her, but I don't. I never used to say that sort of thing when we were married, or at least not enough, so she said when it became apparent that we weren't going to be married for much longer. So it's probably a bit weird to start saying it now. Too little, too late.

Lucia bends down and gives Ben a kiss on his cheek, which he wipes away. 'See you after school, kid.'

'Busy,' says Ben.

'What?' I say. 'You want to be called busy?'

'Bee-Z,' says Lucia with a sigh. 'Bee from Ben, Z from god knows what. Jay-Z probably. Or something else that I'm just too busy myself to keep up with. Oh, he also wants cornrows and a tattoo. I'll let you deal with this.'

'Surely Bee-Zed, in that case,' I say. Lucia gives me a look that I recognise from old; the one that says I'm focusing on entirely the wrong thing in this situation. Then she's gone, out into the cold, dark morning, leaving me alone with Ben. With my son.

I get down on one knee so I'm roughly on the same level as Ben. He's ten, and he looks at me with a pout. We stare each other down for a moment, then I say, 'Bee-Z, huh?'

'I want everybody to call me that. My friends already do. I want you and Mum and Gramma and Mr Singh in the shop and Mrs Lollipop who crosses the road and John and everybody to call me Bee-Z.'

'Ooookay,' I say, patting his bouncy black curls. 'And cornrows? I don't know if school's going to go for that.'

'They're trying to suppress my cultural heritage,' says Ben, sticking out his bottom lip.

I'm impressed. 'Did you get that off YouTube or something?'

'No. I'm going to get dressed.'

When Ben's gone off upstairs I let myself into the kitchen. The breakfast things are piled up in the sink, along with what looks like last night's dinner plates. Lucia never was very tidy. I didn't mind that. I didn't mind anything, really. I'm very easy-going. Too easy-going for Lucia, though. That was the problem. 'You're so laid-back!' she would rage at me, as though that was a bad thing. I always thought it was a positive. I never got angry or sad or annoyed or shouted. I'd had enough of that when I was a kid. I empty the dishwasher and put all the things away. There are still cups and glasses in the cabinets from when I lived here, from when this was our family home. My eyes light on a cracked mug that says *World's Best Dad* in that font everybody hates, Comic Sans. Ben got me that for Father's Day when he was two. Well, obviously he didn't get it. Lucia bought it. I wonder if she ever thought it was true? I set the cup on the worktop and look at it for a moment. I wonder why she's kept it? That was eight years ago, when she got it for me. When we were together and things were all relatively all right. I wonder if it means something, that she kept it?

I've just finished loading up the dishwasher again and am putting a tablet in the little drawer when Ben says from behind me, 'So, can I have a tattoo, then?'

I press the dishwasher door shut and hear it begin to hum satisfyingly. I consider Ben's request. 'What sort of tattoo?'

Ben rolls his eyes. 'Mum said you'd say that. She bet me a pound. She says I need boundaries and you've never given them to me.'

I don't think that can be true. I wouldn't be the World's Best Dad if I'd never done any proper parenting, would I? I ponder whether I should take the cup home so I can use it myself.

'No,' I say, resolutely. 'No, you can't have a tattoo.'

'What about cornrows?'

'No.'

'Will you call me Bee-Z?'

'No.' I smile to myself. I'm pretty good at this boundary business. I've no idea what Lucia is going on about.

'Twat!' shouts Ben, unexpectedly bursting into tears and storming out of the kitchen. I hear him stomping up the stairs. Okay. Boundaries. That's definitely one crossed. I'd better go and deal with this. While I'm working out exactly how to do that, I quietly take the *World's Best Dad* mug and put it back in the dusty recesses of the kitchen cabinet, and close the door.

The frost has gone when we set off, and the mornings are fully light now, but today there's no sign of the sun behind the thick, low cloud that's gathered. I try to take hold of Ben's arm but he shrugs me off, and I'm not sure if that's just because he's ten and doesn't want to be seen with his old man hanging on to him or if it is indeed because he thinks I'm a twat.

Ben has barely spoken to me since we left the house. I followed him upstairs and gave him the hard word about using disrespectful language, especially to his dad, but he didn't seem particularly impressed or contrite. I'm annoyed, and not just because of what he said. I have a nice thing to tell him, but I'm all confused about whether I should or not. I can almost see Lucia frowning at me and shaking her head, and telling me that I'm rewarding bad behaviour.

Still, I say it anyway. 'Guess what?'

His shoulders rise and fall in a shrug beneath his black padded jacket.

'I said, guess what?'

'What?' he says eventually.

35

'I've got two tickets for City. On Saturday.'

Ben always comes to me every other weekend. It's getting so hard to find things to do with him, these days. Time was we could just go to Heaton Park and look at the goats and pigs in the animal centre, laugh at the alpacas, get chased by the peacocks. Or we'd go to the swimming baths, or kick a ball around. Took him to the museum once or twice, showed him Barry the dinosaur. Even got the Metro out to the airport one particularly skint weekend, with a flask of tea, to watch the planes taking off and landing. Now Ben's the grand old age of ten, though, he doesn't seem to want to do that sort of thing any more. I'm not really sure what he wants to do. So when Dorothy, who runs the museum guides, offered me two tickets to the match because her husband's going to be in hospital having his hernia operation, I snapped them up.

'I thought we could go and get a pizza afterwards,' I say, waiting for him to shower me with his profuse thanks.

'Not at that Derek's?' says Ben dourly.

'No, somewhere proper. Pizza Express or something.'

Ben walks on, stamping both feet in a puddle. 'Manchester City,' I say, frowning, in case he thinks I mean something else. 'They're playing Aston Villa.'

'Mmm,' says Ben, rather noncommittally, in my book.

'Do you have other plans, then?' I say, with more sarcasm than I intend. Turns out he does.

'There's a Fortnite tournament on Saturday,' he says slowly.

I've no idea what that is, where it takes place, or what it's going to cost, but I'm determined to accommodate him. 'Fine. What time? Could we go there for a bit and then on to the football?'

Ben laughs. 'You don't *go* to it. It's a game. Online. I thought I could bring my Xbox round to yours.'

'A video game,' I say. 'But surely you can just play that any time? Hey, we could play together, yeah? After the football. And the pizza.'

'You play with other people. Online. That's why it's a tournament. It starts with a hundred and the last one standing is the winner. And it's at three o'clock.'

Three o'clock. Right. Just when City vs Villa should be kicking off. 'But the tickets,' I say, hating the desperate, whiny sound my voice makes. 'Do you know how much these would cost? Do you know the last time I went to a game?'

Back when we were married I had a season ticket. Used to go on the Etihad every week, and Maine Road before that. Not had one for about four years now. It's funny, you'd think that living alone you'd have more money than when you're contributing to a family home, especially when you go out as infrequently as I do these days. But I never seem to have any money at all. That's why I was so pleased when Dorothy gave me these tickets. I thought Ben would be pleased as well.

'You can go to the football,' he offers, as we turn into the street his school is on. 'I'd be all right on my own.'

I consider it for a few seconds, I have to be honest. Is it even legal to leave a ten-year-old on their own, though? But I sweep the thought away. The weekends are supposed to be our time. I'm thinking that maybe I can persuade him to go to the match by the weekend when he says, 'I don't even like football that much.'

I was seven years old when my dad grabbed me by the shoulder one Saturday morning and said, 'United or City?'

I didn't know the answer to that. I had heard older boys talking about football, but I didn't like it, or even understand it, that much. I hazarded a guess. 'United?'

Dad had slapped me against the side of the head, not hard enough to knock me off my feet but enough to make me stagger.

'City,' he corrected me. 'My dad supported City and I support City and you support City. That's just the way it is.' He took hold of my arm and I flinched, making him frown. He rubbed the skin with his rough, calloused thumb. 'You don't get to choose. You're born to it. Like you're born to the colour of your skin. So, what are you?'

'City,' I said dutifully.

He looked at his watch and tossed the *Manchester Evening News* at me. 'I want you to memorise the names of the starting eleven by three o'clock.'

I knew what would happen if I didn't. So I did. And that's how I became a City fan.

'You're a City fan,' I say to Ben as we stop at the school gates. 'Like me. Like your grandad. Like my grandad.'

He thinks about it. 'If I go to the football, will you call me Bee-Z?'

I sigh. I remember what Ben said, back at the house. I want you and Mum and Gramma and Mr Singh in the shop and Mrs Lollipop who crosses the road and John and everybody to call me Bee-Z.

'Maybe it could be—' I pause. 'Wait. Who's John?'

'What?'

'At home you said you want everyone to call you Bee-Z and you mentioned a lollipop lady—'

'Mrs Lollipop.'

'Mrs Lollipop. Then you said "John".'

Ben shrugs. 'John's Mum's boyfriend.'

Then he's off, rushing through the gates towards a knot of boys in padded coats.

Why didn't Lucia tell me she was seeing someone?

6

Daisy

When I get into work I find that somebody has pushed over the Baryonyx skeleton and it's crashed to the floor in a huge pile of bones. Nate is trying to put it all together but he's making a right mess of it; there's a femur sticking out of its neck and the head is hanging from one hip socket and it makes me furious, and I'm telling him to leave it alone, just leave it, leave it, leave it . . .

'Leave it!' I shout. It takes me a moment to work out where I am as my brain catches up, like a submarine breaking the dark waves of a deep, still sea. I'm in bed. Dreaming. I look over at my radio alarm. Seven-thirty-one. Rosie has just left for work. Must have been her slamming the door that woke me up. I sink back on to the pillow. Not like me to sleep in. Must have forgotten to set my alarm for seven. Not like me at all.

I'm halfway through my first coffee, sitting at the kitchen table wrapped in my fluffy dressing gown, staring through the window at the slash of blue sky between the grey clouds when the call comes.

'Daisy! Daisy! Are you there? Daisy!'

You learn to read the calls from Mother, the tone of them, the inflection, the volume, whether it's going to be a request for a cup of tea or a report of pain or help required in finding the telly clicker or just, on her good days, a need for a chat. I can tell immediately that this is not going to be one of her good days. There's a tremulousness to her voice as it floats down the stairs, a weakness, a suppressed tinge of shame. When I get to the top of the stairs and the smell hits my nostrils, I realise with a sinking heart why.

'I'm sorry, I'm sorry,' whimpers Mother as I help her to sit up in the bed. She's soiled herself. It doesn't happen frequently, but it does sometimes. Some side effect of the medication, apparently. Especially if she's been in a deep sleep. The sight and smell of it makes me gag, but I take deep breaths through my mouth and start by dragging the duvet on to the floor. The whole bed will have to be stripped and washed. I hold her against me and pull her nightdress up and over her head, rolling it into a ball and dropping it on the duvet.

'I think we'd best get you in the shower,' I say, inspecting the scene. She nods sadly and allows me to help her off the bed and walk her to the bathroom. I turn on the shower and wait until it runs warm before helping her in, making sure she's steadying herself on the rail set into the tiled wall before going back into her bedroom to take off the sheets and pillow cases. It's got everywhere.

When I've wrapped it all up and left it on the landing – to be honest I'd probably be better off burning it in the garden than washing it, but we can't afford to keep buying new bedding – I go back into the bathroom. Mother is standing under the jets of water, her naked body thin and scrawny, her skin hanging off her bones. She's staring at me and crying, her tears mingling with the shower water.

'I'm sorry,' she says.

'It's all right.'

'It's not.' She takes a deep, ragged breath and lets out a little wail. 'No daughter should have to see her mother like this. It's not right.'

I take the flannel and wash her down with Badedas shower cream, getting a good foam up to cover her body, not just to wash away the stench and the stains, but so I don't have to look at her saggy breasts and her pale, wispy downstairs area.

'You can't help it,' I murmur. It's like a well-worn script we run through, as though we're actors in one of those long-running stage shows, *The Mousetrap* or something. Next she'll tell me that she doesn't want to be a burden.

'I never wanted to be a burden to you and Rosie,' she says, right on cue.

'You're not. Turn around so I can do your back.' It's my turn, my line, and for once I consider not sticking to the script, to see what happens. But it's as though there's an invisible prompter crouching behind the toilet, urging me on. So I say the words I always say. 'Besides, you did it for us when we were little. It's just come full circle.'

'I suppose,' says Mother, as she always does. 'You're a good girl. Both of you are.'

I wonder what Rosie says when Mother soils herself and she has to clean her up? I wonder what their script is like? I'm not bigging myself up or anything, but I'm pretty sure Rosie isn't as patient with Mother as I am.

I wrap Mother in her dressing gown and sit her in the chair in her room while I go to put the sheets and nightie on a boil wash. I spray half a can of Glade in the kitchen and on the stairs but the smell still lingers. Mother watches me as I put clean bedclothes on and a new duvet, and find her a fresh nightie in her drawer. I replenish the little box where she keeps tubes and tubes of Extra Strong Mints by the bedside. Loves her Extra Strong Mints, does Mother. Can't get enough of them.

She's stopped crying now, which is something. I think it's the crying I find worst of all, more than the soiling. Mother was always what Rosie calls a tough old bird. Don't think I ever saw her crying when we were growing up, not even when Dad left, though admittedly I was very young at the time and don't really know what went on behind closed doors. Maybe that's what toughened Mother up in the first place. And it was the cancer that did what even Dad couldn't: made Mother cry.

For one moment during all of this I entertain a wicked idea. An awful idea. Of not sticking to the script, for once. Instead of briskly cleaning up Mother and pandering to her crying and snuffling, I put my face close to hers, my nose wrinkling from the stink of her.

'I have had enough of this,' I hiss at her, and she flinches at the venom dripping from every word.

'Daisy . . .' she says, eyes wide in terror.

Well, that's what I am, isn't it? Terrifying? After the thing that happened, after what I did . . . who wouldn't be scared of me? I did a bad thing. That must mean I'm a bad person.

But I don't enjoy the look I imagine would be on Mother's face if I said those things to her. It makes me feel sad, gives me an unpleasant feeling in my tummy. I wish I had never done the bad thing. Because I don't feel like a bad person, even though I know I am. Of course, I don't say any of those things I'm imagining.

'All done!' I say brightly, instead, folding down a corner of the duvet like they do in hotels. 'Do you want to get back in bed?'

'I think I might stay in the chair for a bit,' says Mother, looking around. 'Have you seen the clicker?'

I locate it on the bedside table and she jabs at it until *Good Morning Britain* comes on the little TV sitting on her chest of drawers. 'What do you want for breakfast?'

'Couple of eggs? Poached? On toast? And a cup of tea.'

The rest of the morning is taken up by hoovering the whole house, cleaning the inside of the windows, polishing the tables and windowsills, and doing an online shop at Asda to arrive tomorrow. At eleven-thirty the post slaps on to the mat. There's a letter from the hospital with the date of Mother's next check-up appointment, which I write on to the calendar in the kitchen before sticking the letter on to the metal board at the side of the fridge with a magnet in the shape of a flower. There's also a white A4 envelope addressed to Mrs Dukes, which could be any of us, really. People often assume that if you're in your thirties you're married. Rosie nearly got married once. She got engaged. It didn't work out. That's why she's back living at home.

I've never been anywhere close to getting married. But I did have a boyfriend once. A proper one. People thought we might have actually got engaged ourselves. Maybe even married. Except for what happened. I think about that app on Rosie's phone, with the men on it. That's how people find boyfriends these days, isn't it? How else would you find one, if you never go out anywhere? There's only work, I suppose. Not a great deal to go at there. I think about Nate, in my dream, trying to put Baryonyx back together in that stupid way, and I get annoyed all over again, even though it didn't really happen.

I make myself a coffee and sit at the kitchen table, turning over the envelope in my hands. I can't see anyone sending me a letter, to be honest. It could be for Mother. Might be from the hospital. I give it an experimental squeeze. Feels like it could be a magazine or something. More than likely, it's for Rosie.

I feel suddenly, giddily reckless, and decide to open it anyway. If it is for Rosie she should have given them her full name for the avoidance of doubt. I go to the kitchen drawer and get a knife to run under the gummed-down flap; I can't stand it when Rosie rips into letters, making a jagged, untidy mess of the envelope.

It's not a magazine, but a brochure. There's a photo of a smiling old lady on the front, sitting in one of those chairs that recline or move forward when you press a button on the arm. She's being given a cup of tea by a friendly-looking young woman in a blue tunic. There's a vase of flowers on a side table by the chair. At the top of the cover it says *Elysian Fields: Award-winning hospice and dementia-specialist care home.*

I stare at it with mounting fury until I hear Mother shouting, 'Daisy? Daisy!', then slap the brochure down by my cup of now-cold coffee and head up the stairs.

When Rosie walks through the door at a little after four I'm already in my museum uniform and ready to go. My bus is at half-past, which gets me into town right in time to start my shift. There isn't much crossover time between Rosie getting in from her work and me leaving for mine. So today I have to make it count.

'This came for you. I opened it by mistake. It didn't have your full name on it.' I push the brochure, back in its envelope, into Rosie's chest as she walks into the kitchen. 'At least, I assume you asked for it to be sent. I know I didn't, and I haven't asked Mother because she's been upset enough today.'

Rosie stares at me with tired, dark eyes. 'What?' she says, pulling the brochure out of the envelope. 'Oh. Right. This. Yes, I did send off for it.'

'Do you think I'm stupid?' I hiss. 'Do you think I don't know what a hospice is? It's where people go to *die*.'

'It's where people with terminal illnesses go for end-of-life care.' Rosie sighs, putting the brochure down on the table.

44

She hasn't even got her coat off and she's rubbing her arm, where her scar is. 'It's not a fucking . . . elephant's graveyard.'

'Don't swear at me,' I say, turning to the sink to fill the kettle. I always make Rosie a cup of tea when she comes in from work, before I leave. 'Don't you think you should have discussed this with me first?'

'I just sent off for more information, Daisy,' says Rosie evenly, dragging off her coat and throwing it over the back of a chair. She sits down heavily. 'It doesn't mean anything. I picked up a brochure for the Algarve last month but I'm not bloody going, am I?'

'You'd like that, wouldn't you?' I say, clicking on the kettle and throwing a teabag with force into a cup. 'Holidays? Probably with some man you met on that phone app?'

Rosie frowns at me, her mouth hardening to a straight line. 'Actually, yes, I would. What are you saying, Daisy? That it makes me a bad person because I occasionally dream of going on a sodding holiday, when I can find five minutes between working all day and looking after *her* all night?'

'Don't call her *her*. She's our mother.'

'She's a very sick woman,' says Rosie, dropping her voice to a whispered hiss. 'She's got *cancer*, Daisy. Terminal cancer. I just thought it was a good idea that we had all the information at our fingertips. Maybe not for now, but perhaps for later. When . . . if things get worse.'

I say nothing, squeezing the teabag on the side of the cup and throwing it into the bin, stirring in the milk vigorously. Rosie says, her voice calmer, 'How has she been?'

'Soiled herself this morning,' I say curtly, putting the tea in front of her.

Rosie rubs her hand over her face. 'Oh, god. This is what I'm talking about, Daisy. We're not . . . we're not *carers*.'

'No. We're *daughters*,' I say.

'My point exactly,' says Rosie. 'It's just that I think that means different things to me and you.'

We don't speak for a long time, the brochure sitting on the table between us, saying everything that needs to be said. Eventually, I break the silence. 'I made a stew. It's in the fridge. Microwave a bowl of it for three minutes for Mother. But put it into a different bowl when you give it to her, because those bowls get hot.'

Rosie nods and sighs, then stands up and goes to the fridge, taking out a bottle of wine. She pours herself a big glass. I say, 'I made you a cup of tea. You haven't touched it.'

She says nothing and takes her wine into the living room. I hear the telly come on and the announcer says the next programme is about to start. It's called *A New Life in the Sun*. I have two minutes to get outside for my bus, so I run upstairs to Mother's room. She's dozing, an open packet of Extra Strong Mints clutched in her hand. I gently prise them from her fingers and place them on the bedside table, then give her a light kiss on the forehead and head out, slamming the front door behind me and not saying goodbye to Rosie.

7

Daisy

It's staying light a lot later now. Won't be long before the clocks go forward. At least that might make Rosie a little less grumpy. I like the dark nights, though. That's another difference between us. Mother always said it was because I was a winter baby and Rosie was born in summer. She loves the onset of spring and the feel of the sun on her skin; I think that's why she's always dreaming of going to faraway places. Her mood lifts considerably from the beginning of April. I'm the other way. I find summer hot and bright and uncomfortable. I feel too . . . *visible* in the glare of the sun. I like the damp days when it barely gets light and night falls early and heavily. I like the mist and the scrunch of fallen leaves under your feet. I like the clear nights when the moon hangs low and the stars feel just that little bit closer. It's easier to hide in the darkness of winter.

The lighter nights are bringing out other elements, though, and I'm not talking about spring lambs and nesting birds. I mean this gang of boys who are often hanging out about the shops on the parade, where my bus goes from. I never look closely enough at them to study them, but there seems to be a rotating cast in a huddle that's never less than five or six strong. If I was pushed, say if the police sat me down and had me give descriptions of them, if they'd done a robbery or something like that, I'd have to say they were aged between about nine and fifteen, though I'm not really the best judge of that. Children seem so much taller these days, than when I was young. And they're what you'd call a very diverse mix. Multicultural. That would be considered a good thing in some quarters, and I suppose it should be, if they didn't bother me so much.

My bus is due in less than a minute and I put my head down and hurry to the stop, hoping they haven't seen me. But they have. One of them shouts, 'Look who it is! Crazy Daisy!'

I don't know how they know my name. I always keep my museum name badge covered up by my coat or jacket when I'm not in work, because you can never be too careful. You don't want random strangers talking to you as though they know you. What I suspect is that one of their parents has told them my name, someone who knows Mother or Rosie. Someone who knows what happened, or think they know. Someone who heard something once. Some old gossip.

I stand at the bus stop with my back to the boys. I don't like doing that. It puts me at a disadvantage. My senses are tingling, on high alert. One of them starts to sing, gutturally and tunelessly. 'Crazy Daisy, give me your answer do . . .' He tails off. He doesn't know the rest of the words to the song. They wouldn't be talking to me like that if I'd got into the police like I wanted.

From being as young as I can remember I wanted to be in the police. I was obsessed, Mother said. Once, when I was about seven, Rosie, who was five, said to me, 'You be a police lady and I'll be a robber and then we can work together all the time.' That made Mother laugh. I used to make myself badges and warrant cards out of the backs of cereal boxes, writing out neatly in felt tip CONSTABLE DAISY DUKES. At school, whenever we had to talk about what we wanted to be when we grew up, I would say a police officer. I used to religiously watch *The Bill* and make notes about all the slang and the jargon they used. Mother even took Rosie and me to an open day they had at the local police station once. I got to see the cells and the interview rooms, where there was a tape recorder on a table. They had a big white-board that was magnetic, like the board by our fridge, and I could imagine writing the names of suspects on it in marker pens and sticking witness statements to it with magnets. The policeman showing us around gave all the kids badges that said *I'm a Crimebuster!* on them. I whispered to him not to give Rosie one because she wanted to be a bank robber. He laughed but Rosie shot me a glare. She got a badge anyway, but I never saw her wear it. I wore mine for months. I still have it in my bedroom.

Of course, after my ninth birthday, nobody ever talked about me going into the police again.

That doesn't mean I've forgotten everything I learned from the TV shows and movies and books, though. I can feel my skin prickling, can hear the whispers of the boys behind me. They're up to something. Along the road I see the bus approaching. I dig into my pocket for my bus pass, and stick out my hand so the driver can see me. As the bus approaches and the driver indicates to pull in at my stop, I sense something and spin round, just as I feel an impact on the back of my coat.

There's a boy there, the wide-eyed shock on his face telling me that he wasn't expecting me to turn around so quickly. He's one of the younger ones in the gang, a skinny slip of a thing, really, not much taller than me. Further behind him, the older boys are hooting and hollering, snapping their fingers together. For a moment, my eyes lock with those of the boy. I want to ask him why he's doing what he's doing. He looks like – and I know this sounds weird – he wants to tell me. He wants to explain. But there's no time for that because the bus has pulled up and opened its doors with a groaning exhalation of hydraulics. I turn away as the boy starts to skedaddle back to his mates, and climb on board.

I show my pass to the driver and twist my shoulders. 'Is there something on my back?' I'm suspecting an egg, or a tomato, or something worse. The driver reaches under the glass partition and plucks at something on my coat. It's a yellow Post-it note, printed with neat ballpoint writing. It says MAD WOMAN DO NOT APPROACH DANGERUS.

The driver gives me a sympathetic look and hands me the note, closing the doors. 'That's not how you spell dangerous,' I say because I can't think of anything else. I walk to the back of the bus, steadying myself on the poles as it jerks away from the stop, and sit on my own, looking at the gang through the dirty windows as they punch the younger boy's arm and rub his hair in celebration of a prank well pulled.

As soon as I get into the museum I remember my dream, but the crocodile-snouted Baryonyx skeleton is as it should be, all its yellow bones present and correct and in the right places, as far as anyone really knows what the thing actually looked like at all. I run through the handover with Nate; as ever, there's nothing to report. I feel very frustrated and I wonder aloud if Nate is really taking as much notice of everything as he should be.

'Daisy,' he says, 'it's a museum. It's not . . .' He appears to be searching for some suitable analogy, settling on, 'It's not *Fort Apache, The Bronx*.'

I frown at him. 'Well, it wouldn't be, would it? That was a film about a police station in New York.'

'You know what I mean, though,' he says gently. 'I'm not sure what you're expecting to happen, but nothing ever does.'

'Fine,' I say, and I admit I'm possibly a bit more abrupt than usual. That incident with the boys has shaken me up more than I thought it would. I wonder if I should tell Nate about it, and then I immediately wonder why I would. But sometimes it would be nice to just have someone to talk to. If I tell Mother she'll either be so out of it on her medication that she won't even hear me, or she'll get upset. If I tell Rosie she'll either give me one of her looks and tell me to get a grip, or she'll head off to the parade and try to find them to bash their heads together. You never know what you're going to get with my family. For once I'd just like to tell somebody something and have them *listen* to me, rather than feel they have to pass comment on how I've handled it or take matters into their own hands to find a solution. Nate looks like the sort of man who would just listen to you. I can't imagine he's got many troubles of his own to be distracted by. I've even gone as far as to take the crumpled Post-it note out of my pocket to show him.

'Daisy?' I blink and realise Nate is looking at me with a furrowed brow. 'Are you all right?'

'Why wouldn't I be?' I say, and I have to say that's what you'd call *snapping* at someone. I wish he'd just leave me alone. I look at my watch. 'It's gone five. You should be going home.'

'Didn't you get the memo?'

I glare at him. What memo? I don't like being out of the loop. I haven't had the chance to go to my pigeonhole yet, or log on to my museum emails on the computer in the security office.

'There's a staff meeting at six, after closing up,' says Nate. 'Seema called it.' He rubs his chin. He still hasn't had a shave. 'I hope it's nothing bad.'

'Why would it be?'

Nate gives me what I can only call a quizzical look. 'Maybe I've worked at too many places where a staff meeting called at short notice is never good news.' He sort of cocks his head to one side and looks at me for long enough to make me feel a bit awkward and uncomfortable. 'I wish I lived in your world, Daisy. You always give the impression that nothing bad ever happens to you.'

I glance down at the Post-it note in my hand. MAD WOMAN DO NOT APPROACH DANGERUS. I shove it back into my pocket. 'There's usually somebody worse off than you,' I say. 'My mother always says that.'

I decide to get a patrol in before the staff meeting, and to my annoyance Nate insists on coming with me. 'I just want to see how you do things,' he says. The patrol takes twice as long as usual because Nate insists on talking to every single person he sees in the museum. I don't know how he has the energy to do it. I don't know how he can just go up to total strangers and talk so *easily* to them.

There's no one to talk to in the Lever Wing, the thick trade-union banners insulating the room from the noise in the rest of the museum. Nate stands and stares up at the embroidery on one particularly intricate banner, as though he's never really seen it before. Does he even do patrols? I begin to wonder what he does in fact do all day.

I'm about to head out to the staircase when something catches my eye. There are four big glass cases in the centre of the room, and I head over to the one nearest the far wall, inspecting it closely. The cases are each devoted to a different industry that was prominent in the north, such as mining, steel production, farming and, as is the case with this one, textiles. As I stare into the cabinet I see Nate's reflection appear, looming over me.

'What's up?' he says.

'There's a gap. Yesterday there was a weaving shuttle there. I'm sure of it.'

Nate leans forward and peers at the shelf. 'Was there?'

'Yes. One of the oldest surviving examples in such good condition. It came from the Cheesden Lumb mill in Rochdale.'

Nate – or at least his reflection – looks singularly unimpressed. 'Maybe they moved it.'

'Well, where to?'

'Does it matter?'

I turn to look at him. 'Maybe they didn't move it. Maybe it's been stolen. Today.' I don't add on your watch because it's obvious what I mean.

Nate frowns. 'Who would steal that?'

'I don't know,' I say, exasperated by his apparent inability to see the seriousness of the situation. 'Plenty of people.' I lower my voice. 'There are museums in Liverpool would kill for a piece of textile history like that.'

He raises an eyebrow and also drops his voice to a whisper. 'What, genuinely kill?'

'Well, perhaps not,' I concede, before seeing the grin he's unable to contain. He's laughing at me. 'Never mind. This is my shift now. I'll deal with it.'

I stalk off to the stairs to continue the patrol and Nate hurries after me, catching me up in the room at the top, with Theodore Malone's effects.

'Daisy,' he says, 'I'm sorry. I was only joking with you.'

'Forget it,' I say. 'I'm going to report it to Seema.'

Nate glances at his watch. 'There's still half an hour to the meeting. I think I'll wait in here.'

'Fine,' I say, glancing at Theodore's boiled skull on its velvet cushion. Rather him than me, sitting in here all alone with that thing.

'I like it in here,' he says, like he's reading my mind. 'It's peaceful.' He must see me looking at the skull, because he crouches down behind the glass case and says in a stupid voice, 'Alas, poor Theodore! I knew him, Horatio, a fellow of infinite jest. A gottle o' gear, a gottle o' gear.'

To my surprise it makes me laugh, but I disguise it as though I'm coughing. Nate's head bobs up from behind the skull case and he smiles broadly at me. 'I'm going to write a report on the missing exhibit,' I say.

'See you at the meeting,' Nate says with a nod, settling down into one of the chairs.

'Well, yes,' I say, frowning. 'You most likely will.'

Then I head back down the stairs, feeling generally puzzled by so much more than the missing shuttle.

8

Nate

I'm pretty sure that Daisy laughed at my ventriloquist act. She made it look like she was coughing, but she was laughing. I'm certain of it.

When she's gone I get the book from the shelf. Annoyingly, somebody's moved the bookmark again. Must have been someone looking at it today. That fella with the sandals, I'll bet. I mean, I know spring is in the air, but who wears sandals in this weather? Without socks? He's going to end up with toes like Captain Oates.

The bookmark is an old postcard of Mykonos, which is quite fitting for a book on Greek myths. No idea where it came from. It's been placed in the chapter on Prometheus, who stole fire from the heavens to give to mankind. Maybe the sandals bloke was wishing someone would steal some fire for him, warm his feet up a bit. I flick forward through the book until I find the story I was reading. Oizys, goddess of misery and discord. Causer of wars and feuds. Purveyor of disputes and dissension.

Why didn't Lucia tell me she was seeing someone?

Not that she should, to be honest. And not that I should be bothered. Which I'm not. Well, maybe a little bit. Because though we're divorced we're both still Ben's parents. Don't we owe it to our son to put up some kind of . . . I don't know, united front?

I can almost hear Lucia saying *It's a bit late for that.* Because we didn't have much of a united front towards the end. Oizys was definitely sowing her seeds of discord in our house. Some days it was positively a temple to her.

Or maybe what's really bothering me is the way Ben was so matter-of-fact about it all. *John is Mum's boyfriend,* as though that was the most normal thing in the world to say. Just how well does Ben know him? How long have he and Lucia been seeing each other? How often does he come round? Does he play Fortnite with Ben? Does he stay over? In what used to be our bedroom? Our bed?

What if Lucia and this John get married?

What if Ben starts calling him *Dad*?

I stare furiously at the book to try to derail my train of thought. Oizys was one of the daughters of Nyx, goddess of night, and Erebus, who ruled from a palace in the darkest corner of the underworld. 'Little was written about Erebus,' I read aloud. 'He does not figure greatly in many of the histories.'

I look up at the polished skull of Theodore Malone. What if that happens to me? What if Ben grows up and I'm just a footnote, like Erebus, not figuring greatly in anyone's history at all?

The meeting is in the Standish Hall, where they've pushed back the displays of the photographs of Manchester's rock history to accommodate three rows of chairs and a lectern at the front for Seema and Mr Meyer. Mr Meyer smiles benignly but it's obviously Seema who is to deliver the news. She is smiling, but I don't take much comfort from that. I'd imagine a shark looks like it's smiling just before it bites your leg off.

We all assemble and wait for Daisy to lock the front doors,

having seen out the last of the stragglers. I smile at her and nod at the empty seat beside me. She bites her lip and looks around at the four or five other empty chairs, and I realise I've created some kind of conflict in her mind. I'm not even sure why I indicated the empty space, but now she's wrestling between wondering why she should sit there, and whether it will hurt my feelings if she doesn't. I can just tell with the look on her face. I can read that Daisy Dukes like a book. In the end she sits down in the seat but one next to me, and seems fairly satisfied with her compromise.

'Are we all here?' says Seema, from the front.

'Harold's not,' points out Daisy.

Seema frowns. 'No, well, he wouldn't be, would he? We didn't think it was worth getting him in for the presentation. I'll be emailing out the full details later to everyone.'

'So why did we need to come at all?' says Daisy, her brow crinkling with puzzlement. It is rather . . . what's the word? Not cute. I don't think she'd like that. Fetching, maybe. It's rather fetching.

Seema ignores her and taps at the laptop on the lectern. Behind her on the white wall the museum's logo appears. Oh, good. A PowerPoint presentation. Said nobody, ever.

'There's something coming up which affects you all,' begins Seema, and Daisy's arm immediately shoots up. Seema takes an audible deep breath and says, 'Daisy?'

'Is it about the thefts?'

Seema pouts and narrows her eyes. 'Thefts?'

'From the Lever Wing. Maybe other places, too.'

Seema glances at Mr Meyer and shakes her head. 'I'll speak to you later about that. No, I've gathered you here—'

Daisy's arm goes up again. 'Are we losing our jobs?' She glances at me. 'Because it's never good news, is it, when a staff meeting's called at short notice. Somebody told me.'

I feel the weight of Seema's stare on me and start to fiddle with the cuff of my shirt. 'No,' says Seema evenly. 'Nobody's losing their jobs. Not today. If I might be allowed to get on . . .?'

Before Daisy can say anything else, Seema slaps the laptop and another slide appears. It says ManMuSH BIG SLEEPOVER. She looks proudly at it for a moment then turns back to us and says, 'We're planning this for before the Easter holidays. It's something that's worked well in other museums. We're going to stay open all night for a ticketed event. We'll have stories about some of the exhibits, some food and drink laid on. It's going to be family-focused, so we'll be expecting children, with adult supervision, of course. It's going to be a fun event.'

'You should call it Nights at the Museum,' says Janice.

Seema looks at her coldly. 'That's a film.'

'Or Behind the Scenes at the Museum,' says Dorothy.

'That's a book,' says Seema.

'What about After Dark?' suggests Daisy. 'I'm reading a book called *After Dark*.'

Seema sighs loudly. 'Look. We're calling it the ManMuSH Big Sleepover. That's not really up for debate right now.'

'Are you reading *After Dark*?' I say to Daisy, mainly because I haven't said anything yet and feel like I probably ought to show willing.

'Yes,' says Daisy. 'By Haruki Murakami.'

'I was thinking of the short-story collection by Wilkie Collins,' I say. Daisy is staring at me with that crinkly brow.

'I haven't read that,' she says, still looking at me. 'The Murakami is good. I can lend it to you.'

'If the book club at the back has quite finished,' says Seema testily, and we both turn back to focus on her. 'To summarise, we'll be expecting all of you to work that night. And to

58

spread the word so that we sell enough tickets to make this a success. I cannot stress to you all how important it is for the museum to more successfully engage with the community, and it is through events like this that we will extend the reach of our brand.' Seema looks at me thoughtfully. 'You have a son, don't you, Nate? Perhaps you could bring him along.'

'If I can get him away from his Xbox,' I say, cheerfully, glancing at Daisy, who quickly looks down at her hands. 'But, yes, good idea, I'll bring Ben.'

I remember the one and only time my dad took me to work with him. Not the odds and sods of jobs he did that never lasted very long, the building sites and the factories and the warehouses. He never considered that proper work, just something to fill the time – and replenish the bank balance – between what he thought of as his proper job and so, by extension, so did I.

I wasn't supposed to be there; I'd never shown any interest in going before and he'd never offered to take me. They were always at nights, mostly at weekends, and I would stay at home with my mum, always asleep in bed by the time he came back, either despondent and unpredictable if he'd lost, or almost maniacally happy and equally unpredictable if he'd won, having usually drunk half the purse.

This time, though, Mum couldn't look after me. She'd got a phone call to say her mum, my grandma, had been taken into hospital, about half an hour before Dad was due to go to work.

'You'll have to get your sister to look after him, Precious,' said Dad.

'Flora will be at the hospital, Terry!' Mum said exasperatedly. 'It's her mother too!'

'What's up with Grandma?' I asked, but nobody answered me.

'One of the neighbours, then,' said my dad, shoving his gloves into a sports bag.

'Terry, can't you just take him with you? You can buy him a can of pop and sit him at the back. He'll be no trouble.'

They both looked at me, eight years old, sitting on the sofa, already in my pyjamas and holding the grubby stuffed bunny whose fur had been worn smooth and which I loved more than anything else. Dad sighed. 'All right. But get him dressed. And he's not bringing that bloody rabbit. I don't want anybody thinking Terry Garvey's boy is some sort of sodding pansy.'

I knew that Dad was a boxer and I'd watched fights with him on the telly, but nothing had prepared me for seeing it live for the first time. Dad sat me on a plastic chair at the back of a big room in a shabby hotel on a ring road, where the ring had been set up in the middle. He gave me a can of Coke and a bag of crisps and told me he'd collect me at the end.

'Will Grandma be all right?' I asked him. He looked at me blankly, shrugged and walked away.

The room was noisy, smelly and much brighter than it was on the telly; so bright it hurt my eyes. Clouds of cigarette smoke wafted in front of the bright lights, and there was an overpowering stench of booze and sweat and embrocation. The audience was mainly men, who seemingly couldn't sit still in their chairs and were always leaping to their feet, punching the air, shouting and swearing. Two flabby men were at the tail-end of their fight when I sat down and watched Dad disappear through a door; both exhausted and leaning against each other, aiming weak, desultory punches at each other's midriffs. It looked more like dancing to me than fighting.

When the fight had finished two ladies in bikinis paraded around the ring holding up cards saying the next match was in ten minutes. The men were all shouting and whistling at them while I sat there, wide-eyed. I knew the word 'fuck', had heard my dad say it plenty of times, and sometimes my mum. But I had never heard it said so loudly and so many times as I did by those men shouting at the ladies.

The crowd had only just quietened down when a man in a black suit and a bow tie got in the ring and said into a microphone that the next fight was starting. I missed what the first boxer was called but never forgot the way the man said my dad's name: 'Terry "The Black Bomber" Gaaaaaarveeeey!'

If what the men had been shouting to the ladies had made me wide-eyed with astonishment, what they started shouting about my dad – and the colour of his skin – made me shrink into my chair, trying to make myself as small as possible, pulling down the sleeves of my T-shirt to cover my bare arms.

I'd never heard people say those things before, just like I'd never heard men shout those sorts of words to ladies. Two firsts in one night. And there was more to come.

The man who Dad was fighting was shorter than him but whereas Dad carried a bulge of fat around his middle the other man had a stomach like a plank of wood. The tops of Dad's arms wobbled a bit when he threw a punch; the other man's were like they were carved from stone. Dad was fast enough to hit me or Mum round the head when we weren't expecting it, but compared to the man he was fighting he might as well have been moving in slow motion.

I wished I had my rabbit, but instead I hugged my Coke can, trying not to look but unable to tear my eyes away as the white man laid punch after punch on my dad's face, into his stomach, under his chin. There didn't seem to be anywhere he didn't get hit. At one point a gout of bright-red blood sprayed out of his nose.

Between the rounds the ladies held up cards with numbers on and Dad had to sit in the corner of the ring while a man wiped the blood off him and seemed to be telling him off. Every time the bell clanged and he got up off the little chair I prayed that it would be over soon and wondered how long Dad was going to stand there while the other man kept hitting him.

Not long, it turned out. I think it was in the fourth round that the other man punched Dad once in the belly, then again, then hit him straight in the chin, spinning him around and throwing him face down on the canvas. I shouted something out – I can't remember what – and everybody on my side of the ring turned around and laughed at me, pointing, until I started to cry. The man in the suit bent over Dad and counted to ten while he tried to push himself up and eventually he gave in and lay down in the ring, his head turned towards me and his eyes meeting mine with a cold stare.

Afterwards Dad, back in his normal clothes, little plasters on his puffed and swollen face, came to collect me. 'Never do that again,' he hissed, dragging me out of the room by my arm.

When we got home Mum and Auntie Flora were sitting in our living room, crying and holding each other. Grandma had died in hospital.

9

Daisy

I never had Nate down as a reader. I don't know why. I suppose, really, I'd never thought about it. Rosie doesn't read much, apart from those celebrity gossip magazines which build pages and pages of articles around a single photograph of a TV presenter or an actor who has been walking their dog in a park and doesn't look at their best. I don't think I've ever seen Mother with a book. I don't remember her ever reading to us when we were small.

I wonder if Nate reads stories to his son? Ben. I wonder if he will bring him to this open evening? I wonder if his wife will come, too?

Not that any of that matters to me, whether Nate brings his son or his wife or whether he is a reader. It's just that I never had him down as being one, that's all. Wilkie Collins, he said. I've never heard of this writer. I resolve to make a note of the name when I get back to the security office, and look up what they've written.

'Does anyone have any questions?' says Seema. She's been talking about the open evening but I've not really been listening. I put my hand up. Seema nods at me, 'Yes, Daisy?'

'It's about the thefts,' I say.

Seema frowns. 'Oh, yes, you said. Let's talk after the presentation. Does anybody have any questions about the ManMuSH Big Sleepover?'

Janice says, 'What's this ManMuSH all about? It sounds rude.' She laughs to drive home her point.

Seema glares at her. 'It's the rebranding, Janice. Manchester Museum of Social History. ManMuSH. You got the memo.' She looks around the room. 'Any questions? About the event?'

Nobody puts their hand up so Seema smiles and says, 'Very good. I'll email you all the presentation slides. Thank you for staying on to attend.'

I have to unlock the doors again to let everyone out. Bonny Sue says she has left me some more cake in the security office – red velvet cake, this time. Mr Meyer and Seema approach and I step sideways to block their path through the door.

'About the thefts,' I say.

Seema rolls her eyes. I don't know if she thinks I didn't see it, or doesn't care if I did. 'What was it again?'

'A weaving shuttle. From cabinet D in the Lever Wing.'

'Perhaps it's gone for cleaning or restoration. We have items out all the time, Daisy. Or maybe it's back in storage.'

'Did you put it back into storage? Or send it for restoration?' I ask. I can tell by the look on Seema's face that my line of questioning is perhaps more strident than I intended.

'I don't know,' says Seema coolly. 'There's a list in my office. Should be in a blue file on the bookshelf behind my desk. Feel free to take a look.'

I nod, and move aside to let them pass. 'And if it's not? On the list?'

Seema shrugs. 'Then . . . come and see me tomorrow. I'm sure there's a normal explanation for it. Good night, Daisy.'

They've all gone except Nate, who seems to be hanging back in the lobby. I point to the door. 'Good evening, Nate.'

He has his coat on but hasn't buttoned it up. He pauses, then says, 'Is the book good?'

How does Nate know about the book? Is that why he mentioned the CCTV? Has he been watching me on the recordings? Taking the book from the Theodore room and reading it in the security office? It isn't as if I've done anything wrong. I'm entitled to a break, and the books in the Theodore room are not off-limits.

'The book you mentioned in the meeting,' clarifies Nate. '*After Dark*. By the . . . is it a Japanese writer?'

'Oh,' I say, with relief. 'Haruki Murakami. Yes, it's good.' I remember I'd said I would lend it to him. 'Do you want to borrow it?'

'If you say it's good, then yes, please.' Nate looks at me curiously. 'I never had you down as a reader. I don't know why.'

It's funny, that's exactly what I was thinking about him. I wonder why neither of us look like readers. I wonder what a reader looks like. The door is open and an icy cold wind is blowing in.

'Well,' says Nate.

'I need to lock up and do my patrol,' I say. 'You should get home. To Ben. Your son.'

Nate looks like he's going to say something, and then changes his mind and fastens his coat. 'Well, goodnight, Daisy. Have a good shift.'

And then I'm finally alone in the museum. I must be feeling all discombobulated – which is a Mother word – by the fact it's almost seven o'clock and everyone has only just left, because for the first time I suddenly feel a strange sensation, as though the emptiness in the museum has weight, as though absence is a thing you can touch.

Mother calls it the black dog, which used to scare me as a child. She would say, 'the black dog's on me', and I would be looking for it, a huge, slavering hound, dark as night, its vast paws on her shoulders, its tongue lolling out of its mouth. I don't know what used to scare me more, the fact that she said it was there, or that I couldn't see it.

I started having the black dog on me when I was nine, after the thing happened. Mother said it wasn't surprising. When Mother had the black dog on her, she said the only thing that would see it off was a bottle of wine, and it used to make me laugh, imagining her running down our street waving a bottle, the dog running away from her, its eyes wide. But obviously I couldn't have a bottle of wine when I was only nine.

I learned a lot later that people say the black dog thing when they mean they are depressed. I always thought being depressed meant being sad, but black dog days aren't about being sad. Sad is what you are when Bambi's mother gets killed by the hunter, or you lose your favourite toy, or when a gang of boys call you Crazy Daisy at the bus stop. The black dog is different from that. It makes you feel tired, lethargic, like you really are carrying a dog around on your back. It makes it hard to sort out everything you have to do in a proper order, so instead of having a list in your head you have a swirling cloud of things and it's impossible to pin down which you should do first. It means you can't concentrate on your favourite book, and just end up staring at the wall as hours tick by, not thinking of anything in particular.

Fortunately, I don't have black dog days very often now. I'm too busy with work at the nights and looking after Mother in the days. I can't afford to have black dog days. Which is why it's a surprise to feel the black dog padding around in the shadows as I go round switching off all the lights.

I do a patrol first, pausing to shine the torch on the empty space in the cabinet where the weaving shuttle should be, then I go to Seema's office to check the restoration list. There are a number of ring binders on the small bookcase and I find the one marked restorations and sit down with it at Seema's desk. The office is a lot brighter and more airy than the security office. It would be nice to work somewhere like this. With plants and a water cooler. And windows. Through the tiny gaps in the slats of the blinds I can see the blackness of night and the glow of streetlights. What would it be like to work with people all day, Seema and Janice and Dorothy and Nate? I suppose I'd have to talk to them, chat, make small talk. I've never been very good at that.

There is a single page in the file of items that have been taken out of the museum for cleaning or maintenance. The weaving shuttle isn't on the list. I check back at the previous three months' lists to make sure it isn't on those, then I copy out on a Post-it note the name and telephone number of the company that does the restorations. Perhaps I can call them tomorrow, see if the shuttle has been sent but not logged. I put it in my pocket and it makes me think of the other yellow note that's there, put on my back by that boy at the bus stop.

I don't honestly think those boys really know what happened when I was nine, because it was all kept really quiet. But sometimes things get out, hints, whispers, and they get passed on, and passed down, and at the end it's just a vague idea that something once happened, and all that's left is a cruel nickname like Crazy Daisy. I haven't even thought about it for ages, years probably. The only reason I'm thinking about it now is because when I was talking to Rosie earlier she was touching the scar on her arm. I don't even think she was thinking about what had happened. I don't think she ever does.

I put the binder back and lock up the office, then go to the security office to check the saved CCTV files. I go back over twenty-four hours and watch in fast-forward, seeing the people skittering around the Lever Wing, looking into the cabinets, talking, even kissing at one point. It's impossible to see whether the shuttle is in the cabinet at this range. I wonder if there's a possibility to enhance the footage, like they do on crime shows. Nate wanders in and out, talking easily to people. I slow the footage down and watch him for a moment, laughing with two old ladies. Then the visitors thin out and disappear, and it's just me doing my patrols, lit by the dim night-lights. The CCTV footage is recorded in eight-hour stretches that correspond to each of our shifts. On the next file there's silence and no movement in the Lever Wing, eventually broken by the arrival of Harold ambling around. I only see him once, shuffling across the polished floor. He obviously doesn't do proper patrols. I see him looking into the cabinets and at one point he adjusts his tie in the reflection in the glass. Then there's nothing for ages, save for morning light starting to filter in through the windows, and then the file finishes.

I load up the next footage, beginning at nine o'clock this morning as Nate appears, striding across the shot, and then the first of the visitors start to trickle in.

Well, that is frustratingly inconclusive. I rerun the footage from Nate's shift, when the museum was at its busiest. There are a couple of times when a few people are crowding around the cabinet in question, when conceivably someone could have removed the shuttle, but the cabinets are all locked. Unless, for some reason, Nate had left it open. I'll have to speak to him about that. But that would involve everybody either being in on the crime, or turning a blind eye to someone blatantly stealing the shuttle.

Well, there's no use spending any more time on the CCTV. I do another patrol, and then decide to take my break a little early. I take the book from its shelf in the Theodore room and read it in the security office, being careful not to get

68

any crumbs from Bonny Sue's red velvet cake on the pages. Annoyingly, someone has moved the Mykonos postcard again. I had no idea the book was so popular during the days.

The next story after the Prometheus one is about King Midas. Everybody knows this story, but I read it anyway. This is what they call a 'cautionary tale'. A lot of the Greek myths are just about gods and people killing each other or having sex but this is the sort of story that has a moral, and that is that you have to be careful what you wish for. Personally, I think being able to turn things to gold by touching them would be the sort of thing you could manage pretty well if you were more careful than Midas was. It's not like there's actually any need to go around touching other people, is it? I think my favourite bit, though, is not about turning things to gold, but later on, when Midas find himself judging a music contest between the gods Pan and Apollo. Midas thinks Pan is best and the angry Apollo gives him donkey's ears. Midas has to cover them in a turban and only shows them to his barber, swearing him to secrecy. But the barber is bursting to tell someone, so goes and digs a hole in a field and tells the secret into it. He thinks he's got it off his chest, but when the grass that grows over the hole blows in the wind, it whispers, 'Midas has ass's ears.'

It's funny, but not really, because Midas kills himself after word gets out. Maybe Midas had the black dog on him that day. Maybe shame does that to a person. Sometimes I wish I could talk to someone about the thing that happened.

I take the book back to its case and as I lock it away my eyes fall on the polished skull of Theodore Malone. No wind to blow through here and give the game away. It's a daft thing to do, and not my sort of behaviour at all, but on a whim I unlock the top of the cabinet and lean in − the skull smells of beeswax and, faintly, of bleach − and whisper my secret.

Nate

'It's not a secret,' says Lucia. 'It was just never the right time to tell you. With only seeing you for five minutes in the mornings.'

I have made sure I am early this morning, so I can give Ben his breakfast and not feel like I'm being accused of anything. I wasn't going to mention John, but pretty much as soon as I got through the door I blurted out, 'Why didn't you tell me you were seeing someone?'

'I suppose you told him. Bigmouth Strikes Again,' Lucia says, pulling out her tongue at Ben. He giggles. I feel a stab of envy at this easy way they have with each other. Why are me and Ben so much more awkward together?

'Is it serious?' I say.

'He's nice,' says Lucia, which doesn't answer my question. She pulls on her coat and gets her bag. 'Maybe you could meet him sometime?'

I grunt noncommittally. Lucia gives Ben a peck on the cheek and tells him she'll see him after school. When she's gone I go to get Ben his breakfast, which he eats in front of some cartoons in the living room. Then I set to tidying the kitchen.

I frown when I open the dishwasher. Everything's stacked wrong. The cutlery basket is at the wrong side. The bowls are where the cups should be. The plates are facing the other way! I never fill the dishwasher this way and I lived with Lucia long enough to know that when she actually bothers to do the dishwasher, she does it the same way as me.

John has done this. Which means John was round yesterday. For his tea. Maybe for something else, as well. Maybe he stayed over. Maybe Lucia ushered him out of the door five minutes before I arrived.

I resolve to turn up even earlier tomorrow.

Walking to school, Ben seems chatty, but it doesn't feel like the right time to ask him if John stayed over last night. He might not even know, and I don't want to freak him out. He's telling me about what happened at school yesterday, how everybody had to say what their mums or dads did as a job, and what the kids would really like them to do. Feels a bit like putting a bit of undue pressure on already hard-pressed parents to me, encouraging the kids to have unreasonable expectations about what they do for a living, if they've even got jobs.

'It was dead funny,' laughs Ben. 'Kaden Reynolds said he wished his dad was a bank robber.'

'Why is that funny?'

'Because his dad is PoPo,' says Ben, almost doubling over.

'PoPo?'

'Police. Fed.'

'When did you start using this gangster talk?' I say with a frown.

Ben shrugs and stops to look at a dead sparrow in the gutter. 'What about my tattoo?

'It's still no.'

'Cornrows, then.'

71

'What did you tell them about my job?' I say, by way of changing the subject.

'I told them Mum was a nurse at the hospital,' says Ben, walking on in front of me. 'And that you were a security guard.'

'And what jobs did you wish we both had?'

Ben cocks his head to one side as he walks. 'I said that Mum should just still be a nurse because she saves people's lives and makes them well and there wasn't anything better than that.'

'I bet she loved that,' I mutter, but under my breath. 'What about me?'

Ben turns to face me. 'A detective!' he beams.

'A detective? What, like Kaden's dad?'

'No!' says Ben, laughing again. 'Not a police detective. A detective like Pikachu.'

Now I'm totally lost. I thought Pikachu was the yellow rabbit thing off Pokémon. His job is basically to live inside a little ball and just come out to fight other creatures, isn't it? Now I think about it, there are a few animal rights issues around that whole Pokémon thing that Ben loves. That's probably a conversation for another day, though, as we're turning into the street where the school is. So I just say, 'He's a detective now, eh?'

'He sure is! With a little hat and a magnifying glass and everything. He solves crimes and mysteries.'

'And that's what you wish I did for a job?'

Ben shrugs as we stop at the school gates. 'It's cooler than being a guard at a boring old museum.'

I decide to leave off telling him about the ManMuSH Big Sleepover until another time. Instead I just lean in to give him a kiss on his cheek, which he nimbly dodges and runs off into the playground.

★

'Good morning, Harold!' I say, shrugging off my coat and hanging it on the hook in the den, the hook recently vacated by Harold's grey mac, which he's wrapped up in and sitting in the desk chair, glowering at me.

'You're late,' he says.

'Three minutes,' I say cheerfully. 'There was an accident at the bottom of Deansgate.'

He grunts and takes his woolly hat out of his pocket and jams it on his wispy white hair. He's a bit of a wonder, is Harold. Never looks tired, despite working through the night. I suspect he spends most of his time asleep in the den. I know I would. Wouldn't do for me, working those hours. I like my sleep.

'Anything to report?'

Harold raises an eyebrow at me. 'Is there ever?'

I put the kettle on and spoon some coffee into the *World's Best Dad* mug I decided on a whim to liberate from Lucia's house. 'Didn't you hear, Harold? There's been an incident. A heist. Crime of the century.' I wink at him as he wraps his scarf around his neck. 'Weaving shuttle gone missing from the Lever Wing. Surprised Daisy didn't mention it to you.'

'That she did,' says Harold, gathering up his carrier bag with his lunchbox in. 'Wrote three pages about it in the report as well.' He nods towards the desk. 'It's in the bin if you want to read it.'

I jiggle the jar of Coffee Mate to get the last scoops of it out. 'I'll get some more of this on my break. No, I'm good with the report. I had chapter and verse on it yesterday. You really should put paper in the recycle bin, though. We're all supposed to do our bit to save the world. They say we only have ten years or so to solve climate change.'

Harold sniffs. 'Reckon I'll be gone before that has to worry me.'

Cheery. To change the subject I say, 'So what do you reckon to her, then? Daisy?'

'Don't reckon I think much one way or the other,' Harold says with a shrug. 'Why?'

I don't really know why, to be honest. I plough on regardless. 'Doesn't it feel like she . . . I don't know, doesn't give much away? That we don't really know a lot about her?'

And then I realise that I don't really know very much about Harold, either. I don't know why he works such an awful shift at his age, don't know whether he lives on his own or if he's got family, don't even know where he lives. He gives me a curious stare. 'Why do you want to know more about her?'

'I don't!' I say. 'I'm just interested in people, I suppose.'

'That's what we used to call being a nosy parker,' says Harold with a shake of his head as he walks to the door. 'I'll tell you one thing about Daisy,' he adds. 'She always makes me a brew when I clock on. So see that you buy a new jar of Coffee Mate before you go home.'

It's funny, I think, as Harold leaves. All these people pass in and out of our lives, and we never really know them at all, other than the faces that they choose to show us. Then I take a big swig of coffee from my *World's Best Dad* mug.

Some people, though, you just know that what you're seeing is exactly what you're getting. Take Janice on reception. I've only passed by on my way to do a wander around the halls and I've already learned that her sister's husband is going in for his prostate seeing to, her cat has worms, she's got tickets to see *Bambi On Ice*, and at lunchtime she has to take a six-pack of knickers back to Debenhams because there's absolutely no way they're a size twelve like it says on the packet.

'I mean to say, Nate,' she says, dropping her voice to a

confidential whisper so I have to lean in to hear, 'they make my backside look like two footballs in a string bag.'

Janice does that funny little high-pitched laugh of hers, and while I'm leaning over the reception desk she takes the opportunity to unexpectedly squeeze my upper arm.

'Blimey,' she says. 'Do you work out?'

'No,' I say, straightening up and fiddling with my tie, a little flustered. 'I work here.'

Janice laughs again, so hard that she has to take her glasses off and wipe her eyes. 'You are funny, Nate,' she says. 'And I'll tell you what else you are. Naughty.'

I blink at her uncomfortably. 'Am I?'

'Yes you are,' she says, replacing her glasses. 'Didn't I tell you to tell Daisy about the staff do?'

'Oh, yeah,' I say, screwing up my face. 'Clean forgot. Sorry. I'll tell her later.'

'It's fine, I've already done it.' She drops her voice again, forcing me to lean over the desk to hear her. 'Don't you think she's a bit . . . odd?'

'Daisy?' I say, stalling for time so I can work out how to have this conversation.

'Yes, Daisy,' says Janice, rolling her eyes and tapping me reproachfully on my forearm. 'Don't you think she's a bit . . .' Janice stops making sounds altogether now, just forming the words with her lips. It takes me a moment to work out what she's mouthing at me. *A bit soft in the head.*

'Janice!' I say. 'That's a terrible thing to say! Daisy's lovely!'

Janice looks disgruntled. 'All right, Mr Muscle. Don't get your knickers in a twist.' She suddenly grins. 'Not like me with them ones I got from Debenhams. Size twelve my arse.' Then she erupts into a gale of trilling laughter again. Janice is divorced, and I briefly wonder if that laugh of hers was partly to blame.

Fortunately, I'm saved from further conversation by the entrance of a middle-aged couple pushing a buggy, who want to show their little boy the dinosaur.

'Ah, you want to see our Barry!' I boom, leading them to the lift. 'Keep your hands in your pockets though, young man. He hasn't bitten anyone for a while, but you never can tell . . .'

As I jab the button to call the lift and wink at the wide-eyed toddler, I silently curse myself for over-egging the pudding with Janice. Why did I have to go and tell her that Daisy is *lovely*? Where did that come from? I don't even know Daisy. Not really. Not at all, in fact.

After I've given all my spiel about the Baryonyx I leave the couple and their boy looking at the dinosaur skeleton and take a stroll through the other halls. The museum is filling up nicely. It does get a decent number of visitors, I have to admit. I think it's the fact that we're so . . . what's the word? Eclectic. You'd think that a museum of social history would be a bit dry, especially if you were a kid. Especially if you were my kid, I think, still a bit stung by what Ben said earlier, about wishing I had a more exciting job. But the fact is, all history is social history, really. History is just the stories we tell ourselves about what happened to make us what we are. Sometimes the stories are true, sometimes they're not.

I direct two old ladies to the toilets, and join the back of a small group of Japanese tourists being shown around the Malone Room by one of Dorothy's guides. Then I head into the Lever Wing, and straighten one of the trade-union banners that's become curled round at the bottom.

It's then that I notice the cabinet near the back. The one with the weaving shuttle that Daisy is convinced has been stolen. Except it hasn't. It's back, right where it belongs, on its shelf. It must have just been taken for cleaning or restoration, just like I said.

Daisy will be so pleased when I tell her.

I I

Daisy

I'm not quite sure what Nate expects of me when he ushers me up to the Lever Wing before I've even taken my coat off and stands beside the glass cabinet with his arms out like he's showing off the prizes on a telly game show, and says, 'Ta-daa!' Maybe he thinks I'm going to do a cartwheel or something.

'So it wasn't stolen after all,' he says. 'It really must have just been off to be cleaned or something.'

I peer into the cabinet. The shuttle doesn't particularly look like it's been restored, or refurbished, or that there's anything at all happened to it other than it's been taken out of the cabinet and then replaced.

'Fine,' I say. 'Can I go and take my coat off now?'

'I thought you'd be chuffed,' says Nate. His face falls like he's a little boy who's done a drawing he thought was really good but his mum has said it's not going on the fridge door.

'You should have just saved it for the handover,' I say. I really don't like things being done all out of order and haphazardly like this. There's a time and a place to do everything and bundling someone off up the stairs to show them a weaving shuttle when they've not even got through the door properly isn't it.

I realise I'm probably being a bit grumpy, considering, but it's not just Nate rushing me around. It's those boys at the bus stop. They've been at it again.

I don't notice them at first because to get to the bus stop I have to walk along the parade where the shops are, and because I'm a little bit early today I stop to watch some work going on at the takeaway. There are two men on ladders taking down the red, white and blue sign that said *Derek's Dominoes* and replacing it with a green and white one that says *Big Macs*. The 'M' in 'Macs' is two yellow arches.

A thin, wiry man is overseeing the operation and talking to a short lady with a brightly coloured turban, leaning on a tartan shopping trolley.

'So, they got you then, Derek,' says the woman, with a deep, rumbling laugh. I have never been in Derek's because I don't like the things they serve: pizzas and fried chicken. I heard this story about a takeaway once where someone bought some fried chicken and it turned out to be a rat. Or maybe it was that they were eating the chicken and their teeth crunched on something and when they took it out of their mouth it was a wedding ring. And the chicken was actually someone's hand. Or maybe that was in a book I read. Now I come to think of it, yes, I think that was a story. It was the rat that was the true thing, that's definite.

'No, they have most certainly not!' says Derek, who I assume is the Derek of Derek's Dominoes, as was. 'I am merely pre-empting the game and changing the name of my very own accord.'

'To Big Macs,' says the woman, shaking her head. 'Out of the frying pan, into the fire.'

'As I told you last time you graced my establishment with your presence, dear Marina, Mac was my grandfather's name—'

He is interrupted by a dirty white van pulling up at the kerb. A young man jumps out, opens the back, and drags out a big cardboard box. Some money changes hands between Derek and the driver and the van zooms off.

'What's this?' says Marina as Derek opens the box with the edge of a key.

'Well, you know my cast-iron defence for calling my shop Derek's Dominoes was because I sold dominoes?' says Derek, delving into the box. He pulls out a beige raincoat, holding it up triumphantly. 'The food is just a side hustle. Behold my new line! Only in sizes of XXL or above! My latest business venture is selling *big macs*, do you see?'

'You're an idiot,' says Marina, grasping the handle of her shopping trolley and walking away.

I glance at my watch and hurry to the bus stop a few yards away, only then noticing the gang of boys leaning on the concrete bollards nearby. I try my best to commit their descriptions to memory, just in case. There are five of them. The two oldest I would say are about fifteen. One is white with short, shaved hair, wearing a blue anorak and grey jogging bottoms. The other is Afro-Caribbean, and wears a thick gold chain hanging over his T-shirt, beneath a black coat. There is an overweight white boy, and a skinny Asian kid, both a little younger. The last one is a small, slight, Afro-Caribbean boy, a good couple of years younger again.

I have to stand with my back to them, which I don't like. Even above the afternoon sounds, the cars on the damp road, people getting in the last of the afternoon shopping, I can hear them talking in low, guttural voices.

'Do it.'

'I don't want to.'

'You wanna be in the gang, blood?'

'I did it last time.'

'Do it again.'

My every muscle feels tense and tight, and my fists are clenching and unclenching, the hairs on the back of my neck standing up. It's as if I can almost feel the approach of one of the boys, sense every step he's taking towards me. I force myself to stare straight ahead at the dark road, waiting until the very last second before whirling around and shouting, 'Ha!'

It's the small one, the black one, and he jumps as I shout, his eyes wide. He's only tiny and young and I almost feel sorry for him, until I see what he's got in his hand. A small blue plastic bag, tied in a bow at the handles, heavy with dog poo. He – or one of his mates – has obviously got it out of the bin fixed to the lamp post. He stands frozen for a moment, staring at me. I shudder to think what he was going to do with it. Then my hand darts out and grabs his wrist, twisting it until he shouts, 'Ow!' and drops the bag.

I don't say anything, just stare into his eyes. He's frightened. I'm furious. I don't say anything to him, but try to drive the message home to him with my eyes. *You don't want to mess with me, little boy. Do you even know why you call me Crazy Daisy? Do you even know what I did? When I was younger than you? Do you want me to tell you? Then you can run home crying to your mummy?*

We stand like that for what seems an age, me gripping his wrist, until I hear the swish of the bus's tyres on the road and I let him go, turning away from him. A chorus of 'Crazy Daisy!' starts up as I climb on to the bus, and I only realise I've been holding my breath when the doors sigh shut behind me.

Nate follows me to the security office where I hang up my coat and survey the desk. There's a coffee-stained cup on it that says *World's Best Dad*. He picks it up apologetically and says, 'I was just going to go and wash that. Oh, and I got some new Coffee Mate.'

'Did you take the money from the kitty tin?' I say.

'It's fine. It was on offer.'

'You should take the money from the kitty tin,' I say, reaching for it on the shelf. 'That's why we have a kitty.'

It's actually an old coffee jar, not a tin. I think it was Nate who started calling it the kitty tin. He always has to come up with a name for something rather than calling it what it is. I start to unscrew the lid but my hands are shaking and I don't know why. Actually, I do know why. I'm still all tense and angry from that encounter at the bus stop. I can see Nate frowning at me as I struggle to open the jar.

'Daisy, it really doesn't matter. It was only a pound.'

'Yes it does!' I shout. 'It matters! Things have to be done properly!'

Then it's like I'm two people, an invisible copy of me but then also me, and the invisible version is looking at the real me, appalled, as I start to sniffle and cry.

'Daisy,' says Nate softly, taking the jar from me and putting it down on the desk. What is wrong with me? I never cry. Especially not in front of strangers. 'Are you all right?'

Of course I'm not all right. People who are all right don't start crying for no reason. But I'm not about to tell Nate that. And then, the invisible me looking on aghast, that's exactly what I do. I start to tell him everything about the boys at the bus stop. It all comes spilling out. Nate unwinds a length of paper from the kitchen roll on the shelf and hands it to me, and I blow my nose into it noisily and wipe my eyes.

I look at him, and at the mug on the desk. 'You're a dad,' I say. 'Why are children so horrible?'

He shakes his head. 'I don't know.'

'I mean, what makes them want to do things like that? What makes them want to hurt people?'

He shakes his head again. 'It's hard to say. You don't know what their home lives are like, you don't know what troubles they've been through. For some kids, being in a gang is more like family than they ever get at home.'

I blow my nose again. 'It sounds like you're making excuses for them.'

'I'm not, I'm really not. It's horrible what you've been through, Daisy. I'm really sorry this has happened.'

Nate puts his hand out and places it on my forearm. I stare at it for a long moment. I'm not used to people touching me. He sees me looking and removes his hand, murmuring an apology. Even under my white shirt, my arm feels like it's burning from where his hand was.

'I don't think you can blame upbringing and parents for everything,' I say. 'Some children who have really happy childhoods do bad things.'

Nate nods. 'Ah, the old nature versus nurture argument. Do you think kids can be born bad, then?'

'I think children can do really bad things for no reason,' I say quietly. There's a long pause. I fold up the paper towel and drop it into the bin. Where Harold has dumped the report I left him from last night.

'Maybe you could use another bus stop,' suggests Nate brightly.

I frown at him. 'Why should I?'

He pulls a face. 'So the kids don't bother you.'

'But why should I change what I do because they're behaving badly? Shouldn't they change their behaviour and let me carry on as normal? I'm not the one doing anything wrong.'

'Well, no,' agrees Nate. 'Yeah, actually, you're right.' He pauses. 'I mean, so far, it's been Post-it notes and dog poo but . . . Daisy, are you worried? That they'll go further? Do something more serious? Do you think it's maybe something you should report to the police?'

It's then I realise that Nate and I are talking at complete cross-purposes. He has completely misconstrued the real reason that I am upset. I feel stupid for showing this display of emotion in front of him. Now he just thinks I'm weak and foolish. I turn to my bag. 'I brought that book in for you. The Murakami.'

He takes it off me and flips to the back, then opens up the front cover. There's a pause as he reads my bookplate. I put bookplates in all my books. They're just printed pieces of paper, really, that I had photocopied at the corner shop. They say *This Book is the Property of Daisy Dukes* and then there are two columns like what you'd find in a library book. I'm very particular about my books and who I lend them to. That's why it says at the bottom of the bookplate *Please return this book in the condition it was lent to you or you will be expected to provide a replacement.* I have written today's date in the first column and a second date in the second column.

'I've given you a week with it,' I say, pointing at the dates. 'That should be long enough. It's a pretty short book.'

Nate looks a little nonplussed. 'Right,' he says, one eyebrow raised.

He's been kind to me, if a little misguided, so I say, 'If you need it for longer, just let me know. I'll put a different return date on it.'

Nate smiles, but it's one of those odd, forced smiles that people do. He puts the book in his coat pocket. I look at my watch and say, 'Time for you to go.'

Nate nods and puts on his coat. I reach for the kitty tin and as my hands aren't shaking any more I easily take off the lid and pluck out a pound coin.

'You're sure it was a pound?'

'Sure,' says Nate, putting it into his trouser pocket. He pauses, then says, 'Daisy, I am worried about you. After what you said. You will be careful, right? And if there's any more trouble with those boys . . . look, I'd hate for anything to happen to you.'

'Why?' I say.

He frowns. 'Why what?'

'Why would you hate for anything to happen to me?'

Nate looks perplexed. 'Because . . . because . . . well, it's just what you say, isn't it? And it's true.'

I consider this for a moment. 'OK.'

Then it's time for me to let everyone out and close up the museum. I see them all out, Nate and Janice and Seema and Dorothy and Mr Meyer and the guides and I'm finally all alone. Just me and my thoughts.

I think about that gang, and the look on that boy's face when I grabbed his wrist.

I think about the scars on Rosie's arm.

Nate had it all wrong.

I wasn't upset because I was worried what those boys might do to me.

I was upset because I was worried what I might to do *them*.

12

Daisy

I do a patrol, pausing in the Lever Wing to inspect the weaving shuttle. I unlock the cabinet and take it out, though no one is really supposed to touch the exhibits without wearing white gloves. I turn the shuttle over and look at it this way and that. It looks exactly like it did before. I can't see any reason why it would have been removed and then replaced. I put it back and lock the cabinet. It's a mystery, I suppose, but not a very exciting one.

After the patrol I review the CCTV footage from Nate and Harold's shifts. There's nothing much to report, especially on Harold's watch. There he is again in the Lever Wing, shuffling across the floor, checking his reflection in the cabinet. I can't see any images of anyone returning the shuttle, whether officially or not. Then again, it's not a very good system. The footage is always grainy and out of focus. On those crime telly shows they always say things like, 'Get this enhanced!' and it happens almost immediately. No chance of that with this creaky old system.

The only interesting thing occurs when I click on the file for the recordings from the Malone Room. It's just a constant snowstorm of static. Frowning, I go there and stare up at the camera mounted in the corner of the room. There's a tiny red light flashing on top of it. I check the cameras in the other rooms; they all have a light as well, but those are solid green.

Back in the Malone Room, I trace with my fingers the cable that runs down the wall from the camera, which disappears into the skirting board. Right at the bottom, the lead has been pulled roughly out of the wall, exposing the bare wires. That's a hazard, that. I go to find some electrical tape in the den . . . I mean, the security office, and seal it up. Some kid must have done it, presumably during Nate's shift. Either that, or we have a vermin problem. I go back to the security office and send Seema an email about the camera.

When I get home after the shift Rosie is still up, sitting in the kitchen, drinking a big glass of wine, scrolling through her phone.

'How's Mother been?' I say.

'All right, actually,' says Rosie. 'Good, even. Quite bright.' She taps a cigarette out of her packet.

The news cheers me, after the day I've had. I say, 'You should get off to bed. Work in the morning.'

'It *is* the morning. And thank Crunchie it's Friday.' She looks up from her phone. 'I've got a date on Saturday.'

'Anyone I know?' I say as I put the kettle on and plop a teabag into a cup.

She waves the phone at me. 'No. Off here. Finally found someone who doesn't appear to be a one hundred per cent bullshitter.'

Rose goes to the back door to smoke her cigarette and hands me the phone. 'What do you think?'

His name is Ian and he is thirty-five years old. He is a plumber and he lives in Didsbury. He is divorced, no kids, and supports Manchester United. He likes *Peaky Blinders*, Indian food, Formula 1 and Peter Kay. He is looking for friendship and possibly more, and enjoys nights out at the pub and cosy nights in with Netflix. He has a bald head and a beard in his photograph, which looks like it has been taken on a Spanish beach.

'I think you could do better than that,' I say, giving Rosie back her phone.

She barks a laugh. 'How can you possibly know that based on what you've just read? He might be really nice.'

I squeeze out my teabag and drop it into the pedal bin. '*Might* be. That's the thing. You won't really know that until you meet him. And by that point it's too late.'

'Oh, Daisy,' she says, but not unkindly. 'You don't make some sort of commitment to marry them by agreeing to meet them. If you don't get on, you just don't see them again. It's called taking a chance on something. You should try it yourself.' She takes a long drag of her cigarette and blows the smoke out into the cold night air. 'When's the last time you went out with a man?'

'Not since Darren,' I say quietly.

Rosie coughs and bangs her chest with her fist. 'Jesus, Daisy, that was years ago! Don't you ever want to . . . you know. Just be with someone?'

I think about the heat from Nate's touch when he laid his hand on my arm in the security office. It has been a long time since I've even just spoken to anyone who wasn't Mother or Rosie or the brief interactions I have at the museum.

'Oh, when would I find the time? I'm at work all night and with Mother all day.'

'There's always the weekend,' says Rosie, stubbing out her cigarette. 'Give me your phone.'

'Why?'

'I'm going to download this app to it.'

'I don't want to, Rosie.'

She holds out her hand. 'Give.'

It takes her a minute to instal the app, and then she starts to input my details. She looks at me critically, then says, 'Five foot four? Five five?'

'Five foot four and a half.'

Rosie takes the end of my hair in her fingers. 'Auburn.'

'Mousy brown.'

'Hobbies?'

'I don't have any.'

'You like to read.'

I frown. 'That's not a hobby. That's just something I *have* to do. Like breathing, or eating.'

Rosie looks at me like I'm from another planet. 'I'll put gym, socialising, cinema, pub.'

I don't do any of those things.

'Stand back,' she says, fixing me in the lens of the phone's camera. 'Hmm. Not your best look, to be honest. A bit . . . harsh.' She changes her mind about taking a fresh picture and scrolls through the camera roll on my phone. She looks up at me. 'Why are there so many photos of birds?'

I shrug. 'I like birds.'

Eventually she says, 'This'll do. It's a bit old but you haven't changed much. You're actually wearing make-up on this one. And you're smiling.'

'Let me see,' I say, holding my hand out for the phone. It is an old one, from one summer that feels like a thousand years ago. It was taken in Castlefield, in the amphitheatre. By Darren. The day he broke my heart.

'Smile,' says Darren.

'I am smiling,' I say through gritted teeth.

'Smile more.' He stands stock-still for a second, then hands my phone back to me.

'Why did you take it on my phone and not yours?' I say as I slide it back into my handbag.

'Because you look pretty. And happy. And I want you to remember what that feels like.'

I can put myself back in the memory as easily as I can conjure up a scene from one of my favourite books. The sky is blue, without a cloud in it, and the sun is beating down, blanketing the pale stones of Castlefield in a treacly July heat. The bars around the bowl are busy, and someone drops a tray of drinks with a clatter and crash and a volley of cheers goes up. Someone shouts, 'Sack the juggler!' There's the merest of warm breezes, and buoyed upon it is the sound of a brass band.

I think what Darren has said is a funny thing to say. Not, as Mother would say, funny ha ha, but funny peculiar. I tell him so. He looks at me through his glasses, and wipes his hands on his *League of Gentlemen* T-shirt.

'I'm sorry,' is all he says.

'What for?'

'Because I can't stop thinking about what you told me. About what happened.'

'You don't need to feel sorry for me,' I say. My mouth is dry. I glance over at one of the bars. I don't really drink much but I want more than anything for Darren to ask me if I want a cold beer.

'That's not what I mean when I say I'm sorry,' he says. He is staring down at his belly pushing the T-shirt out, as though it's the first time he's noticed it. I notice it all the time, but I don't mind it. It's just who he is. He isn't what you'd call handsome. He's not very funny, or witty. He doesn't dress stylishly. He can be very awkward with other people. He values things, books and DVDs and comics and vinyl records. He understands them. Better than he understands people. We go to quiet pubs where we talk to each other, mainly about the things he likes. Sometimes we sit in silence. We have, sporadically, what I imagine is unremarkable sex, though I haven't got very much to compare it to. He does not know that I found on his laptop, in the bedroom at his parents' house which he fills with things he loves, some pornographic photographs in a hidden file, downloaded from the internet, of women dressed in superhero costumes. I never said anything because while Darren is all those things that I have said he is, I am not and never will be Wonder Woman or Catwoman or Power Girl, who seems to be his particular favourite. We are lucky to have found each other at the factory where we work on zero-hours contracts, locating and finding items bought by people on an online shopping site and despatching them within the requisite 24-hour delivery period. We spend our days fulfilling other people's wishes, and our nights comfortably tolerating those of each other.

Until now.

'Then what are you sorry for, Darren?'

'I can't do this any more,' he says, still staring at his belly, making it sound like a line from a film, which it probably is. 'Not after what you told me.'

I don't say anything and finally he looks up at me. 'You make me feel scared, Daisy.'

'Yes, that picture's fine,' I say, giving my phone to Rosie so she can upload the photograph. It's not like I'll ever use the stupid app anyway. But I learned a long time ago that it's easier to just go along with my sister rather than kick up a fuss. You never win an argument with Rosie Dukes.

'All done,' she says a moment later. 'Now you just have to wait for all the hunks to message you, and if you're impatient you can contact them, but I wouldn't recommend it. You don't want to look desperate.'

She puts the emphasis on look, as though she means to say, you don't want to *look* desperate, even if you *are*.

'Thank you,' I say, though I'm just being polite. She drains her glass of wine and yawns. I say, 'It's recycling day tomorrow. Did you put the bin out?'

'I forgot,' she says, stifling another yawn. 'I'll do it now.'

'It's fine, I'll do it. You get to bed.'

She nods and gives me a weary smile. 'Like the old song says, things can only get better, eh? Chin up. And have a bit of fun, Daisy. You deserve it.'

I wheel the heavy, clanking bin to the bottom of the yard and open the gate, dragging it along the dirt track of the back alley to the dark side street, where all the other bins are clustered haphazardly under the orange glow of a streetlight. It would be much easier for the bin men if people put them in more ordered ranks. I ponder doing it myself, but I'm tired as well. Instead I open our bin to take a look to see why it's so heavy. It's perhaps three-quarters full, mainly with empty wine bottles. There are two or three whisky bottles in there as well.

There's only Rosie drinks in the house. The bin men come for the recycling every two weeks. I do some maths, based on a rough estimate of the number of empty bottles in the bin. That's a lot of alcohol consumption. I take my phone out of my pocket and Google how many units of alcohol are in a bottle of wine, and how many units it is safe for a woman to drink in a week.

I do the sums in my head. It isn't pretty. I knew Rosie liked a drink, but not this much. And that doesn't even take into account the bottles of whisky.

Just one more thing to worry about, I suppose. And yet Rosie always seems so . . . okay. So in control of her life. So confident in herself. But then, appearances can be deceiving.

While my phone's in my hand, I take another look at the photograph Rosie uploaded to the dating app. I'm happy, smiling, and I do look pretty in my summer dress as the sun shines down. And yet, five minutes after it was taken I was standing alone, tears streaming down my face, while a brass band played, oblivious to my pain. We never know as much as we think we do, especially about other people.

Or how they behave and react. Darren was scared of me and fled. Because he could. Maybe Rosie's scared of me as well. And maybe because she can't flee, she does something else to push me away. Drinks.

After what happened, I shouldn't really blame her for that.

13

Nate

'It's great to meet you at last, Nate. I've heard so much about you.' He squeezes my hand harder than is strictly necessary. He's as tall as me, but broader, his chest and shoulders wide beneath the purple shirt and black suit. His skin is shining, his beard is immaculately trimmed. He's a pound-shop Idris Elba if ever I saw one.

To be honest, I'm not too sure I'm very enamoured with John.

'Lucia tells me you're a security guard at a museum. Do the exhibits come alive at night, like that movie? Ha ha.'

In fact, I don't think I like John at all.

'Me? Property. Making an absolute killing at the moment. Especially places like Moss Side. No, don't laugh. Couple of years ago they sold off all the social housing to private land-lords and now they're getting rid, so we're buying it up and gentrifying the place.'

Actually, I am pretty sure I actively dislike John.

'Yeah, that's my Audi out front. Full electric. Not much change from eighty-five K, between you and me, ha ha.'

Scratch that. I positively loathe John.

'Bee-Z! My man! Brought you a present. Detective Pikachu plush. Limited edition. They put one aside for me at Geekchester.

Yeah, I know the guy who owns the shop. They only got two of these in.'

I am seriously considering whether I can kidnap John, tie him up and drop him down a very deep well somewhere far away.

Ben is hugging the soft toy like it's the best thing he has ever been given in his entire life. Lucia emerges into the living room, in a slinky blue dress, fastening her earrings.

'You going out?' I say, immediately feeling stupid. She's not dressed like that, with her hair done, with that red lipstick on, to sit in front of the telly on a Friday night. Or maybe she is. Maybe that's how her and John roll.

'No shift tomorrow, and as you're having Ben for the weekend, thought I'd seize my chance.' She grins. There's something odd and unfamiliar about her manner. It takes me a while to put my finger on it. She's *happy*, I realise.

'Mate of mine just opened a new Thai-Caribbean fusion restaurant in the Northern Quarter,' says John. Well, that sounds awful. 'It's his opening night. Invited guests only. Some of Manchester's very big hitters will be there.'

'What are we doing for tea, Dad?' says Ben, putting the Pikachu on top of the little wheeled suitcase he always brings to mine. In a carrier bag beside it are his Xbox and a spaghetti of tangled cables.

'I thought maybe Derek's Dominoes,' I say. 'Family Box? Your favourite?'

John guffaws. 'Sounds tasty! Hey, Nate, speaking of big hitters, Lucia tells me your old man was the Black Bomber.' He shadow boxes with Ben, who laughs. 'Remember my dad watching him fight a couple of times. Had a mean right hook, your pops.'

'Yes, he certainly did,' I say, standing up. 'You ready, Ben?'

Ben pulls a face. 'Do we have to walk, Dad? It's miles.'

'It's one mile, if that. The fresh air'll do you good.'

'But I've got my case and my Xbox.'

'I'll carry that. Come on.'

John is waving his hands. 'Whoa, whoa, you guys don't need to walk. I'll run you down in the motor. Take me five minutes.'

'Yay!' shouts Ben.

'No!' I say. 'We're walking.'

Lucia is giving me one of her looks again, this time the one that says I'm fighting a losing battle and should know when to give up. That's what she always said to me when we were married. 'Don't be like your dad. Don't keep going when you're getting battered. Just go down and have done with it.'

'Fine,' I say with a sigh. Ben cheers. John grins and mimes holding a steering wheel. He makes a *vrrrm-vrrrm* sound and laughs. 'To The Beast!'

I groan inwardly. People who give their cars names are only trumped in the Worst People in the World stakes by those who give their cars names like The Beast.

At the front door, Lucia gives Ben a kiss and tells him to be good for Dad, then he follows John to the car parked outside to put his case and his Xbox in the boot.

'He seems . . . nice,' I lie.

Lucia raises an eyebrow. 'I know you don't mean that. But that doesn't really matter. What matters is that he makes me happy.'

I look at Ben climbing into the car and John turning on the engine, which purrs into life with barely a hum. 'And Ben?' I say. 'Does John make him happy, too?'

'That doesn't matter either, really. It's nice that they get on, it makes things easier. But that's not why I'm seeing John. I'm doing that for me. I'm not looking for a new dad for Ben. He's already got one. A good one, who he loves.'

I can feel tears prickling my eyes and my mouth wobbling. It's a combination of being told that Ben does love me, when I had begun to wonder, and of finally accepting that me and Lucia are definitely not a thing any more, that she's properly moved on.

As if reading my mind, she says softly, 'You should try, you know. To meet someone. If that's what you want. You're a lovely, handsome man, Nate. It just wasn't meant to be, for us. Not forever.'

'Oh, where would I meet anyone?' I say airily, blinking away my tears.

She shrugs. 'Where does anyone meet anyone, these days? Online. At the pub. Doing hobbies. At work.'

'Hmmm,' I say, not convinced. There's a sharp peep of a horn.

'You should get off. See you Sunday,' says Lucia. She gives me a quick kiss on my cheek and I hurry down the path to where John and Ben are waiting in the sleek, black Audi.

The ride is every bit as luxurious as I expected, and thankfully it does only take a couple of minutes to get to my house, so I don't have to make much small-talk with John. As he pops open the boot and tells Ben to go and get his things, though, he seizes the opportunity for a bit of a man-to-man.

'Nate, I just wanted to say . . . I'm not trying to take your place, you know. With Ben.'

'Right,' I say, thinking, but you've already taken my place with Lucia. And then I think that's stupid, because we've been divorced for years.

Ben appears at the passenger side and taps the window. John sticks his hand out and I cautiously take it, bracing myself against his solid handshake.

'Later, Nate, Bee-Z,' says John, and we watch him burn away from the kerb, Ben shaking his head in admiration.

'That is a cool car,' he says. 'You should get one, Dad.'

'Yeah, maybe I will,' I say, picking up his bag. Not much change from eighty-five thousand. 'Let's get these inside then I'll phone through to Derek's for some chicken.'

What got me through my teen years was the knowledge that one day my father would be an old, shrunken man whose muscles had atrophied and whose fists had lost their power, and eventually I would not fear him but pity him, and I'd somehow come to terms with what an utter bastard he had been to me and Mum.

And then he robbed me of that when I was eighteen, by quietly nursing a brain aneurysm for years that spectacularly burst during what proved to be his final bout with his family.

He should have retired from boxing years before, but as the nineties entered their final leg he became increasingly desperate to cling on to the glory years, and he began to spend more and more Saturday nights fighting in fleapit venues, facing off against equally washed-up old fighters or helping younger boxers get up the ladder by taking a solid beating from them.

More often than not he'd have drunk away whatever few quid he'd got for the bouts before he got home, and brimming over with rum and self-loathing he'd inevitably start to take it out on Mum.

I'd been working in a builder's merchants since I'd left school, but I hadn't left home, even though I had friends who wanted me to share a house in Chorlton and embrace Manchester's nightlife and music scene. I just felt like I couldn't leave Mum alone with him, not as his behaviour became more and more erratic. Neither of them were spring chickens any more, but while Terry Garvey was content to take blow after blow to the head and stomach every weekend, I genuinely worried that Mum couldn't take much more of his violence. I worried that he would kill her.

My job was low-paid and involved humping bags of cement and sand and planks of wood around all day and in all weathers in the open yard behind the merchants. One unexpected side effect was that my body, always tall and stringy, began to fill out and harden up, to the point that even the Black Bomber sometimes quailed and backed down when I inserted myself between him and Mum on those Saturday night rows. The tide was turning and I could see light at the end of the tunnel, a time not too far in the future when the fight would go out of Dad once and for all.

It happened more suddenly, and finally, than I was expecting, though. He'd taken one hell of a beating that particular Saturday night, his left eye swollen, his lip fat, a bruise blossoming on his cheek. I can't remember what started the argument – I never could, really, by this point – but he was standing in the lounge, in front of the telly, ranting and spitting and waving his arms while Mum cowered in the chair and I faced off against him, wondering if this time, this time, I'd be forced to actually hit him, and give him a taste of his own bad medicine.

And then he just stopped shouting, stopped talking, and his eyes rolled back into his head, and all eighteen stone of him crashed backwards into the telly, and everything went quiet.

The coroner recorded a verdict of death by natural causes. The aneurysm had been biding its time in his brain for years, more than likely, the result of countless blows to the head. Had he been to the doctors, and had an MRI scan, it could perhaps have been caught and treated. Had he been a better fighter and not let himself get hit in the head so much, he might have never got ill at all.

His funeral was packed, a large photograph of him in his prime, head down, gloves up, on an easel at the front of the church, near his coffin. The pews were stuffed with big men filling out cheap suits, all cauliflower ears and broken noses. A succession of promoters and fighters took to the microphone to give little eulogies about The Black Bomber. My mum cried throughout the service and afterwards, at the Labour club where we held the wake, she said to me, 'Don't you see, Nathaniel? It was never his fault. It was the brain damage. That's what made him treat us badly. I knew it couldn't be him. I knew it had to be something.'

I was so disgusted I left the wake, to stop myself saying something once my tongue got loosened by drink. For Mum's sake I wouldn't speak ill of the dead, but there was no way that Dad was going to get such an easy pass for all the things he'd done to us.

Mum died two years later, after suffering a massive stroke. In the hospital, all small and thin and connected with wires and tubes to machines and drips, she held my wrist in a feeble grip and whispered, 'He was a good husband to me. He was a good dad to you.'

I had just met Lucia and knew that at some point in the very near future I was going to ask her to marry me. And all I was absolutely certain of in my life was that if she said yes, I would never be the sort of husband that Terry Garvey was to my mum, and if we had children, I would never, ever, in a million years, be the sort of father he was to me.

'Nathaniel!' bellows Derek as I go in to collect the Family Box which, for once, I'll share with my son, as the name of it suggests, rather than scoffing all by myself.

'You've changed the name, Derek.'

'Welcome to Big Macs!' he guffaws. He points to the far

side of the shop, at a rail of beige raincoats. 'There is my core business! Probably have one in your size!'

'The chicken will be fine.'

'So long as you realise the food is just a sideline,' says Derek, tapping the side of his nose and winking theatrically. 'So, you have your boy this weekend? What plans do you have?'

'Two tickets for City versus Villa,' I say.

'Wonderful! Some bonding for the boys!'

'Exactly!' I say, collecting the food. 'That's what I thought. I mean, Ben wants to play some video game thing, but . . .'

'Pshaw!' says Derek. 'He can play a video game any time. Now football, on the other hand, that is the beautiful game!'

That settles it, I think as I head back home with the feast. It's like Ben himself said to me. He needs boundaries. He needs to be told what's best for him. We are going to the football. We are going to have fun. Together. My mind is made up, and I'm not having any arguments.

14

Daisy

When I arrive at the museum Nate already has his coat on and is heading out of the door. 'Taking an early dart,' he explains. 'Got to pick my lad up.'

'But what about the handover?' I say.

'Nothing to report,' he says hurriedly, 'but they're looking at the cable in the Malone Room.'

Well, at least Seema acted quickly on my email after I discovered the vandalism on the CCTV wire. I hurry up there after dropping off my coat in the security office, to find two men in overalls and a tall stepladder, and a hole in the ceiling above the security camera. Seema is there too, jabbing at an iPad cradled in the crook of her arm.

'What happened?' I say. 'Was it deliberate?'

Seema scowls at me and one of the men rubs the back of his neck and says, 'It does look like someone did pull that cable out of the wall,' he says. 'To be honest, it shouldn't have been exposed like that anyway. Should have been behind the plaster. If some kiddie did it, they could have got a nasty shock.'

Seema types rapidly on her iPad screen, her fingernails tapping on the glass.

'But that's just the tip of the iceberg,' says the man. 'In fact, whoever pulled it out probably did you a favour. The entire wiring for the system is completely shot. A lot of it's corroded. It's a fire hazard. We're going to have to rip the whole lot out and start again with it.'

'Yes,' says Seema icily. 'Someone really did us a favour. How much is that going to cost?'

The man sucks air in through his teeth and glances at his mate. 'We'll send you an estimate. Probably not going to be pretty, mind. And the system's going to have to stay offline until it's all replaced.'

'What?' I say. 'No CCTV?'

'Well, that's not a huge problem,' says Seema, glancing at me. 'We have round-the-clock security personnel Monday to Friday. It's the weekend that's the issue. We only have an external company doing occasional patrols.'

The man glances around the Malone Room. 'Well, it's not like you've got the Elgin Marbles in here, is it?'

'Elgin Marbles, good one,' pipes up the other man at last.

'Aren't we getting a new weekend security guard?' I say.

'Maybe,' murmurs Seema. 'We're just finalising the budget for the new financial year.'

The man starts to fold up the stepladders. 'We'll get back to the office and email you the estimate. Don't dilly-dally too long over it, though, if you want us to have a chance of starting it before Easter.'

They leave Seema and me standing in the Malone Room, her lost in whatever she's looking at on her iPad. She looks up and stares at me in a curious, narrow-eyed fashion that makes me wonder what's going on behind her gaze. 'How long have you worked here, Daisy?'

'About six months,' I say.

She nods and taps something on the screen. I say, 'Why?'

She gives me one of her thin, forced smiles. 'No reason. Right, better get on. Lots to think about.'

As her heels tap on the polished floor, I try to decide what to do. Do I go back downstairs and start the patrol from the ground floor, or carry on from here? I don't like having my routines disrupted like this. I dither for a moment and then decide I'll go back and start from the beginning, when something catches my eye in one of the long glass cabinets that form a square in the centre of the room. Or rather, it's the absence of something that catches my eye.

There's a display of items from Manchester during the Second World War years. Ration books and newspapers, some fragments of a bomb and photographs of some of the Manchester regiments that fought. The case nearest me is all about how the war affected children, and right in the middle of it is a space where there should be, according to the little label, a gas mask made for a child. It was supposed to look like Mickey Mouse, with two round black ears on the straps that go over the head, and an elongated, upturned nose. But with the glass eye goggles it always looked a bit grotesque and scary to me. And not a lot like Mickey Mouse. I'm not sure what would have given me more nightmares when I was small, the threat of a gas attack that never came, or that horrible mask hanging up on the back of my bedroom door.

The mask that is now gone.

'Not this again, Daisy.' Seema sighs. 'Haven't we already been through this with the weaving shuttle? The weaving shuttle that hadn't gone missing at all?'

'It did go missing, but it came back,' I say. 'You can come up to the Malone Room with me if you like. It's obvious where the gas mask was.'

'Maybe it's on loan. Or being cleaned up. Or we've lent it to a school for a project or something.' Seema continues to tap at her keyboard. 'Daisy, would you say that you're busy on your shift?'

'Extremely busy,' I say. 'What with the patrols and the handovers and the reports.' Why is she asking that? Is she suggesting I'm not doing my job properly with these things going missing? 'If the gas mask has gone out wouldn't it be recorded somewhere? Can I check your file again?'

At that moment Mr Meyer comes out of his office and smiles benignly at Seema, me and Dorothy, at her desk at the other end of the room. 'Hello,' he says, then looks at me, frowning slightly. 'Oh, are we talking to—'

'Daisy was just leaving, Mr Meyer,' says Seema quickly, pushing the blue file into my hands. 'You can go and check this in the security office at your leisure. I've got a meeting with Mr Meyer.'

He leans over Seema's shoulder and squints at the monitor. 'Is that the estimate for the CCTV rewiring? Oh dear. That is expensive. I think your long-term suggestion that—'

'Thank you, Daisy,' says Seema firmly with a tight smile. 'Mr Meyer, perhaps we can continue this in your office . . .?'

The Mykonos postcard has been moved again. Who is doing that? It seems someone is reading the book every single day, before I come on shift. Or moving the postcard deliberately, randomly, just to annoy me. Perhaps the same person who's stealing things from the museum. Maybe it's like a game to them, someone who thinks they're the Moriarty to my Sherlock Holmes.

I feel all out-of-sorts today. I think it's a combination of the boys at the bus stop – just a volley of 'Crazy Daisy' shouts this afternoon, no creeping up on me, thankfully – and the items going missing from the museum. And the strange way that Seema was behaving. And Mr Meyer. Like they have secrets.

Secrets never do you any good, Mother always said. They always come out eventually.

It's all adding up to making me feel . . . perturbed. Finding all those bottles in the recycling bin didn't help. As if I didn't have enough to concern me, now I have to worry that Rosie is drinking too much. While I'm still trying to be annoyed at her for sending off for that hospice brochure.

Because of everything, I can't really concentrate on the book. I feel like one of the characters in the Greek myths . . . one of the mortals, constantly at the whim of the capricious gods. It's as though there are higher powers at work here and I'm not in control of anything that's happening. I don't like that. I don't like feeling like I'm not in control. If I'm not in control, who would be? Who would put the bins out and bring them in again, who would organise the online shopping delivery? Who would do the handovers and the reports?

And yet, there are things happening all around me which I have no power over.

I close the book. I'm not going to be able to concentrate on it tonight. I'll take it back up to the Theodore room when I've finished my break. First I'll take the file back to Seema's office. No gas mask has been logged out for cleaning, lending, or anything. Just as I expected. Just like the shuttle.

I let myself into the office and return the file, and another folder catches my eye, just by Seema's keyboard. It says *RATIONALISATION* on it. I wonder what that means. I think it must be because I'm not feeling myself that I do what I do. I'd never normally look at something that wasn't any of my business. It's just not me. But as I flip open the folder on a whim, I discover that it's very much my business after all.

It's a single sheet of paper with a couple of typed paragraphs on it and a handwritten note from Mr Meyer, which says, *This all looks sound, Seema. It's a shame, but I think we're going to have to seriously consider it.*

The two paragraphs detail how the museum could save money over the next financial year by extending the terms of the contract of the external security firm that does the patrols at the weekends, to cover the rest of the week. And by 'letting go' the current full-time security team. Meaning, Nate, Harold and me. Furthermore, it says, there would be further significant cost savings as Daisy Dukes has been employed for less than a year and there would be no obligation to offer the standard redundancy package.

They want to get rid of me. They want to get rid of all of us.

I return the book to the Theodore room and do what I can only describe as a desultory patrol, barely taking anything in. I stop for a long while and stare at the empty space where the Mickey Mouse gas mask used to be. Then, which is quite unlike me, I just go back to the security office and think about things for a long while.

Letting go, the note said. Like the three of us are . . . ballast weighing down a ship, or bags of sand stopping a hot-air balloon from taking flight. Letting us go. Casting us adrift. And that's exactly what it would be like, for me at least. My entire life is structured around my shifts. What would I do if I lost this job? Everything at home is so finely balanced. We cannot afford to run the house without my wage. I would have to try to find a new job with exactly the same hours, and the same travelling time. What are the chances of that? How many jobs are there for me where I could work from five in the afternoon until one in the morning?

My mind is whirling. I'm not supposed to have seen the

memo, and I wish for all the world that I hadn't. But once a genie is out of the bottle, it's terribly hard to get it back in. I wonder when they were going to tell us about it? Before the start of the financial year? They'd want to get their ManMuSH Big Sleepover event out of the way, certainly. They've already told us we're working that.

This feels too big to keep to myself, but I know I can't really tell Rosie about it, or she'll be talking about seeing solicitors or union reps or something like that, and it'll all come out that Daisy Dukes is a little old sneak who looks at things she's not supposed to.

I realise that the person I really want to talk to about this is Nate. And I don't quite know why, other than the fact that he's as affected by all this as I am.

On the wall of the security office is a sheet of paper with everyone's home and mobile phone numbers on it in case of emergency. I look at it for a long moment and then find that I've taken out my phone and already pressed ten of the eleven digits before I cancel the call.

What am I thinking of? Nate told me that he had to go and pick up his son. Probably from some event or something. They are doubtless going out on some family occasion. Even if not, he won't want to be taking a call from me on Friday night. That's when people spend time together, when families have quality time. Normal families, that is.

Not like mine.

15

Daisy

Rosie always lets me lie in a bit on Saturday mornings, to catch up on my sleep, which is good of her. But this morning I'm awake early, listening to the birds outside, watching the sunlight coming in through the gap at the top of the blinds. I can hear Rosie get up and go in to see to Mother. I want to get up and take over, but force myself to lie there a bit longer. Rosie will only have a go at me, saying I'm interfering and she's quite capable of getting Mother a couple of slices of toast and a cup of tea.

I have a sensation of what I think they call impending doom. I feel vaguely anxious, and obviously a lot of that is from what I read at the museum, the rationalisation proposals that could see me out of a job. But it's also all mixed in with my worries about Mother, and all those empty wine bottles that Rosie had thrown in the wheelie bin. The things that keep going missing at the museum. And in and out of everything Nate seems to walk, which I find perplexing. I'm sure he'll be all right if he loses his job; it'll be easier for him to get a day job than it will be for me to get another night shift somewhere on the same money. I don't know why I'm worrying about him.

And into this mix my stupid brain keeps stirring memories of that day. When we were small. In the kitchen. With Rosie.

I push the thoughts away. I can hear Rosie in Mother's room. She must be getting her dressed. Their voices are slightly raised, but I can't quite make out what they're saying. Then Rosie goes downstairs and I hear the kettle boiling. The back door opens, and I hear the clank of empty bottles being thrown in the bin. Oh, Rosie.

I'm about to get up when my phone on the bedside cabinet makes a beep. I frown. Nobody ever messages me. The screen displays a notification that makes my eyes widen. I jump out of bed, find my dressing gown, and run downstairs to find Rosie.

'What do you think?' I say.

'It's more what you think,' says Rosie.

We both look at the screen of my phone on the kitchen table. His name is Alfie and he lives in Bury, but works in a warehouse in Salford. He is thirty-six, unmarried, enjoys reading and going for walks, and has a dog. Crucially, he works from four to midnight every day.

'He ticks a lot of boxes, I suppose,' I say, a little doubtfully.

Rosie laughs. 'That's the app's job, to tick the boxes. You're supposed to . . . I don't know. Use your instincts. Follow your heart.'

Algorithms are easier to understand than hearts. But I inspect his photograph again. He's not exactly Brad Pitt or George Clooney. But who is, apart from Brad Pitt and George Clooney? If I had to compare him to anyone, I'd say probably Benedict Cumberbatch. If Benedict Cumberbatch was shorter and chunkier and had thinning hair, and a slightly lazy left eye.

Rosie seems to be struggling to find anything hugely posi- tive to say about him – I mean, he's certainly not her type. But she gives me an encouraging smile. 'I think you should arrange to meet him. Just for a drink, or a coffee. I mean, what's the worst that could happen?'

I consider this. 'That he's a serial killer who kidnaps me and puts me in a pit in his cellar to fatten me up so he can wear my skin?'

She taps out a cigarette from her packet. 'I was more thinking that you don't really like him so you just don't meet him again.'

'It's your date tonight,' I say, putting the kettle on as Rosie goes to the door to smoke. 'Ian, thirty-five, likes *Peaky Blinders* and Formula 1. What are you doing?'

'Going to meet him in town at seven. At the Wetherspoons. I want you to ring me at half-past, just in case he's an absolute dick. Then I can say I've got an emergency at home and clear off.'

'We should have a codeword,' I say. 'Just in case he's a kidnapper. If you say it I'll know you're in trouble.'

'Good idea,' Rosie says with a nod, though she rolls her eyes. 'How about *life is not a fucking film, Daisy.*'

I'm making a note of it on a piece of paper before I realise she's being facetious. 'I'm only trying to help,' I mutter.

'Sorry,' says Rosie. 'I might nip into town this afternoon, pick up something to wear in the spring sales. Will you be all right with Mother?'

I nod. 'I'll go check on her now, see how she's doing.'

Five minutes later I'm running down the stairs again, screaming Rosie's name.

'She can't have gone far,' says Rosie as we hurry up the high street, against the flow of football supporters in blue and white heading out for an early start for the Manchester City game.

'How could she have even got out at all?' I say for the fifteenth time. I'd gone into Mother's room and it was empty, her bed neatly made. Rosie had got her dressed so at least she wasn't wandering about in her nightie. Her little boots had gone from the hall. My best guess was that she slipped out while I was in the bathroom and Rosie was having a smoke. I glare at her. Or a drink, for all I know.

I'm starting to panic as we get on the parade. It's so busy. We'll have no chance of spotting her among all these people. I drag Rosie into the first shop, a bakery, and give them a description of Mother, but they just shake their heads.

'Wait, Daisy, we can't just run around like headless chickens,' says Rosie as I'm heading out of the bakery and into the butchers next door. 'We need to think this through. Logically.'

'Logically, the front door should have been locked,' I say coldly.

'I had to get the milk in,' says Rosie, glaring at me. 'I didn't realise the house was bloody Colditz.' She rubs her chin. 'She took her purse. Maybe you're right, maybe she has come on the front to buy something.' She looks at me and bites her lip.

'What?' I say, crossly.

'Nothing,' says Rosie. 'It doesn't matter.' She pauses, then says, 'She's ill, Daisy. She's not suddenly made of bone china. She's got all her faculties. We can't keep her prisoner, you know.'

A bus chugs past and my hand flies to my mouth. 'What if she's caught a bus? She could be anywhere!'

It's weird, but I don't really remember much about Mother before the thing that happened when I was nine. I remember her, of course, but I don't remember her being very motherly, if that make sense? It was only afterwards that she seemed to do more hugging and more holding of both of us, me and Rosie, being more affectionate. I think she was trying to tell us both that she still loved us equally, no matter what had happened. That was when I really remember my own love for Mother sort of . . . solidifying. Rosie is younger than me but always seemed more switched on, even when we were very little. She tells me that before what happened happened, Mother was still very sad and angry about Dad leaving us. It's almost like the thing that brought us all together snapped her out of it. They say every cloud has a silver lining, and though that was a terrible thing that happened, maybe if you believe in that then you can think that out of it did come some good.

'Rosie! Daisy!' I blink and realise there's a woman standing in front of us, weighed down with shopping bags, smiling broadly.

'Hello, Mrs Jackson,' says Rosie, and I then recognise her as the lady who lives in the next street, used to be very friendly with Mother. She looks a lot older than I remember her, though.

'I saw your mum a bit back,' she says, and then I'm suddenly fully alert.

'What? Where was she?'

Rosie puts a hand on my arm to calm me down, and I realise I was shouting.

Mrs Jackson doesn't seem to have noticed, though. She says, 'I was coming out of the fishmongers and I saw her walking down the street and I thought, is that Barbara Dukes? I didn't realise it was her at first because she's lost so much weight! I mean, she was never what you'd call a big lady but she's so thin now!'

'That'll be the cancer,' I say, my voice shaking.

Mrs Jackson pulls a face. 'Ooh, I know. She told me. I wondered why I'd not seen her for a bit. Awful thing, cancer.'

'Mrs Jackson,' says Rosie. 'Do you know where she went?'

'Yes, love,' says Mrs Jackson. 'She got a taxi, didn't she? From the rank outside the betting shop.'

Rosie thanks her and I head off at a run towards the line of cars, looking over my shoulder as Mrs Jackson shouts, 'Lovely to see you both! Hashtag fuck cancer!' and waves at us.

I start gabbling at the driver of the first car but Rosie pushes me to one side and more calmly explains the situation. The driver remembers a woman fitting our description of Mother getting into the car parked in front of him at the rank. He gets on his radio to his office to ask where Sadiq took the fare he picked up half an hour ago. When he tells us I glare at Rosie.

'Don't, Daisy,' she says firmly. 'Not now. You can give me a row after if you want, but not now.' She leans in to the car again. 'Can you take us there?'

We find Mother sitting on a bench outside Elysian Fields, the award-winning hospice and dementia-specialist care home. From the brochure that Rosie sent off for. It's a low, modern building, set back from the main road, in big, well-maintained grounds. I suppose it looks nice. I'm not taking that much notice, though; I'm rushing over to Mother and crouching down in front of her, while Rosie asks the taxi to wait.

'We were out of our minds with worry!' I chide her. 'What on earth were you thinking, just going out like that?'

She looks pale and a little unwell, but she still manages to give me a Mother look. 'I'm not a child, Daisy. And I'm not a prisoner in that bloody house.'

'Told you,' says Rosie, appearing behind me.

'I felt good this morning, and thought I'd like to enjoy a bit of the spring sunshine,' says Mother.

'You should have said something! I could have taken you to the park.'

Mother sighs. 'I just wanted to get out on my own for a bit.' She looks up at Rosie. 'Decided to come and look at this home you're planning to put me in.'

'It's not like that,' says Rosie gently.

I stand up and pull a vicious face at my sister. 'It is though, isn't it? Admit it! You just want her out of the way so you can . . .' I don't mean to say what I say, but I say it anyway. 'So you can just sit there in that house and drink yourself to death!'

Rosie's mouth becomes a hard line and she glances at Mother. 'I don't think this is either the time or the place, do you, Daisy?' she says quietly.

'I quite agree,' says Mother. 'I'm not having you two going hammer and tongs in the street like a pair of fishwives. Besides, I'm not feeling as good as I did when I set off this morning. Is that cab waiting to take us home? You might as well have a row when we get there than do it here while his meter's running.'

'I'm sorry,' says Rosie, helping Mother into the taxi. 'I wasn't going behind anyone's back.'

Mother glances up at Elysian Fields. 'It looks a nice place, to be fair.' I help her buckle her seatbelt and she takes a packet of Extra Strong Mints out of her bag and pops one in her mouth. She gives us both a weary smile. 'But I'm not quite ready for the knacker's yard just yet.'

'This is the last fucking straw,' says Rosie when Mother has gone back to bed.

'Don't swear at me,' I say. 'It wasn't me that let her get out.'

Rosie gives me a look and shakes her head. 'She's not a dog, Daisy.'

'No,' I say, putting the kettle on. 'She's our mother. Do you want a tea? Or is it wine o'clock already?'

Rosie glares at me and opens the fridge, dragging out a half-full bottle of wine. 'It is now you've said that. Think I'll just . . . drink myself to death, was it?'

'You are drinking a lot,' I say quietly as I squeeze the teabag in my cup.

Rosie laughs. It's not a nice sound. 'You don't know the fucking half about anything.'

'Stop swearing.'

Rosie waves the wine bottle at me, quite nastily in my opinion. 'Fuck fuck fuckity fuck.'

I feel on the verge of tears. All this with the rationalisation. What if I lose my job? What if I can't get another night shift somewhere? We can't survive on Rosie's wage and if I got a day job who would look after Mother? We've already seen she can't be trusted.

And I'm standing there. Right at the spot where it happened. The bad thing. And I try to summon up the memory of it but it's all noisy and spiky and confused. But it happened. I know it happened, even if I can't remember it very well.

Rosie is starting to speak, saying, 'Look, Daisy, maybe this just flags up the need for Mother to have proper care—'

I cut her off. Make my voice as low and menacing as I can. If I can't quite fully put myself back there, I can at least summon up the feelings that a bad person who did a bad thing would have. I say, 'No, Rosie. No. She's not going anywhere.' I look at her with hooded eyes. 'You know what I'm capable of. And I say no.'

Rosie looks at me for a long time. She doesn't look scared. She looks something I can't recognise. Then she turns on her heel and takes the bottle of wine and a glass to her room.

Rosie goes out to buy herself a new dress in the afternoon and when she comes back neither of us mention what happened at the kitchen sink, which I suppose is what passes for a truce. She looks nice in her new dress when she's done her hair and put her make-up on, but I'm not quite ready to tell her that just yet. I just say to her to enjoy her evening as she leaves. Mother is asleep after her exertions so I watch *Pointless Celebrities* then make myself some tea. I have some spicy parsnip soup from a can and some crusty bread with butter on.

I'm still angry enough at Rosie for sending off for that stupid brochure in the first place to consider not ringing her at seven-thirty like I'd promised. Would serve her right if she was thrown in a pit in some serial killer's cellar. But of course I do, and Rosie is already merry and bubbly with drink, even after just half an hour in the pub. I feel a momentary and unfamiliar pang of something – a little like loss, a little like envy – at the sounds of music and talking and tinkling glass in the pub behind her.

'No worries, he's fine,' says Rosie. 'More than fine, actually. He's just gone to the bar. Think it might be his lucky night. Don't wait up. And don't be surprised if I'm not there in the morning.'

When I ring off I look at the picture of Alfie, thirty-six, from Bury, on my phone again. Having watched *Pointless*, I revise my opinion of him to being a shorter, chunkier Richard Osman rather than a Benedict Cumberbatch. Still, no Brad Pitt, no George Clooney. What was it Rosie said, though? *Life is not a fucking film, Daisy.* I hesitate for a moment longer, then message him back to arrange a meeting, before I change my mind.

16

Nate

Well, that weekend was what you can only call a disaster.

It starts at breakfast. I'd gone for a shower and when I come down Ben is glued to that game he was going on about on the telly where he'd plugged in his Xbox. I stand in the doorway, watching him sitting in my chair pulled right up to the screen, hunched forward, his thumbs dancing over the buttons on his controller. I am there for a while, trying to understand the game, which mainly involves a character jumping about some kind of island landscape, in the hope of understanding my own son a little better. Eyes still focused on the screen, he reaches out with his hand to get his glass of juice, and I suddenly realise what it is sitting on, balanced on the arm of the chair.

'Ben, no!' I call, and he jumps at the sound of my voice, his hand brushing the glass and knocking it over. On to what he is using as a makeshift tray. Daisy's book, *After Dark*.

'Bloody hell, why can't you be more careful!' I shout, picking up the book. It's soaked with orange juice, the pages already warping and swelling. It's ruined.

'It's just a book,' says Ben with barely a glance. 'Besides, it was your fault. You made me jump.'

'It's not just a book!' I say, exasperated. 'It's someone else's book. And there's no such thing as just a book anyway.'

'Books are boring,' says Ben, his eyes grazing back to the TV, his fingers making the avatar on the screen climb a mossy rock outcrop.

I look around the living room. I've got a small bookcase near the back, and there are small clusters of twos and threes of paperbacks scattered around the room. I always have at least two books on the go. It occurs to me I've never seen Ben reading.

'Books are not boring,' I say.

'You only say that because you've nothing else to do. I don't have time to read books.'

Suddenly angry, I snatch the controller from his hands. He looks at me, aghast. 'What are you doing?'

'Switching this off,' I say, turning the controller around trying to find an off button.

'I'm dead!' shrieks Ben in horror. I look at the screen to find two other characters beating his with sticks.

'Good,' I say. 'It's time to go and get a shower before the football.'

'I don't want to go to the football!' shouts Ben, standing up. 'I hate football and I hate books!' He picks up the juice-drenched copy of Daisy's book and throws it across the room, which makes me even more furious.

'How can you hate books?' I bellow. 'How can you hate football? We're going to the City game and that's that.'

'You only like football because your dad hit you until you did,' says Ben, his eyes narrowed. 'Is that what you're going to do to me?'

'I'm not my father!' I shout.

'And I'm not you!' Ben shouts back, storming towards the stairs and giving Daisy's book on the floor a vicious kick for good measure.

We get the bus to the Etihad and Ben sits in silence, plugged into his earphones, pointedly ignoring my attempts to jolly him along and refusing to allow the atmosphere of the bus, which is largely full of City supporters, to improve his mood.

He's insisted on bringing that stupid Pikachu soft toy that John gave him, which makes me annoyed. I'm not sure if that's because John gave it to him, or because you just don't take soft toys to football matches. It's just not right.

The seats are good ones, right in the home end, and I ply Ben with soft drinks, hot dogs and snacks to try to cheer him up a bit, which he accepts with sullen and cursory thank yous, but no attempt to brighten up.

After ten minutes Ben is asking me how long there is to go, and I have to exasperatedly explain to him that each half of a football match is forty-five minutes, plus stoppage time, and half-time on top of that. He rolls his eyes and puts in his earphones.

Though the day had started off brightly, clouds had started to gather over the Etihad from kick-off, and by half-time they darken and let loose a torrent of rain. Added to that the play in the first forty-five minutes is abysmal on both sides, and the scoreline stands at nil–nil. If even I thought it was a bad game, there was little chance it was going to win over Ben.

He stuffs the Pikachu under his coat to stop it getting wet, and just glowers at the pitch until the change of ends and the whistle for the second half. Then Villa seem to wake up but City continue napping, and there is a flurry of goals from the visitors that leaves us three-nil down. And there the score stays until the final whistle, after seven agonisingly dull minutes of added time, and Ben speaks for the first time in the entire match to ask if we can go home now.

He's more talkative on the bus journey back, relaying to me a series of messages he's received from his friends about how they fared in the Fortnite tournament that he pointedly makes sure I know he completely missed because I forced him to go to the football. I should take the opportunity to engage with him but it's my turn to be surly and reticent, and I just frown and grunt at him until he gives up and, inevitably, puts in his earphones. I can almost hear Lucia saying to me, Ben's a child and you're a grown-up. Only one of you is allowed to behave like a child. And guess which one it isn't, Nate?

By the time the bus gets us back into the city centre I've rallied a bit and ask him where he wants to eat. He shrugs at every option so I decide for him and we get a booth in a Pizza Express. Eventually I coax some conversation about him, and between finishing the dough balls and starting our American Hot pizzas we're almost back on talking terms.

'What do you want to do over the summer holidays?' I say. 'I've got two weeks to take off. Thought we could have some nice days out. Maybe even stay over somewhere for a night or two. Anywhere you'd like to go?'

'Tenerife!' says Ben suddenly.

I give him a pained smile. 'Well, not sure we can stretch to that . . . I was thinking more . . . Blackpool?'

'No, I mean we're going to Tenerife! Me, Mum and John. I forgot to tell you. We're going to this hotel and it's basically carved out of a mountain and the room actually has its own swimming pool on the balcony.'

'That sounds great,' I say, plastering a smile on my face. I've suddenly lost my appetite and throw my balled-up napkin on to the plate with a little more force than I intend. Tenerife. I haven't had a holiday for years. I drift into a reverie, thinking about where I'd like to go. Greece would be nice. After reading all those myths in the book in the Theodore room at work.

I think about that postcard I use as a bookmark. Mykonos. It looks absolutely idyllic. I absently wonder who keeps moving the postcard from the page I'm up to. I wonder who else is reading the book.

Ben has finished his pizza and is slurping his Coke so I grab the attention of a passing waiter and mime writing with an invisible pen on the palm of my hand, the internationally recognised gesture for asking for the bill. I imagine doing it in some taverna on the harbour of a sun-drenched Greek island.

'We could rent a movie when we get back,' I say as the waiter brings over the bill on a little silver plate with two round mints.

'Maybe,' Ben says, shrugging, as I dig inside my coat pocket for my wallet.

Which isn't there.

'Dad,' says Ben, sinking lower into his chair as I check and recheck every pocket for my wallet. Which still isn't there.

'I had it at the game,' I say, patting my trousers. 'I bought the snacks with it. Did I take it out on the bus? No, I had change in my pocket.'

Ben slides lower, evidently mortified. 'Shit,' I say, and the waiter tuts. 'That means somebody either lifted it at the ground, or I left it on the bus. Great.'

'We take Apple or Android Pay,' says the waiter.

'I haven't got that on my phone,' I say, and Ben moans a little. I sit there in silence, glancing from Ben to the waiter and back again. I have lost all my cards, and the cash I'd drawn out, and I have no way of paying for this meal. I suddenly realise I have no idea what to do.

Ben sighs and digs into his pocket and pulls out a debit card. I stare at him. 'You have a bank account?'

'Yes.'

'And you've got money in it?'

'Yes.'

I show him the bill. 'This much money?'

'Just about.'

The waiter gives me a withering look as he hands Ben, hands my ten-year-old son, the terminal for him to insert his card and input his PIN number. 'I'll pay you back when I get home,' I say, feeling wretched.

I'm not sure if the waiter gives Ben a sympathetic glance and a shake of his head or if I imagine it, but as soon as the transaction is cleared I stand up quickly and start putting on my coat. Ben puts his hand in his pocket and pulls out a handful of change. 'I'm guessing you don't have any money for a tip,' he says, and puts it on the table. I follow him out, my shoulders slumped, feeling like everyone in the restaurant is watching me, and judging me very badly indeed.

'You let him do what?' says Lucia.

We're standing in my living room. Ben has gone out with John to put his case and Xbox in The Beast, which I still refuse to call John's car. It's barely ten o'clock on Sunday morning, but Lucia texted me half an hour ago to ask if she could pick up Ben early as she wanted to take him to see her mother. Which, I guess, is so that she can introduce John to her family. I also suspect Ben might have texted Lucia first, pleading with her to come and get him after the disastrous Saturday.

Which didn't end at Pizza Express, apparently. It was after eight when we got back, and dark, but Ben had begged me to let him go out for a couple of hours.

'Out where?'

'Just with my friends. Hanging out. On the parade.'

'It's too late.'

'It's not! I'm ten! You're allowed to stay out until your age, that's the rule. Don't you know that?'

'Is it?' I'd said dubiously. 'Maybe I should phone your mum.'

Ben shrugged. 'If you want. I think she's gone to the cinema with John tonight. Interrupt her if you like. If you think it's a good idea.'

I pondered. 'And you'll be back by ten? No later? And you've got your phone?'

He promised me he would call or message if there was any trouble. I was a bit doubtful, but ultimately felt as though I'd actually done the right thing in trusting him, treating him like a grown-up. Obviously, I was wrong.

'I can't believe you let him bullshit you like that.' Lucia sighs. 'You need to get a grip of your parenting, Nate. One minute you're letting him run wild, then you're shouting at him and making him go to the football, which you should know he hates, the next you're letting him roam the streets after dark. There's no consistency, Nate.'

'I can't win,' I say morosely, thinking ha, Ben did text her this morning, if she knows about the football and the shouting.

Lucia rolls her eyes. 'It's not about winning. You're not in some kind of competition with Ben. You're his dad. Just be his dad. And stop trying so hard not to be yours.'

I open my mouth to retort, but I have nothing to say. There's a moment's silence, punctuated by the beep of a horn from outside.

'Did you cancel all your cards?' says Lucia.

'Yes. And I've transferred the money back to Ben's account on my laptop.'

She nods, and takes out her phone. 'I wasn't joking the other day, you know. When I said you should meet someone. It might . . . I don't know. Give you focus. You're drifting,

Nate.' She hands the phone to me. There's a picture on it of a woman. Blonde. Smart. Pretty.

'That's Sara. She works at the hospital. In the admin office.'

I shrug. 'And?'

'And she's very nice. Divorced.'

I shrug again. 'And?'

'And you've got a date with her on Wednesday night.' Lucia punches her phone and I feel mine beep in my pocket. 'I've texted you the details. See you tomorrow morning when you come for Ben.'

I hear the door slam and the growl of John's car pulling away, but I'm too busy staring at the text Lucia's sent to my phone, along with the picture of the smiling Sara.

Perhaps the weekend hasn't been a total disaster, after all.

17

Nate

It's stupid at my age, but I'm nervous about the date tonight with Sara. We're meeting at nine at some pub in the Northern Quarter, but Lucia has given me strict instructions that I have to go home first and shower and get changed, not go straight from work. And I have to shave, as well.

I can't remember the last time I went on a date. I was so young when I met Lucia, and I wasn't exactly what you might call a Lothario before that. This morning I tried to get Lucia to call the whole thing off, but she refused. 'Just try it, Nate. You never know what might happen.'

'Nine seems late, though,' I say.

'I want to make sure you've got enough time to get home and make yourself look handsome. Sara's got tomorrow off. And you don't have to come to take Ben to school. John and I can take him. Just this once. Stop making excuses.'

So John is staying over then, I think, but I don't say anything because what's the point? Whatever Lucia says, I'm not so stupid that I don't realise she's pushing me into this date so she doesn't feel as bad about me moping around on my own while she lives it up with John.

Besides, there's been plenty of excitement at work this

week to take my mind off it. Seema's been in overdrive about the ManMuSH Big Sleepover event that's happening in two weeks. At least Ben seems to be talking to me now, and is at least not woefully against the idea of going, if not actually outwardly excited. On Monday we had a group from a local school in, sixty of them. And with two of Dorothy's guides down with the flu, that meant I had to step in to help shepherd them round.

Oh, and Daisy's been on her burglary thing again. She reckoned that an old kids' gas mask had gone missing from the Malone Room on Friday, and with the CCTV system out of operation while they strip out and replace all that wiring, there was no hope of catching whoever she thinks might have done it. But then when I got into work on Tuesday the gas mask was exactly where it should have been. Bit of a spooky, horrible thing it is, too. Meant to look like Mickey Mouse, but more likely to give kids nightmares than any threat of a gas attack. You'd think Daisy would be mollified by it, but it only made her worse. She thinks there's some kind of conspiracy.

I tell Ben about the missing things and he thinks it's great. 'Like Detective Pikachu!' he says. 'You should solve the mystery, Dad.'

Wednesday is nice and bright, if still a little chilly. But the clocks go forward next week, and hopefully it'll start to get warmer. I go for a wander on my lunch break, feeling a bit happier about the arrival of spring and the imminence of good weather. Well, we're due a nice summer for a change, aren't we? I think about the postcard of Mykonos in the Greek myths book, about how I'd like nothing more than to be in one of those tavernas, someone handing me a glass of beer, beads of condensation on it. I wonder if that someone could be Sara? I have ten minutes of my break left, so I go up to the Theodore room and take down the book. I don't read any of it, though. I just take the postcard out. Shame for such a lovely view to be locked up in that dusty old tome. It'll look much nicer pinned up in the den. Cheer us all up, that will.

When Daisy arrives at a quarter to five I've already got my coat on and meet her downstairs in the reception lobby. 'I thought we could do the handover here,' I say. 'Got to get away on time today.'

'Going somewhere nice?' asks Daisy.

For reasons I can't quite fathom, I'm a bit vague with my answer. 'Just have to get home and get back into town for something.'

She looks like she has something to say as well, but seems to decide against it. 'So, what's the report?'

Because I'm feeling a bit giddy at the prospect of going out with Sara, I start to spout all sorts of nonsense. 'We had a man turn into a werewolf in the Lever Wing. Didn't attack anybody but did his business on the floor. Awful mess. Then three ninjas abseiled into the cafe and tried to steal all Bonny Sue's Eccles cakes, but Dorothy saw them off with her umbrella. Oh, and Harold's phoned in; he's not coming in tonight, he's won the lottery and is going to live on a Caribbean island with the Manchester Giants' cheerleaders.'

To my surprise, a little smile plays on Daisy's lips. Maybe it's the onset of spring. Cheering everybody up a bit. She gives me a mock-reproving look and says, 'I take that to mean it was quiet today, then?'

'As usual,' I say. 'What's it like out? Still dry?'

She nods. 'Nice.'

I notice Daisy is holding a big carrier bag, with what looks like clothes in it. I nod at it and say, 'What's that?'

She frowns, and I realise I've probably overstepped the mark with her. 'Just something to wear,' she says, a little uncertainly. 'For something.'

There's something different about Daisy, something beyond her laughing at my stupid dad jokes. I peer at her for a moment and then say, 'Have you had your hair done?'

It does look a bit more wavy and done than usual. She touches it self-consciously and says, 'Just a . . . bit.'

'It's nice.'

We look at each other a little awkwardly. 'Well!' I say, unnecessarily loudly. I zip up my coat and head for the door. 'Well, hope it's quiet tonight. See you tomorrow.'

As Lucia instructed, I shower and shave and select the clothes that she chose from memory for me, knowing that I probably hadn't bought any new ones in years. A white shirt and a pair of chinos. 'Tuck your shirt in,' she'd ordered. 'You're not twenty any more.' I polish my black brogues and take all the old receipts and bus tickets out of my best navy-blue coat. I find two bottles of aftershave at the back of the bathroom cabinet. Aramis and Kouros. God knows how long they've been there. They might even have been my dad's. They're both half full and the tops are a bit crusty. Do aftershaves have use-by dates? I cautiously sniff them both and neither smells like vinegar, and in the end I opt for Kouros, because it sounds a bit Greek and reminds me of the Mykonos postcard I pinned up in the den. I wonder if Daisy's seen it yet. I splash a liberal amount of the Kouros on, then a bit more for good luck. And then it's time to go for my big date.

By ten o'clock I would be fully prepared to chew my own leg off like one of those wild animals caught in a steel trap, if it allowed me to escape. Sara is not only dull, she is positively awful. But I have realised this too late, when I have committed to the night, and now I can only ride it out.

I honestly can't understand what Lucia was thinking, hooking me up with this woman, unless it's some kind of deliberate act of revenge. Lucia is smart and funny and emotionally intelligent. Sara is none of these things. In fact, she is the negative of these things. I can't believe that she and Lucia are friends, even just work friends.

It starts promisingly enough, to be fair. For about ten minutes. I make sure I'm early and I stand around outside the pub – it's a new place run by people with moustache wax and braces but it's made to look like an old spit and sawdust boozer for some reason – until Sara comes around the corner. She's wearing a long beige coat and heels that make it difficult for her to walk straight. She clocks me and waves, almost going over on her ankle.

'Sodding hell,' she says, bending over to rub her leg when she reaches me. 'I got these from Primark at lunchtime and they're absolutely crucifying me.'

'Buy cheap, buy twice, my mum always said,' I say, and immediately bite my lip. What on earth possessed me to say that?

But Sara seems to find it funny and slaps me playfully on the arm. 'Ooh,' she says. 'Muscles. No idea why Lucia sacked you off. You're a bit of a catch.'

'Well, she didn't exactly . . . is that what she says? That she sacked me off?'

'Ooh, we're not here to talk about her. Are we going inside? I'm gagging for a drink.'

Inside the pub we find a corner table and Sara shrugs off her coat, revealing a tight red dress. She's got a good figure. She catches me looking and slaps my arm again. 'You're a right one, you, I can tell I'm going to have to keep my wits about me. Lucia never told me that.'

I stand up to go to the bar but one of the moustache-and-braces guys comes over with a phone to take our order. 'Porn Star Martini for me!' announces Sara, kicking my shin under the table. 'Saucy, or what, Nate?'

'Uh, pint of bitter. Boddington's,' I say.

Mr Braces nods towards a menu on the table. 'Craft beers,' he says. No Boddies, then. I squint at the menu and pick something at random. 'Er, pint of, um, Devil's Munchbox, then. I suppose.'

'Good choice,' he says and goes off to get the drinks.

Sara looks round the dark pub. 'This is nice, eh? Your idea?'

I'm about to say that no, Lucia organised it, but stop myself. That won't look good. Mr Braces comes back with the Porn Star Martini, which also comes with a prosecco chaser, for Sara, and a pint of cloudy-looking liquid for me. I'm about to ask him if he's sure the barrel doesn't need changing but he's gone.

Sara takes a sip of her martini then says, 'Bottoms up!' and necks the prosecco in one. I take a sneaky look at the drinks menu and shudder a little at the prices. I take what I hope is a reviving swig of my beer and almost spit it out. It's absolutely rank.

'And you've booked us into Chillibobs at half eleven as well!' says Sara. 'You certainly know how to treat a girl.'

'Have I?' I say before I can stop myself. Sara laughs uproariously. What on earth is Lucia playing at? I've seen that Chillibobs, it's not far from the museum. I've no idea what sort of food they serve. All I know is that it looks bloody expensive. This is looking more and more like some sort of vengeance on Lucia's part. I wish I knew what for.

The next two hours are excruciating. For me, at least. Sara doesn't seem to notice, because she doesn't stop talking. She has an opinion on absolutely everything, and all of them are the exact opposite of mine. Or rather, as I come to realise, she doesn't have any real opinions at all. We have three rounds in the pub and the bill makes my eyes water.

We walk to the restaurant and she links arms with me, ostensibly because her shoes are killing her feet. I feel like I've been . . . I don't know. *Claimed*. Like an old dog at the shelter.

Chillibobs is apparently a fusion restaurant. I catch sight of the specials board and the prices don't make my eyes water this time, they make my wallet weep. We're shown to a table by the window.

We've barely got our food (something Mexican-Thai for Sara, something Indonesian-French for me, a bottle of the house white) and she's off again, this time about Brexit.

'Well, it was only right, wasn't it? The majority had spoken and all these horror stories about what was going to happen never did, did they?'

'Well, if you can call fifty-two per cent a majority, which it is just about—'

'And everybody really wanted it, even if they weren't saying that. I mean, nobody's bothered about whether chicken is chlorinated or where the beef comes from, really, it was all the foreigners.'

'Foreigners. Right.'

She reaches over and touches my hand. Well, more rubs it really, with her thumb, as though she's subconsciously trying to see if my colour comes off. 'Not like you.'

'I was born in Chorlton.'

'Well, obviously. I mean the foreign foreigners. The ones who can't speak English. The ones who just come over on dinghies for the benefits and houses.'

'My grandfather came over on the *Windrush*, you know, Sara.'

'Windrush! Sounds like something you get after eating a curry!' She makes a *parping* noise with her mouth and laughs. Then she reaches over and, astonishingly, rubs my hair. 'Ooh, it's lovely. All fuzzy.'

I pull back. 'You shouldn't do that without asking.'

Sara looks at me in a way I can only describe as coquettish. 'Oh, we're friends, aren't we, Nate? Maybe . . . more?'

Something across the road has caught my eye. The window is misty with condensation but I could swear . . .

'Nate,' says Sara, somewhat stridently. 'Are you listening to me?'

I stare through the window a little longer. I can't imagine *why* I'm seeing what I'm seeing, but I'm sure I'm right. Two people, across the road . . .

I turn back to Sara. 'Do you like Greek myths?'

She shrugs at me and laughs. 'No, but I like mythters! Get it?'

I press on, one eye on the scene unfolding across the road. 'There's a story about Echo, who was an Oread. Which is a type of mountain nymph—'

'Nympho!' she cackles. 'I told you that you were naughty!'

'Nymph. Like a . . . spirit. Hera, who was the queen of the gods, suspected her husband Zeus was monkeying around with the nymphs, so she made it so that Echo could only ever speak the last words that were spoken to her.'

I turn away from the window, and scribble with my invisible pen on my hand at the nearest waiter. Sara frowns. 'We haven't had pudding yet.'

'You're like Echo,' I say, pulling on my coat. 'You read all this . . . this crap on Facebook and in the tabloids, you get told rubbish second and third hand, and you just parrot the last thing you heard. You don't think about anything. You just talk.'

I pay the bill without looking at it, without even bothering to hope that my replacement debit card, only arrived yesterday from the bank, is good for it. Then I toss two tenners on the table. 'Hope this can cover your taxi home, Sara. If you'll excuse me, I have to go.'

For the first time tonight, Sara is speechless. I take one look at her appalled face then head for the door, and across the road.

18

Daisy

The first thing I see is that someone has taken the postcard from the book in the Theodore room and stuck it to the wall of the security office with a drawing pin.

I am furious.

That is my postcard of Mykonos, from Rosie. It can only be Nate or Harold who has put it there, because no one else has access to the security office. Whichever one it is, what are they doing messing about with my things? Why have they been poking around in the book. I mean, granted, it's not exactly my book, but I'm the only one who ever bothers with it. Apart from whoever's been moving the postcard around in it, of course. As I stash my bag of clothes under the desk I suddenly wonder if either Harold or Nate have been reading the book as well. It doesn't seem likely. It must be someone coming in when the museum's open, and perhaps they've given the postcard to Nate, thinking it shouldn't be there, and he's pinned it up in the office. That seems the most reasonable explanation. I wish I'd seen this before Nate left for whatever he's got planned.

I was in quite a good mood before I got to work. Even that gang of yobbos (as Mother would call them) hanging about the parade, with their shouts of 'Crazy Daisy!' couldn't make me upset, even when they sent that little one over again to try to snatch my hat off my head. I don't usually wear a hat but seeing as I'd had my hair done (how funny of Nate to notice that, though?) I thought I'd try to protect it from any wind and rain we have today.

It was Rosie who made me get my hair done, obviously, made me an appointment at Jennifer's salon on the parade for this afternoon. I was a bit dubious about leaving Mother alone after what happened at the weekend, but she promised not to go anywhere. We've all been dancing about the incident a bit, to be honest, not really addressing it directly. Especially what I said about Rosie and her drinking. We're all trying to ignore that and Mother's little jaunt brought on by the hospice brochure but it's always looming on the edges of everything like a big shadow that we all pretend we can't see.

It was Rosie who found me something to wear, a blouse from my own wardrobe and a skirt from hers, from when she used to be a little bigger than she is now. The skirt is black and a lot shorter than I'd usually wear, but Rosie bought me some opaque black tights from town. I tried it all on after I'd had my hair done and it did feel good to be wearing something nice for a change.

It was even down to Rosie that I'm getting off an hour earlier from work. She made me give her Harold's mobile number and she called him and said that there was a family situation and I had to finish at midnight, and could he possibly come in a little earlier? I'd never have been able to lie like that – my face goes all red and my eyes swivel round if I don't tell the truth. So I never don't tell the truth. But Rosie said it wasn't really a lie. We do have a family situation. We have plenty of family situations.

All of which means I am in a fairly good mood. Or was, until I saw the postcard. Which, I recognise, is a little illogical. It's my postcard, yes, but I did leave it in a book that anyone can read. I suppose I'm lucky that whoever handed it in to Nate didn't just pocket it or throw it in the rubbish bin.

I decide to leave the card where it is. It does brighten up the security office a little, after all. As I busy myself with seeing everyone out and locking up and getting on with my first patrol, I think about Alfie, who lives in Bury, but works in a warehouse in Salford, who is thirty-six, unmarried, enjoys reading and going for walks, and has a dog. He is getting off work a little early, too, and we are meeting at a quarter past midnight in a bar chosen by Rosie, not too busy but not too quiet. She has asked if I want her to stay up and phone me half an hour into the date, to give me an excuse to leave, but I say no. If I decide I want to leave, I just will.

I suppose I'm not surprised when I notice, in the Standish Hall, that something has gone missing again. Earlier this week they took down the black-and-white photos of sulky pop stars and replaced them with a mini exhibition about Manchester fashion through the ages. There are mannequins dressed in nineteenth-century millworkers' clothes, First World War uniforms, that sort of thing. The mannequins are, I suppose, a little creepy after the museum is closed and empty. They have white, featureless faces and you sometimes feel as though they're watching you, though they don't have any eyes.

One of the mannequins is dressed in women's clothes from the sixties, a very short miniskirt and a striped knitted jumper. She used to wear a corduroy hat, one of those peaked ones that's a bit baggy on top. It always makes me want to sing that old song, 'Georgy Girl'. Anyway, it's gone. I don't bother making a note to ask Seema for the list of items out for refurbishment, because the exhibit's only been up a couple of days. Someone's stolen it, for sure.

I go to the office and make some notes. Three items stolen: the weaving shuttle, the gas mask, and now the hat. What links them? I tap my pencil against my teeth, while I think. Nothing obvious, apart from the fact they are all items here at the museum. And that the shuttle and the gas mask were both returned after a few days. It's possible that the hat isn't linked to the other two; the Standish Hall being located near the main doors, and the mannequin not being behind glass, it could be that someone's just grabbed it and made off. Especially if there have been a lot of school parties in, as Nate said.

I decide to keep this one to myself. One reason is the rationalisation; I don't want to give Seema and Mr Meyer any more ammunition to use against the security team. If they think we're not doing our job properly, that we're letting items get stolen, it will make it easier for them to get rid of us.

The other reason is that I'm starting to think that this must be what they call in the movies an inside job. Seema, Mr Meyer, Janice, Dorothy, the guides, the Sues, even Harold and Nate.

They're all suspects.

The shift goes off without incident, and Harold duly turns up an hour early at midnight. He looks me up and down in my flowery blouse and black skirt, and sniffs. 'Family situation, they said.'

I wonder if I've made a mistake by getting changed before he arrived, but what else am I supposed to do? Rosie had said that if I go out in my security-guard uniform she'll change the locks before I get home and won't let me in. I think about coming clean to Harold but he's already ushering me out of the door.

'Have a nice . . . situation,' he says, glaring at me.

It's only when I'm outside on the street that the enormity of what I'm doing hits me. I'm going on a date. With a man I've only ever seen a photograph of. I feel giddy and sick all at the same time. I ponder just going home and sneaking in to the house and telling Rosie in the morning that the date went fine, but she'll know I was lying. The red face and the swivelling eyes are a dead giveaway.

So I take a deep breath and force myself to walk along the street towards the bar that Rosie has chosen for us because it stays open until three. It's on a fairly busy stretch of the Northern Quarter, with a couple of other bars and restaurants on both sides of the road. I pause outside the bar, not sure if I'm supposed to meet him on the street or go in. In the end, I decide to wait indoors. It's chilly and there are a few knots of drunken people staggering around. My phone tells me it's ten past twelve. Five minutes early. With a bit of luck, he will be, too.

The bar is busy enough that nobody gives me a second glance when I push through the door, but not so packed as to be uncomfortable. I scan the people but can't see anyone who looks remotely like Richard Osman or Benedict Cumberbatch. Am I supposed to go and get myself a drink? Or is that bad form? And what should I have? What looks good? What looks bad?

I'm still pondering when I feel someone brush past me, and I yelp as something digs into my bum. I spin around to see a man who is shorter and chunkier than either his photograph or profile suggested, and looks absolutely nothing like anyone off the telly or films in the flesh. Yet, here is my date.

'All right! You must be Daisy! I'm Alfie!'

He holds out his hand. The one I'm pretty sure he just used to goose me. I take it warily and he lets his sit in mine, like a limp, dead fish. Alfie looks around the bar. 'Never met anybody here before. Don't usually go so posh.'

I look around too. Is it posh? 'Do you meet people a lot?' I say. 'Where do you usually go?'

Alfie shrugs. He's wearing a creased gingham shirt over a black T-shirt, and shapeless jeans that are hanging off his wide hips. His Converse sneakers are unlaced and grimy. 'Pubs, sometimes. Sometimes we just meet up outside.'

I plaster on a smile. 'Shall we get a drink?'

'If you're buying!' he says.

I get myself a gin and tonic, because that's what Rosie suggested, and Alfie a bottle of beer. We find a table in the corner and sit down. He seems to be inspecting me, which makes me a little uncomfortable. I try to remember his profile, think of something to say. Eventually I settle on, 'What sort of dog do you have?'

'A dead one!' he says. Alfie seems to speak in exclamation marks all the time. 'I really should update that profile.'

'Oh,' I say. 'I'm sorry. How was work?'

'Shite!' He drains his bottle. 'Shall we move on?'

I still have most of my drink left. I desperately cast around for more conversation. 'What sort of books do you like to read?'

'Serial killers!' says Alfie, his eyes shining, even the lazy left one. 'Love serial killers, me!' He looks at my glass. 'Come on, drink up!'

'Where are we going?' I say.

I think he's having a seizure or maybe a stroke, then I realise he's trying to wink at me. 'I'm easy, me. Where do you usually go?'

'Well, I don't . . .' I frown. 'Go for what?'

Alfie's shoulders slump a little and he puffs out his cheeks. 'You know!' He winks again and then makes a circle with the thumb and forefinger of his left hand and pokes the forefinger of his right in and out of it.

Oh. My. God.

I put my drink on the table, smile as politely as I can, and stand up. Alfie grins. 'Here we go! Let the dog see the rabbit and all that.'

I turn quickly and head for the door, panicking. I should stay in the pub, I realise too late, as I push out on to the street. Tell the bar staff. Get them to call the police or something. But I'm already out, and the street is suddenly quiet, devoid of any other people. And here comes Alfie, bustling out of the door behind me.

'Peachy keen, I like that,' he says. 'I don't need owt fancy, though. Have you got a place? I'm in Salford and we can go back there but you'll have to pay for the taxi.'

He takes hold of my wrist and I pull away from him, but he's stronger than his limp handshake suggests. His face darkens to a frown. 'Come on, Daisy. Be friendly, eh? Is that your real name? Daisy? Or your working name?'

'You've got this all wrong!' I say, tears prickling at my eyes. 'I'm not a . . . a . . . what you think I am!'

''Course you are!' says Alfie, keeping tight hold of my wrist. 'Said so on your profile. Night-worker.' He winks at me. 'Very subtle. I like it.'

I drag my arm away from him forcefully. 'This is all a hideous mistake. That isn't what I meant. I work at the museum.'

He ponders this for a moment, then shrugs. 'Well, we're here now, aren't we?' He lunges towards me and reaches a hand around to squeeze my backside. 'I've come all this way. Let's not make the night a total washout.'

I have had enough. I push him, hard, in the chest, and he staggers back a little, but his low centre of gravity keeps him upright. He scowls at me. 'Oh, you want to play rough, do you?'

'I doubt she does, but I'm game,' says a voice. A voice I recognise, but I can't process. Until a tall shape puts itself between Alfie and me, and gives him a forceful push on his chest.

It's Nate.

Alfie looks up at Nate. 'Who're you? Her pimp?'

'Fuck off,' says Nate calmly.

Alfie bobs around Nate's big frame to glare at me. 'Prick-tease.'

Nate balls his fist and shows it to Alfie, who backs away. 'All right, all right, I'm going. Fucking time-waster.'

And then he's off, scuttling along the street. Nate turns to me. 'Daisy? Are you all right?'

I don't think I've ever seen him wearing anything except his uniform. He's got on a white shirt and a pair of chinos and I suddenly feel all disconnected. The adrenaline floods out of my system and I stagger, and fall into him, my head on his chest.

When Nate folds his long arms around me, I suddenly and unexpectedly start to sob.

19

Nate

I don't know why I put my arms around Daisy. I'm not normally a hugger. But when someone's as upset as she is . . . well, you have to be kind, don't you? And as I hold her to me, not caring that she's sobbing tears and snot into my white shirt . . . It just feels the right thing to do. For her.

And for me.

Before I can process that any further, Daisy pushes away from me and starts to wipe her nose with the sleeve of her blouse. I dig into my jacket pocket and find her a tissue; she sniffs a thank you and starts to apologise.

'It's fine,' I murmur. 'Are you all right? That idiot didn't hurt you or anything?'

'Only the idea that I can have a normal life,' says Daisy. I look at her curiously. I've never seen her out of work, never heard her speak so candidly about herself before. She seems different, somehow. Like her security guard uniform is some kind of armour she puts on every day, and without it she's . . . not vulnerable, perhaps, just not as . . . hidden away.

She's got herself under some kind of control, now, and says quietly, 'I was on a date. With a man I met on some stupid app that my sister made me download to my phone. It was a disaster.'

I glance over at Chillibobs across the road, and Daisy follows my gaze. 'Yeah, I'm on a date and my evening has been a bit of a washout as well.'

'Oh,' she says, and I can immediately see she's misunderstood me. 'You should get back to your meal.' She pauses. 'Date? With your wife?'

I laugh. 'My wife? No, she's the one who set it up.' Daisy looks perplexed and before she can think I'm in some kind of weird seventies open relationship I quickly add, 'My ex-wife, I should say. She fixed me up with someone she works with. I'm not sure if she realises, but the woman was an absolute, utter nightmare.' Across the road I can see Sara putting on her coat, through the restaurant window. 'In fact, she's coming out now. Would you mind if we moved on a bit? I really don't want to have to speak to her again.'

We lose ourselves in the crowds that are emerging from the bars, calling it a night, and when we're at what I consider a safe distance from wherever Sara went I say, 'Do you, I don't know, want to get a drink or something? Calm us both down a bit? There'll be some places open for a while yet.'

Daisy considers it. 'What I'd really like is a cup of tea.'

'You read my mind,' I say. 'Not sure that there's anywhere that—' We pause, and stop, and glance at each other. We're just up the road from the Manchester Museum of Social History. I say, 'Don't suppose you have your keys with you?'

'Of course,' says Daisy. How did I guess she would always be prepared?

When we quietly let ourselves into the museum there's a noise that sounds like someone sawing wood reverberating around the ground floor. 'Are the workmen here so late fixing the CCTV system?' I say.

Daisy frowns. 'No. It's coming from the security office.'

'Let me go first,' I whisper, stepping in front of Daisy. I push open the door to the den and we see the source of the sound. Harold, sprawled in the chair, head thrown back, snoring fit to wake the dead.

Daisy shakes her head. 'He's not exactly doing his job, is he?'

'At least we know how he gets through this godawful shift now, though,' I say, unplugging the kettle and taking it over to our little sink to fill it. Even with the gush of water Harold continues to snore, so I stop whispering.

'Do you think we should report him?' says Daisy. I look at her, and I have to say I'm quite shocked.

'No! He'll lose his job!'

She shrugs and digs into our tea caddy to fish out two teabags. I watch her for a moment and say, 'You like following the rules, don't you, Daisy? Like . . . regulations, and such.'

She pours the water into the cups before answering. 'Where would we be without rules and regulations?'

'You like to be in control, don't you? Don't you ever cut loose a bit?'

She gives me a look. 'I have to be. Nate, you don't know anything about me or my life. If I wasn't in control of everything . . . I'm not sure what would happen.' She looks like she's about to say something else but instead turns to squeeze out the teabags and drop them in the bin. She tuts. 'Look, Harold's just thrown my report away without even reading it. And not even into the recycle bin.'

I don't know why, but I want her to carry on talking. I want her to tell me about her life. It's like she's the exact polar opposite to Sara, who had a million opinions that she hadn't even thought through, and was more than happy to spout off about them. Daisy is far more . . . mysterious, I suppose. She's not one of these people who documents every cough and spit of her life on social media, or shares every single thing with her colleagues at work, whether they want to know or not. And whereas I spent the last hour with Sara praying for her to shut up, with Daisy I feel like I want to know more. I'd never really thought about her having a home life before, which is stupid because everybody has one. I just thought of her as Daisy who does the shift after me. Daisy who is funny peculiar, not funny ha ha. Who has a place for everything and puts everything in its place. But when she spoke just now, it was like . . . I don't know. A chink in her armour was showing. I watch her as she pours milk into the teas. She suits those clothes. Her hair looks nice. She looks like Daisy, but not.

Daisy turns around with my tea, and I realise I must have been staring at her. She realises it, too, and her brow crinkles.

'Who are you, and what have you done with Daisy Dukes?' I say sternly.

Daisy glares at me. 'What do you mean by that?'

'It's a joke,' I say.

'Jokes are meant to be funny,' she says, as though her brain is a computer trying to work something out. 'Why is that funny? What does it mean?'

'It's sort of . . . like in an old film? Where people have been taken over by alien pods and look like themselves but are acting a bit weirdly? That's what a character would say to them.'

There's a long pause, punctuated only by Harold's snoring.

'You think I'm weird?' says Daisy eventually, handing me my tea.

'No!' I say quickly. This is spiralling out of control. A joke is not a joke if you have to explain it to this degree. 'It's just that I'm not used to seeing you like . . .'

'Like what?' says Daisy, suspiciously.

I'm digging myself deeper into a hole here and need to get out of it. 'It doesn't matter.' My eyes fall on the Mykonos postcard. 'Ooh, did you see what I pinned up? Thought it might brighten up the den a bit.'

Daisy follows my pointing finger and then looks at me with a hooded glare. 'You put that there?'

I smile brightly, but she doesn't look very impressed.

'It's mine,' says Daisy.

'Well, you can have it if you want . . .'

'No, I mean it belongs to me. Rosie gave it to me. My sister. She went to Mykonos. She didn't bother to post it so she just brought it home for me. It's mine.'

'It was in the book,' I say. 'I thought it was just . . .' I trail off, and now it's my turn to frown.

'Are you reading the book?' says Daisy.

'Are you reading the book?' I say at the same time.

'The book on Greek mythology? In the Theodore room?' says Daisy.

'Yes, I am. On my lunch break. I wondered who kept moving the card.'

'Yes,' says Daisy, looking at me with a curious stare. 'So did I.'

We look at each other for a long moment. Then we both jump as Harold says, 'I was only resting my eyes!' then snuggles deeper into the chair and resumes his snoring with gusto.

'I didn't know you liked Greek myths,' I say. I realise I don't know anything about Daisy. Nothing at all. But it's as though she's cautiously reeling out twine, like Theseus used to mark his progress through the labyrinth of the minotaur, and I have this sudden crazy notion that I've a mind to follow the trail, into the mysterious maze that is Daisy Dukes. She's looking at me thoughtfully, tapping a fingernail on her cup of tea.

'Come with me,' she says, putting down her mug on the desk. 'There's something I want to show you. Two things, really.'

'Are you sure we should be doing this?' I hiss. I don't know why I'm whispering again. Harold's still deep in dreamland in the den. Daisy is sorting through her keys, eventually finding the one that unlocks Seema's office.

'The CCTV is out of action. So is Harold.' Daisy finds the right key and unlocks the door.

'I thought you were all about rules and regulations!' I say. I'm still whispering.

'And I thought you liked cutting loose a bit,' she retorts. 'Well, somebody might be cutting you loose whether you like it or not.'

Daisy opens the door and leads me to Seema's ordered and neat desk. She searches on the bookcase behind it and finds a file. She flicks through some papers and hands one to me. It's headlined *RATIONALISATION*. I read it swiftly, then read it again more slowly, then I look at Daisy.

'They want to get rid of us? You, me and Harold?'

'I'm not sure they actually want to. It's just business.' Daisy gives a little shrug. 'I thought you should probably know, that's all. So you can look for another job.'

'I like this job,' I say, and I realise it's true. I'd never really thought of it before. As something I enjoy. But I do. I read the note again. 'It doesn't look like it's set in stone, yet. They might decide not to go through with it.'

Daisy nods, taking the piece of paper from me and carefully replacing it in the file, which she puts back on the bookcase. 'That's why I said I had two things to show you.'

We're back in the Standish Hall, Daisy having carefully locked up and, which makes me laugh inside, wiping the door handle with one of the paper handkerchiefs I gave her earlier. She stands me in front of the fashion exhibition, before a mannequin dressed in sixties gear. For a moment I wonder what she's trying to show me. The model is wearing a miniskirt, and for a crazy second I think she might be asking my opinion on whether she should wear something like that. Daisy's wearing a skirt tonight and to be honest she does have good legs. That security-guard uniform does nothing for her figure. Then I push the thought away, and try to focus. We're about to lose our jobs. Maybe. This must be connected.

'Have you got it yet?' she says.

I stare at the mannequin a bit longer, then shake my head.

'It's the hat. It's missing. Another thing that's been taken.'

I sigh. 'Daisy, with the greatest of respect, I'm not sure that's of much importance any more.'

But she's counting off on her fingers. 'The weaving shuttle. The gas mask. And now the hat. What's the connection?'

I shake my head, still trying to process the information I've received tonight. 'There isn't any. Two of those items were just taken away and returned. Maybe the hat will be as well. It's not the crime of the century, Daisy.'

'It's still wrong,' she says. 'Taking something without asking, even if you give it back.'

'Haven't we got bigger problems, though?'

Daisy grabs my arm and looks up at me. 'Don't you see? If we can solve the mystery, we could perhaps show them—'

'Show them we're indispensable!' I say. I can feel my eyes lighting up. And something else, as well, something other than saving my job. Maybe something more important. 'We can be detectives! Like Pikachu!'

Daisy frowns again. 'What?'

'Nothing,' I say. 'Just something my son said. But yes, I'll help you! How do we start?'

'I'll formulate a plan.' Daisy looks at her watch. 'I'm going to get a taxi home.'

'Me too,' I say. 'Where do you live? Are we going in the same direction?'

Daisy gives me her address and I gape at her. 'That's literally round the corner from me! I live at the other end of the parade! I had no idea.'

We decide to leave Harold dozing. Daisy even washes the tea cups so he doesn't have any extra work to do. Then we get a cab on the edge of the Northern Quarter and ride in silence, stopping first at Daisy's street. As she gets out I put a hand on her arm and say, 'Thank you for asking me to help you with the mystery. It means a lot.'

She shrugs. 'I was just going to do it on my own but . . .'

'What changed your mind?'

Daisy gets out of the idling cab and takes out her keys. She leans back in and looks at me. 'The book. The Greek myths.'

I want her to explain further, but she slams closed the cab door and bangs the roof twice with her hand, and the taxi driver pulls away. I twist around and watch Daisy letting herself into the terraced house, and keep watching after she's gone in and shut the door, until the cab turns out of her street.

20

Daisy

Of course, the next morning Rosie wants to know all the gory details of how my date went. I tell her the truth and she stares at me, incredulous, over her morning coffee and cigarette, standing a little way into the yard. It's a clear, bright morning and actually feels like it might be a degree or two warmer, like spring is actually here.

'He thought you were a *prostitute*?'

'Well, he didn't actually say the word,' I say primly. 'But he made it abundantly clear that he was only after one thing.'

'And he made you pay for the drinks? What an absolute twat. Daisy, I am so sorry.'

'Well, needless to say, I've deleted that app from my phone.'

Rosie stubs out her cigarette and comes in, giving me a hug which I awkwardly stand and suffer, wrinkling my nose at her smoky breath.

'You shouldn't give up, Daisy. They're not all like that. You just got a bad one.' She pauses. 'You were back late, though. Are you sure you're all right? What did you do?'

I pause for a moment, then say, 'I met Nate. Who I work with. The day security guard. He was having a meal across the road and he saw Alfie grabbing my arm. He come over and saw him off.'

Rosie's eyes shine. 'Ooh, a proper knight in shining armour! Tell me about Nate again.'

I shrug, buttering Mother's toast. 'There's not much to tell. He works days and I work nights. Janice off reception always makes a joke of it. She says Daisy should work days and Nate should work nights. I only see him for fifteen minutes every day, when we do the handover.'

Rosie is sitting me down at the table. 'No, what's he like? Is he tall? Handsome? Married? Funny? Nice?'

I stand up again and get Mother's toast and cup of tea. I cock my head to one side while I consider Rosie's quick-fire questions. 'Yes, he's tall. He has an ex-wife, and a son. He thinks he's funny. He's always making jokes. I don't really get them, though. He said to me, *Who are you and what have you done with Daisy Dukes?* because he said I was different out of work.'

Rosie laughs delightedly. I scowl. 'It's not funny. It's not even a joke.'

'And what about handsome? And nice?' presses Rosie, tapping another cigarette out of her packet.

'He was nice enough to leave his date because he saw me in trouble,' I say with a shrug.

Rosie's eyes widen. 'Wow! And handsome? Come on, Daisy. You must know if he's handsome or not.'

'I suppose,' I concede, heading out of the kitchen with Mother's breakfast before the toast turns into cardboard. 'Shouldn't you be getting ready for work?'

As soon as Rosie comes in through the door after her shift she starts on me again, not even bothering to ask how Mother is. For the record, Mother has had a fairly good day. She actually came downstairs and watched TV in the living room for most of the afternoon, which gave me the chance to wash her bedding and air out her room a bit. I gave the windows a good clean on the inside, and hoovered the carpet.

'Maybe you should go in to work a bit early,' says Rosie. 'Catch up with Nate.'

'There's nothing to catch up with Nate about,' I say. Though, of course, there is the matter of our investigation. I'm not sure how I feel about asking Nate to help me, and him accepting. It wasn't a normal situation. I was all at sixes and sevens (as Mother would say) after that date with that horrible Alfie. And Nate was, as Rosie kept pressing me to admit, being quite nice. I sort of regret sharing so much with him now, but what's done is done. I've now convinced myself he was just being polite, though, and has no real intention of solving the mystery with me properly.

I'm polishing my shoes when Rosie walks in, and she takes the opportunity to box me in at the kitchen table, pulling her chair up against me so I can't escape. 'So,' she says. 'I've been thinking. About Nate.'

'I haven't,' I say, and put my head down so she can't see my red cheeks and swivelling eyes, because I'm lying, I have been thinking about him, because he was very nice to me last night. I'm not used to that. Not from strangers. I suppose he's not really a stranger, because I see him every day, but really he is. I don't know anything about him and he doesn't know anything about me. We learned more about each other last night than we have in six months of working together.

But that's where it has to stop. Because the only things to know about me are either not very interesting, or they're none of anyone one else's business.

Or they're bad.

I have a flash of Darren, walking away from me in Castlefield that gloriously sunny day. I can't do this any more. Not after what you told me. Darren looks over his shoulder at me one last time, but suddenly it's Nate, not Darren. And then it's that horrible Alfie. And then it's a blur of faces half glimpsed on that stupid dating app, all of them walking away from me, all of them hating me when they find out what I did.

'It's that all-night event coming up next weekend, isn't it?' says Rosie, puncturing my little daydream. Well, day-nightmare, really, if you can have one of those. I blink and look at her, and start polishing my shoe again. 'Will Nate be there?'

'I think so. I think he said something about taking his son.'

Rosie rubs her chin. 'Hmm. Not necessarily ideal.' Then a smile lights up her face. 'Or maybe it is, if you can be nice to the kid. Show Nate your softer side.'

I put my shoe down on the page of newspaper I've spread out on the kitchen table and pick up my other one. As I start to smear polish on it I say, 'What do you mean? Ideal for what?'

Rosie, evidently sure I'm not going to flee, goes to the fridge to pour herself a glass of white wine. 'For getting to know him better.'

I consider this for a bit. 'I'd have thought you wouldn't like Nate. Because he's divorced and has a son. I thought you said—'

'I know what I said. But not every man is like Dad, you know. Nate obviously still has a close relationship with his son.'

I buff up the polish on my shoe. 'Rosie,' I say. 'Why do you think Dad left us?'

She peers into her wine glass. 'I don't think he did, not really. He left Mum. We were just . . . what do they say on the films? Collateral damage.'

'But why have we never seen him since? Why didn't he want us in his life?'

'You'd have to ask him that,' she says. She takes a big glug of wine. 'He walked out, Daisy, and he never walked back.

Never phoned. Not after he got with that other woman. He never sent us a birthday card, he never gave Mum any money to help with us.'

'Aren't you interested, though? Have you never thought of finding him?'

Rosie gets up to fill her glass again. 'No. Not for years. I don't think I could trust myself not to lamp the bastard. For what he did.' Then she looks at me, dead in the eye. 'For what he made you do.'

I put my head down again, polishing my shoe furiously even though I can see my reflection in it. I want for more than anything else in the world not to talk about this. About what happened. The good mood that Rosie floated in on like a cloud has dissipated, or maybe turned grey and stormy. When I risk a glance up she's rubbing her forearm beneath her jumper.

'Just go to work, Daisy,' she says, her voice dull and flat.

The boys are shouting at me at the bus stop again. I feel this is all I deserve. I can sense the black dog padding around, sniffing at the bins and slinking between the parked cars, infecting me with its tendrils of inky nothingness. That's how it feels when the black dog is on you. Nothingness. An absence. Not of anything specific, just a void that your energy and your thoughts fall into, that grows and grows inside your head. I just stand, staring ahead, trying to blot them out when they start singing Crazy Daisy at me. They've sent the little one again, this time he's dancing in front of me, and he turns around, looking over his shoulder. Our eyes meet. He looks a little afraid, and I'm not sure if that's of me, of Crazy Daisy, or of the bigger boys who are egging him on with shouts and whistles. There's also a glimmer of something else in his eyes. Shame, maybe. Because then he swiftly drags down his joggers, baring his thin buttocks at me, and runs off as the catcalls reach a crescendo and my bus turns up just in time, before I whirl around and completely lose my rag. I sit on the bus and stare at the boys, and my eyes meet the little one's again. I hate him. I hate them all, but most of all I hate him. Because he knows what he's doing is wrong. But he does it anyway.

When I get into work, Nate is very excited. He doesn't even let me go into the den – I mean, the security office – to take off my coat, but instead steers me to the fashion exhibition in the Standish Hall.

The hat is back on the mannequin.

'Did you see who did it?' I ask.

Nate shakes his head. 'I only noticed it an hour ago.'

'But it wasn't there when you came in on your shift? It's been put back at some point during the day?'

Nate pulls a face. 'Well, I can't be sure, to be honest. I should have checked when I arrived. But I forgot.'

I sigh loudly. Perhaps bringing Nate in on this was the wrong decision. If he's not going to exercise due diligence he might be more of a hindrance than a help. Nate gives a little giggle. 'Harold was funny when I got in. I asked him how the night shift had gone and he was like, yes, fine, nothing happened, boring as usual. He'd absolutely no idea we'd been in.'

I nod and head to the security office. Nate follows me, his face cloudy with concern. 'Daisy? Are you all right?'

'Fine,' I say. The black dog followed me on to the bus and sat beside me all the way into town, and I can still feel it, lurking behind the exhibits and cabinets.

Nate seems a little crestfallen. 'Oh.' Then he brightens up. Nothing seems to keep him down for long. I wish it was so easy for me. 'I made a list!'

He picks up a piece of paper from the desk. On it he's written the name of everyone who works at the museum. 'Suspects,' he declares in a whisper.

I scan the names. 'We aren't on it.'

Nate frowns. 'Well, we're the detectives, aren't we? I know I didn't do it and you know you didn't do it.'

'But I don't know you didn't do it, and vice versa,' I say, handing the sheet back to him. 'Why would you think it's someone who works here?' I don't tell him that I'd begun to have my own suspicions that it was an inside job; I'm interested to know his own thought processes.

'Well,' says Nate with a confidential air. 'Seeing Harold asleep got me thinking. If he's doing that every night, then it would be easy for someone to come in and take things, and put them back. We both saw how deeply he was zonked out. And anybody in the museum could theoretically have access to a set of keys.'

When the black dog is on me it's hard to shake me out of it. I just have to let it run its course. In some way, I don't want to get out of it. I feel like I deserve it. But despite myself, I find Nate's sudden enthusiasm is quite infectious. He has such an easy manner with people; I've seen him talking to the museum visitors, like they're old friends, when they are in fact complete strangers. I feel quite envious of that ability. I've never been very good with people. I take the list back from him and study it again.

'Hmmm. Well, the CCTV is out, and we don't want to tip off Harold because if he starts staying awake, then that'll put off whoever's coming in. If it is someone coming in at night.'

'I was thinking that exactly!' says Nate, his eyes bright. 'That's why I think we should do a stake-out.'

21

Nate

Ben is gratifyingly delighted when I swear him to secrecy and tell him that I've been promoted to detective at work and am investigating the Mystery of the Missing Exhibits. His eyes go wide when I make him promise not to say anything because it is a deeply undercover role.

'Whoa!' he says, a spoonful of Weetabix paused between bowl and mouth. 'That is brilliant!'

It's a somewhat better reaction than the one I get from Lucia. Yesterday I didn't see her because she and John had arranged to take Ben to school. This morning she's had the benefit of stewing over the chapter and verse she got from Sara at work yesterday, and is blazing mad. 'You walked out on her?' she says again, incredulous, coming into the kitchen, all kitted out for work. She's already harangued me about it as soon as I walked in the door, but she's obviously been getting radged up even more while upstairs.

'I told you, it wasn't exactly like that,' I say, realising that it was, in fact, exactly like that.

'And you threw twenty quid at her for her taxi? And you went out and started talking to some random woman on the street? Who do you think you are?'

Ah, so Sara had seen me with Daisy. 'It wasn't a random woman. It was someone from work. I just happened to see her. She was having a bit of bother.'

Lucia isn't for listening. 'Do you know how embarrassing this is for me? I'd told her you were nice.'

I can feel anger and resentment building up inside me, and I let it out with a shout. 'But what you failed to tell me was that she is a bigoted motormouth airhead! Jesus, Lucia, I mean to say . . . what were you thinking of, hooking me up with her?'

'Don't fucking shout at me!' shouts Lucia. And all of a sudden it is like we are still married again. Ben is sitting at the kitchen table with his Weetabix, impassively watching us hurl insults at each other, like he is a spectator at a tennis game.

I catch his eye and murmur, 'Not in front of Ben.'

'Ben knows what an arsehole you are!' yells Lucia. 'The sort that makes him go to football matches he doesn't want to go to and lets him stay out until god knows what time roaming the streets!'

'Not this again! Jesus!'

'I'm going to work!' shouts Lucia. She pauses to give Ben a kiss on his head and then shoots a dagger-filled glare at me, and slams the door behind her.

'Sorry you had to hear all that,' I say.

Ben shrugs. 'It's just what you do. Shout at each other.'

Is that all he remembers from our time together as a family? I feel a yawning pit inside of my stomach, a shame at the way we failed him. At the way Lucia and I failed each other. Even now, I can't do anything right. Even now, I'm just the boring old estranged dad with a boring old job who—

As if reading my mind and coming to rescue me from falling into that widening pit within me, Ben suddenly gifts me the most brilliant, heartbreaking smile. 'Detective, though. That's amazing, Dad.'

'You looking forward to the ManMuSH Big Sleepover next Friday?' I say as we walk to school. 'It'll be loads of fun!'

'Will I meet your partner?' says Ben. 'I won't say anything about the detective work, I promise.' He taps the side of his nose, just like I did when I told him that I was working with a colleague to solve the mystery.

'You might well do,' I say, winking theatrically at him. 'But remember. Top secret. We don't know who's behind it all and we don't want to tip anyone off.'

At the school gates, Ben gives me a big wink and I tell him I'll see him on Monday. It's not my weekend with him, though I wish it was after the disaster with the footy last Saturday. Lucia and John are taking him to Blackpool Pleasure Beach, apparently. Whoopee-do.

Well, I'll trump a quick turn on the Big Dipper when I tell him on Monday that I'm doing an overnight stake-out at the museum. I've kept that one back from him for now, which I'm quite proud of. As soon as Daisy was talking about investigating the mystery it all fell into place for me. Yes, John might have the flash car and the smart clothes and the good looks, but he'll never replace me in my son's affections. Not when I'm an honest-to-goodness *detective*. I really do have Daisy to thank for all this. I mean, it's not as if anyone really cares about those trinkets going missing and turning up again, but if I can play the game for a little while it might go some way towards . . . well, towards making my son love me again.

I have to admit that I was thinking about helping the whole mystery thing along a bit and actually taking something from one of the exhibitions, just for a couple of days. Just to keep things moving. As it turns out, though, I don't need to. Late in the afternoon I'm having a stroll around when I notice a gap in one of the cabinets in the Lever Wing. Not the one the shuttle was in, but one nearer to the door. A small label says there should be a teapot there, in one of those orange and brown designs they loved in the seventies. Despite myself I feel a bit of excitement at the prospect of another thing missing, and am itching to tell Daisy when she comes on for her shift at five.

'I took some photos of the crime scene on my phone,' I say, showing her. She nods approvingly, and that makes me smile. It's nice to actually do something right for a change.

'What's the link?' says Daisy, furrowing her brow. 'A weaving shuttle, a gas mask, a hat, a teapot.' She rubs her chin so I do the same, and we both walk up and down the tiny space of the den, pondering it all very hard.

'Nothing older than, what, seventy-five years?' I say. 'Do you think that's relevant?'

'Possibly a connection,' says Daisy. 'Unless we come in on Monday to find Baryonyx missing.' She smiles uncertainly.

'Daisy Dukes, was that a joke?' I say.

She looks at me hopefully. 'Was it a good one? I'm not really used to them.'

'It was excellent!' I declare.

She smiles and blushes, and says, 'The items are usually missing for a couple of days. That means maybe we should do the stake-out on Monday or Tuesday, if the teapot hasn't come back by then?'

'Brilliant!' I say. Ben is going to love this.

It was sunny the day of Dad's funeral. It's not supposed to be sunny at a funeral. It's supposed to rain, to have roiling grey clouds smashing up against each other in the sky, to match everyone's mood. Perhaps the weather that day mirrored my own state of mind. Terry Garvey was gone; the Black Bomber had thrown his last right hook. The sun had come out at last.

After all the cauliflower-eared boxers had paid their respects at the graveside and my mother had been helped into a car by a pair of aunties, when they'd all gone off to the Labour Club for the cheap beer and curling-up sandwiches, I stayed behind at the graveside, all alone, staring into the pit where his coffin lay, waiting for the gravediggers to shovel dirt over it.

I'd imagine Mum was thinking I was paying my final respects, making my peace with Terry Garvey. I wasn't, though. I was making peace with myself. Or, at least, trying to. All my life I'd been a prisoner of Dad's moods and temper. Even after I could have left, I stayed on to try to protect Mum, a self-imposed incarceration in a jail that was really just an extension of his own head. His state of mind spilled out and over, filling the house with either his rage or his ebullience, which was just as tiring for those caught up in his emotional tsunami.

But now, for the first time, I was free. Free to try to stop worrying about Mum, free to try to forge my own life out of the toxic space that was our family home. I never realised then, of course, that I would be back in that house, long after both parents had passed, living alone except for every other weekend when my ten-year-old son came to – grudgingly, I increasingly suspect – stay for a couple of days.

I made a vow to Terry Garvey as I stood by his fresh grave. I promised him and anyone who was listening that if I ever became a father, I would not be the sort of dad that he was. I would love and cherish and support my children, unconditionally.

It being a Saturday without Ben, I find myself at Terry Garvey's grave again. Well, not really; strictly speaking I come here for Mum, to tidy the leaves and twigs blown by March winds on to the plot, put down a fresh bunch of daffs. But as they're buried there together, you can't have one without the other. Just like in their lives. In my head I talk mainly to Mum, telling her about my fortnight, updating her on how Ben's getting on at school and what Lucia's been up to. As if she's really listening, I offer sanitised, edited versions of events. She doesn't need to know too much about my disastrous date, I mention in passing that Lucia is seeing someone called John (adding that I don't think it's very serious), and I underplay last weekend's disastrous visit from Ben. As I clean the pot of rainwater and arrange the daffs, I realise with mild surprise that I'm telling Mum – or really just thinking towards the headstone – quite a lot about Daisy Dukes.

'She had a skirt on, and this blouse,' I find myself saying aloud. 'She looked quite lovely.'

If I can imagine the spirit of my mother quietly listening to what I'm thinking, then I can also feel the shadow of Terry Garvey behind her, earthy-scented and as black as a rook. A malevolent presence, shackled to her in death as much as he was in life.

'Idiot,' I say out loud to myself. Mum is gone. Dad is gone. I'm free. So why can't I shake the feeling that Terry Garvey isn't quite done with me just yet?

'No teapot?' says Daisy when she comes in for her shift on Monday evening.

'No teapot,' I say.

'Right, if it's not back tomorrow . . . do you still want to do the stake-out?'

I have to admit, that between watching *Match of the Day* on Saturday night and *Call the Midwife* on Sunday evening I'd begun to have doubts about the whole enterprise. It was being away from Daisy, and the almost infectious quiet enthusiasm that I don't think she really knows she exudes. I began to wonder what I was thinking, a grown man of nearly forty, planning to run around a museum in the middle of the night looking for a thief who probably didn't even exist. It was all faintly ridiculous – not even faintly, Lucia would think, which is why I'd sworn Ben to secrecy about the whole matter, under the spurious pretext of it being an undercover operation. I could just imagine Lucia's withering look if she found out I was actually doing this. But then again, maybe Daisy's right. Our jobs are on the line and this might actually work in our favour.

'I think we should,' I tell Daisy. 'Do the stake-out.'

'Tomorrow night, then?'

'It's a date,' I say, and Daisy gives me a curious look for a second, one I can't quite read.

Any doubts I might have about it dissipate on Tuesday morning when, on the walk into school, I confide to Ben that tonight is the night.

His eyes widen, all his thoughts of telling me what a brilliant time he had in Blackpool suddenly forgotten. 'You're really doing it? You and your partner? You're going to stay up all night and catch the villain?'

'Maybe we'll catch him,' I say, winking at Ben as we stop at the school gates. I haven't told him Daisy's name. I'm not really sure why, other than to make it all a bit more mysterious and detective-y by just referring to her as my partner. 'Or maybe his cunning will prove too much for us and he'll evade capture. But we'll get him, you'll see. Dogged determination and detective work will save the day.'

Then, to my astonishment, Ben gives me a hug. He never does that. Far too cool at the age of ten to give his dad a cuddle in public. Even he realises this, that he's slipped, and he pulls away quickly. But it's there. It's done. I am doing good parenting, and I have been rewarded. Stick that in your pipe and smoke it, Terry Garvey. I'm not like you.

I'm not like you at all.

22

Daisy

'You're doing what?' says Rosie.

'I'll be home before you leave for work,' I say. I watch her pour boiling water into two cups of coffee. She puts sugar in one. Rosie doesn't take sugar. Neither do I.

She catches me staring and says quietly, 'It's for Ian.'

'Ian, thirty-five, likes Indian food and Peter Kay?'

'And, as it turns out, cunnilingus. For hours.'

Rosie gives me a coy smile but I'm shocked. I can feel myself blushing on her behalf. 'Rosie! He's here? In your bed? What if Mother heard you?'

'She did. She knocked on the door about midnight to tell me to shut up.' Rosie gives me a slightly exasperated but not unkind look. 'Oh, Daisy. We're all grown-ups. And Mum's had two kids, remember. She's not a nun.'

I think about what Rosie said days ago about Uncle Alan, who wasn't our uncle at all. I don't really like to think of Mother doing . . . well, doing things like that. Not when she's lying there in bed, ravaged by the cancer. It doesn't seem right, somehow.

'What about you?' says Rosie, adding milk to the cups.

'I've got one,' I say, holding up my mug.

'I'm not talking about a brew. I mean Nate.'

'I don't know what you mean,' I say. I briefly imagine Nate lying in my bed and me taking him a cup of coffee. Maybe after he's been . . . what Rosie said. For hours. That's stupid. I push the image away. I don't even know if Nate drinks coffee of a morning. 'Nate and I are just work colleagues.'

'A work colleague who's giving up his night to spend it with you running around a museum like something off *Scooby-Doo*,' says Rosie, with a knowing smile. She picks up the drinks. 'Better get this up to Ian. He's running me into work. Might just be time for a quickie, if he's lucky.'

I'd wondered why Rosie wasn't up when I got in from work. I'd assumed she was just tired. Turned out she was, just not from working. Why is she so fixated on Nate? I decide to go for a shower so I can be ready for when Mother wakes up. She'll no doubt be in a grumpy mood if Rosie and Ian kept her awake after midnight.

At the top of the landing I pause outside Rosie's closed door. I can hear the creaking of bed-springs and my sister making a noise like a cat meowing to be let in from the rain. It's been so long, for me, since Darren. I feel a dull ache down there, like when your tummy rumbles when you're hungry. As I get in the shower, I think of Nate again, the way he put himself between me and that Alfie. I think about his skin and his height and his bright eyes. I turn the shower to cold and stand there under it for a long time.

Ian seems nice enough. He wears jeans and a T-shirt that says *Garlic bread?* on the front. He shakes my hand in the kitchen and says hello, and then goodbye as he and Rosie leave to go to her work. I have time for one more coffee before I hear Mother getting up and shuffling to the bathroom, and then my day starts again.

The plan is that after my shift I will leave the museum and meet up with Nate around the corner. We will wait an hour for Harold to doze off in the security office then let ourselves in, and . . . well, after that, it gets a little vague. Too vague for me. I like things to be planned out properly. Nate has left right on time at five, giving me a wink on his way out, and I'm just waiting for the rest of the visitors to leave, while I try to formulate some kind of plan for tonight. There's a little boy staring at the dinosaur skeleton in the Horridge Wing. I look around and see who I assume are his parents, peering into one of the glass cabinets a short way off. Perhaps we could hide ourselves in the Lever Wing, as that's where the teapot is missing from. Or we could stay in the security office, but then we risk waking up Harold and that would all be a bit awkward.

'What's this dinosaur called?'

I vaguely realise the little boy is looking up at me.

'Cunnilingus,' I say, distractedly.

'That's a funny name.'

With horror I realise what I've said. 'Baryonyx!' I say wildly. 'Baryonyx!'

'That's a funny name, too,' says the boy. Oh god, his parents are walking over now. 'I think I like the first one better.'

'We call him Barry!' I say loudly. I smile at his mum and dad. 'Barry. The dinosaur. That's what we call it. It's short for Baryonyx.'

'You could call it Connie, as well,' says the boy. 'To be short for the other name.'

'Other name?' says his mum.

'Look at the time!' I say. 'Museum closes in fifteen minutes! Best to start making your way downstairs!'

Nate is waiting for me around the corner from the museum at one o'clock, just as he said he would be. He's wearing his security-guard uniform. 'I thought it might be best, in case there's any awkward questions from anyone,' he says.

We stand there together for a moment, as though neither of us can quite believe that we're actually going through with this. In the cold light of day – well, the cold dark of early morning, I suppose would be more accurate – it does seem a bit like a silly thing to do. But we're here, now. And if it does help to save our jobs, well, it'll all be worth it.

'I think we should give Harold a good hour,' says Nate.

'What should we do in the meantime?' I say. The burgeoning spring of the days hasn't yet penetrated the nights, which remain cold with sometimes even the hint of a frost.

Nate makes a show of thinking for a moment, then says, 'What about a drink? There are plenty of bars open in the Northern Quarter at this time.'

'Maybe just one,' I concede. It would be good not to spend the next hour standing in the street. 'We need to be on the ball for the stake-out, though.'

'You said it was called *what*?' says Nate, his eyes wide, his mouth gaping.

'I'm not saying it again,' I say firmly. 'Oh, Nate, I could have died. I wanted the ground to open up and swallow me. Especially when his parents came over.'

Despite what I said before, we are on our second drink. It will have to be our last, though. We are the only people in the bar and at the back the staff are stacking stools up on tables and starting to mop the floor. I wasn't going to mention the Baryonyx thing at all but the first glass of wine seems to have loosened my tongue a bit. This is why I don't drink much. You can't stay in complete control when you've had a drink, can you?

'It's possibly the most hilarious thing I've ever heard,' says Nate, then drains his glass of beer. I glow a little, inside. Nobody's ever told me I'm funny before. Even if I didn't mean to be. It's not like with the boys at the bus stop. Nate's not laughing at me. He's laughing with me. And it's the most wonderful thing in the world, to laugh with someone. I don't really remember Darren and I laughing about much at all.

It might be the wine talking, but I find it all really quite liberating.

The bar staff close up behind us as we leave and Nate and I make our way back to the museum. The cold air brings me up short a little, makes my head feel all bubbly. The wine as well, I suppose, not just the cold air.

As Nate's putting his key into the lock on the main door of the museum I grab his arm, and hiss, 'What if Harold's not asleep?'

Nate considers this for a moment, the key paused in the lock. Then he says, 'We'll tell him it's a training exercise. And that he should have got an email about it. Harold never checks his emails. Or say it was in the report you gave him tonight. Which will be unread and in the bin, covered in teabags.'

With exaggerated slow movements, Nate turns the key in the lock and pushes open the door. It creaks mournfully and we both wince. Nate holds the door while I sneak in under his arm and then he closes it again, painfully slowly, and locks it. He puts a finger to his lips and cocks his head on one side. The silence in the museum is dry and dusty, the silence of sleeping history. But then we hear it, low at first and rumbling like distant thunder, but getting louder.

Harold snoring from the den.

I mean, the security office. Nate grins broadly at me and points to the stairs and I follow him, copying his tiptoe walk and long steps. I have to stifle a giggle; it's exactly like Rosie said this morning. We're just like something from *Scooby-Doo*.

Nate leads me to the Lever Wing, where the teapot is, of course, still missing. 'There's no real reason that it should be replaced tonight,' I say.

Nate shrugs. 'It's never been longer than three or four days between something going missing and it being returned, has it? So tonight's as good a time as any.'

We stand there for a moment, staring into the empty space where the teapot should be. Nate says casually, 'Do you do that often? Go on dates?' He pauses. 'I'm sorry, that came out wrong. I didn't mean it to sound like that.'

'It's fine. And no. That was the first time. For a long while, anyway. My sister Rosie made me download this app to my phone. I won't be using it again.' I wait for a moment. 'What about you?'

Nate shrugs. 'Not since I got divorced. Like I said, my ex-wife fixed me up with someone she works with. It was a nightmare.'

'Sounds like neither of us are any good at dates,' I say. 'Why did you get divorced?'

I can feel Nate looking at me sidelong. Perhaps I shouldn't have said that. I'm never quite sure what's acceptable and what's not in light conversation. But I do want to know, as well. People get divorced for all kinds of reasons, but it's usually because somebody did something wrong, isn't it? That's why people split up. It suddenly occurs to me that I don't actually know whether Mother and Father got divorced. It's never actually been mentioned, as far as I can remember. I wonder if Nate left his wife or his wife left him. 'I'm sorry,' I say. 'None of my business.'

He leans on the cabinet, looking at me. 'It's fine. It was just . . . one of those things. It happens a lot. It wasn't really one big thing that happened. Lots of small things, I suppose. Microscopic things. But they all mount up, don't they? Come together until they do seem to make a thing that's too big to get around any more.'

I can feel him watching me. He says, 'What about you? Have you been with anyone for any length of time?'

I feel like he's being polite, that he doesn't think I'm the sort of person to have a long relationship at all. That's what most people think when they see me. But there doesn't seem to be any mockery in his eyes, no harshness to him. He seems genuinely interested. I say, 'There was Darren. A while ago.'

'What happened?' he says softly. 'Lots of little things, yeah?'

'No,' I say, sounding distant to myself. I look at myself in the faint reflection in the cabinet. 'One big thing.'

Nate looks as if he's about to ask me more but then his eyes widen. I'm about to ask him what's up when I hear it, too. Whistling. Coming up the staircase. Nate looks around wildly, but there's only one way out of the Lever Wing, and that's through the main doors.

'Quick,' I whisper, grabbing Nate's arm. 'Follow me.'

I rush over to the trade-union banners that line the back wall and pull one aside. There's space behind them, enough for us to stand against the wall. I push Nate in and slip in beside him, letting the heavy banner go and shrouding us in semi-darkness. Nate is breathing loudly. I nudge him in the ribs.

As the whistling gets louder, I chance a glance around the draped banner. I nudge Nate again and he bends sideways towards me. 'It's Harold,' I say, barely louder than a breath.

'What. Is. He. Doing?'

I peek around the banner again. Harold is trudging up and down the room, glancing into the cabinets and whistling tunelessly. He turns and I think he's going to leave, but then at the last second he changes course and heads for the chair that stands beside the doors, where Dorothy's guides usually take a seat when they're staffing the exhibition rooms. Harold reaches into his pocket and takes out a slim paperback. I groan audibly, and Harold glances up sharply, then returns to flipping through his book.

I beckon Nate to bend down again and whisper as loudly as I dare into his ear to tell him what Harold's doing. He sighs as well. We could conceivably be here for hours. And nobody's going to come in and replace the teapot if Harold has decided that tonight's the night he's going to stay awake, for once. The stake-out is now more of a wash out.

We stand there in complete silence, listening to Harold turning the pages of his paperback. Even now, in this situation, I'm riven with curiosity as to what he's reading. I time in my head how long it takes him to read two facing pages. Three minutes, on average. I can feel Nate getting restless beside me, shifting his weight from foot to foot. I can feel the proximity of his body alongside mine. It feels odd. Having someone so close. I'm not used to it. Not since Darren, and even with him I never felt as though . . . as though we were close. We were merely two people who sometimes occupied the same space. And at home, with Mother and Rosie, we're like satellites, orbiting each other but never making contact. It suddenly occurs to me that I can't remember the last time Mother hugged me. Certainly not since the thing that happened.

Here, with Nate, it all feels somehow different. Like I'm more aware of him, of the closeness of his body to mine. Like we're two human beings who are not merely passing by each other, but instead are somehow . . . I'm not sure how to describe it. Connected, maybe. And then something quite extraordinary happens.

Nate takes my hand in his.

And then something even more extraordinary happens. As Harold's head nods and bows, as he dozes off over his book, Nate moves to sneak out from behind the banners but I stay put and hold him back.

'Wait,' I whisper. 'There's something I want to tell you.'

It feels right to say it, here, hidden in the darkness, the touch of his hand on mine. It feels right to tell him before things go any further. It feels right to say this, where I can't see the reaction on his face.

'What is it, Daisy?' says Nate quietly.

I take a deep breath.

'I stabbed my sister,' I say.

23

Daisy

So here it is, the thing that happened. I was nine years old and Rosie was seven. I have replayed the scene in my mind so many times that it is now like a movie in my head, an old film that clatters through the projector, whirring around and around and picking out the details of our kitchen, twenty-five years ago.

It's the same kitchen in the same house we all live in now. The worktops and cabinet doors are different; it would be some years before Mother replaced them and here they are shabby and unkempt, the corners of the yellow and brown floral linoleum on the floor curling up. There is a transistor radio on the cracked tiles of the windowsill that looks out into the tiny, flagged yard. It is always tuned to Radio 1. Mother always had music playing when we were smaller. This afternoon there is a live broadcast from a music festival; I looked it up online years later and it was Donington. Heavy, frenetic, fast rock, that probably didn't contribute very well to the mood in the house that afternoon. Though I'm just making excuses.

It is early summer, June, and the sunlight is slanting in through the dusty windows. Saturdays were always tense; it was the day Dad came to visit us. Usually not for long; an hour at most. He was sometimes maudlin and weepy, and sometimes a little drunk, and the two might have gone hand in hand. As far as I can surmise, it was a casual arrangement hammered out between the two of them, not a formal access order put in place by the divorce courts.

Even now I can barely remember Father. In my memories there's a shape, a shadow, a scent of tobacco and sometimes beer, a spicy aftershave. A rough, green coat, something from an army surplus store. I don't remember him leaving us; the shape, the shadow was there, and then it wasn't. I sometimes get flashes of his face, lined and craggy, a cigarette hanging out of his mouth, his hair dark and mop-like, suddenly illuminated by the sun as he throws me up in the air on a summer's day. I must be younger than two, because I have the sense that it's just me and him, that Rosie has not arrived yet. There is the seed of something in that thought that I am sure led to what happened.

But my father doesn't come that Saturday. We never usually knew what time he was going to arrive: sometimes before he went to the pub (best); sometimes after he'd been to the pub (worst). It usually began with him and Mother being frostily civil to each other, and ended with her screaming at him and throwing something – we never had a full, matching set of crockery in those early years – that would explode on the door frame and hasten his departure, tossing insults over his shoulder as he left. That Saturday, though, that is the day we get the phone call.

The scene is set like this: Mother is sitting at the kitchen table, smoking and tapping her ash into a saucer long since divorced from its cup, probably smashed to smithereens inches from Father's head. She has a tall glass in front of her. I don't know what is in it. I am at the sink, washing up, which is one of my jobs. We all have jobs to do in the house. Rosie is useless at hers, whether it is hoovering or washing up or polishing the table with Mr Sheen. I always have to take over and finish it off. Today my job is washing up and I am gazing out of the window at the sharp shadows from the roofs and gables of the surrounding, tightly packed terraced houses, that are moving around the garden like a sundial that it is impossible to decipher.

Rosie is having a tantrum. She is standing by the kitchen door and screaming, her face red and furious, tears and snot streaming down her face. Her tiny fists are balled and white, she is stamping her feet on the curling lino.

Rosie does not want to wait in for Father's Saturday visit. She wants to go to the park to play with her friends. Mother is visibly annoyed but quiet. That's the worst sort of annoyed for Mother. When she is angry and shouting she is like a storm that blows itself out quickly. When she is angry and quiet she is like a distant growl of thunder, a hum of electricity on the air, a taste of copper on the breeze. I concentrate on the sunshine dappling the dishwater and on carefully stacking the washed pots on the draining board.

The phone is in the hall, on a little table by the front door. It is a green trimphone that is old and obsolete even then. It does not so much ring as shriek for attention, and it always puts everyone on edge. It is very often people demanding money, or making threats over unpaid bills, or trying to sell us things we do not want or need or can afford. I sense Mother jump a little when it bursts into its trilling song.

'Shush,' I say to Rosie as Mother heaves herself up and goes to answer it. Rosie walks over to me, pouting. I hold a glass up to the sun to check it's clean and put it upside down on the draining board.

'I want to go to the park.'

'After Daddy has been.' I hold up a plate to let the suds drip from it then stack it with the others.

'Now!'

I can hear Mother's voice, low at first and then angry, and then a tone I haven't heard before. Sort of . . . desperate, I suppose. The phone hits its cradle with a slam. I can feel my heart beating faster and my breath seems to be coming short and shallow. 'Rosie,' I murmur as Mother comes back into the kitchen. 'Stop it.'

Mother lights a cigarette and goes to the fridge to get another glass of whatever she's drinking. I concentrate on the washing-up. Plate. Saucer. Cup. Glass. Carving knife.

'That was your father,' says Mother. She stands behind me as I'm doing the washing-up, and Rosie, standing beside me and looking up at her. 'He's not coming.'

'Can I go to the park then?' says Rosie hopefully.

'No, you cannot go to the fucking park!' screams Mother.

Rosie puts her arms on the worktop, which she can only just reach, and buries her head in them, crying all over again.

'Shut up!' screams Mother, which makes Rosie cry all the harder. 'He's not coming today and he's never coming again! He's met some slag and he's moving in with her and she's got two kids herself so that's the lot of us dumped, all right?'

I slowly wash the carving knife, rubbing the blade with the scouring pad. I am thinking of that snatched image of Father throwing me up in the air, the blue sky whirling around me, his arms outstretched to catch me again.

'It's your fault,' says Mother, slowly. Her voice is low and not sounding like her at all. 'We were happy until we had kids.'

I am spinning in the air again, laughing half in terror, half in elation. Father is holding out his hands to catch me, to keep me safe. I lift the knife from the water and watch the bubbles drain from the blade.

No. Not our fault. Not my fault. Rosie's fault. Father was happy when it was just me. I can remember him being happy. It was after Rosie came that everything started to go wrong; I'm sure of it.

'It's all your fault!' Mother screams suddenly. Rosie goes quiet and looks at her, eyes filled with fear.

What happens next I can't quite remember properly. I seem to think that Mother made a grab for the knife, but I don't know if that was to stop me doing what I did, or after I'd done it. Everything is just black from that moment. The next thing I can recall is that we're all in the ambulance and it's got its lights and sirens on and we're whizzing to hospital. A tiny little part of me is excited that we're in an ambulance but mostly I just feel like I'm going to be sick and never stop.

The thing that happened is that I turned around and slammed the carving knife down hard. The blade went into Rosie's right forearm and through the other side and embedded itself in the kitchen worktop. I never said a word. There was a stunned silence and then Rosie started screaming and Mother ran to phone 999 and all hell broke loose. I remember none of it. I learn it all from the conversations between Mother and a serious-looking man who I'm told is a doctor, but he doesn't wear a long white doctor's coat or has one of those light things on a strap on his head like in my picture books. He doesn't even have a stethoscope around his neck. I am sitting in a chair next to Mother and facing the doctor across his desk. The doctor is asking lots of questions about what happened and Mother is telling him. Rosie had to have an operation and is now in a bed on the children's ward.

The doctor nods a lot and makes notes. After a while he turns to me and looks at me over the top of his glasses. 'Daisy,' he says in a serious but soft voice, 'what do you think about what you did?'

I couldn't remember any of it but I put my head down and say I am very sorry.

'Do you understand why you're sorry?' presses the doctor.

'It was a bad thing to do,' I say, hoping this is the right thing. I think about what Mother has been telling the doctor. 'I was upset because our father is never going to see us again.'

The doctor nods and puts his pen down and turns back to Mother. 'These are obviously very stressful times for you all. I'm satisfied that this was a one-off incident and that there are no safeguarding issues that really require me to refer this to the social services.'

I feel Mother relax beside me. 'Thank you, doctor. It's going to be tough but we'll get through it. Together.'

On the way out of hospital I try to hold Mother's hand and at first she pulls away from me, but then relents. 'Jesus Christ,' she mutters. 'I need a drink.'

Rosie stays in hospital for three days. She comes home with a big bandage around her arm, which is taken off a week later. She has to wear a pressure bandage to stop the scar bubbling up, for some months. Nobody ever talks about what happens. Things are just the same as they were before, except everything is completely different.

My throat is dry after talking for so long. Nate has not said a word throughout my story. I feel a little empty, and a little strangely giddy. I am simultaneously elated that I have got this off my chest, and nauseous about what Nate will think of it. I glance at the outline of him in the darkness.

'Wow,' he says quietly.

'Yes,' I whisper. 'Wow.'

At some point during my story Harold snored, farted, woke up and shuffled off. But I kept talking. And holding Nate's hand. Now I unhook my fingers from his. I can almost sense

Nate trying to formulate some kind of response beside me, so I put him out of his misery.

'It's all right, you don't have to say anything. I just wanted to tell you, that's all. Before . . .'

'Before what?'

I pull back the drape to make sure Harold has gone. 'Before . . . I don't know, Nate. Before this goes any further. It's better to know now. To save us all a lot of bother down the line.'

Nate follows me out from behind the banner. 'Wait. Daisy. I am so glad you told me. Opened up. It can't have been easy for you.'

'Easier this than standing in Castlefield Bowl while somebody tells you they can never feel safe around you again,' I say quietly. 'I think I'm just going to go home now.'

Nate is still trying to process everything. 'Castlefield Bowl?' he says helplessly. I don't have the energy to tell him about Darren, about our life together, and how that ended. I just don't want to be standing there, or anywhere, with Nate telling me the same thing in different words.

'Goodbye, Nate,' I say. 'I'll see you tomorrow for the handover.'

'Wait,' says Nate again. He puts out a hand and places it on my arm.

Our gazes meet.

Something changes in his eyes. Something so subtle you would never notice it, if you weren't looking for it. But I am looking for it. I've seen it before. I'm not sure he even realises he's done it, but as I am seeing something in his eyes, he's seeing something in mine. As though I am a line drawing that has now been coloured in. The picture is complete. The secrets are out. He lifts his hand, only a centimetre, but it's enough.

It's there.

I can't do this any more. Not after what you told me. You make me feel scared, Daisy.

I give Nate a smile that is sadder than I am expecting it to be, and walk across the gallery without looking back.

24

Nate

Well, I wasn't expecting that.

I could feel my feet going numb, standing there behind that banner. I was hopping between them, and could feel Daisy alongside me. It was strange. Almost like I was seeing her with fresh eyes, which was ridiculous because I couldn't see her at all in the darkness behind those thick drapes. I could smell her, though, shampoo and soap. And it was hot behind the banners, so hot I could feel sweat prickling on my forehead. I could hear us breathing, in unison, as lightly as we possibly could. And then it happens.

Daisy slips her hand into mine.

We stand there like that, holding hands, literally holding hands, and it's obvious neither of us know what to do next. It's as though we're two jump leads connected to a battery. I can feel something like energy or electricity coursing through me. It's a feeling I've not had since . . . well, if I'm honest, since ever. It's a strange, beautiful, frightening sensation.

And then she tells me that.

By the time I've sneaked out of the museum, the streets of the Northern Quarter are eerily still and quiet, and Daisy has gone.

'How did it go?' says Ben. 'The stake-out? Did you catch the villain?'

I stifle a yawn as I steer Ben along the pavement. It was four o'clock when I got in to my bed, and I was up at seven. I feel like death warmed up. I've no idea how I'm going to get through work today. I hadn't thought this out very well. It took me a while to find a cab. I wondered if Daisy had got home all right. Wondered how she felt about telling me about her sister.

Wondered how I felt about what she had told me.

'Well?' demands Ben.

'Oh, it went fine,' I say airily. 'But we didn't catch the baddie.'

'Are you going to do it again?'

'Maybe. But probably not on a school night.'

'Do you think you'll have caught the thief by next week? Then we can talk about it at the Big Sleepover thing? Or will it still be a secret?'

A secret. I'm barely listening to Ben because all I can think about is what Daisy told me. I'm not even sure why she told me, or what I'm supposed to do with the information. On the one hand, it was a long time ago. On the other . . . she stabbed her sister. And all this is mixed up with the holding of our hands. And how good that made me feel. The breath catching in my throat. The sensation that I could feel my own blood coursing through my veins. The electric touch of her hand on mine.

The hand that plunged a knife into her sister's arm.

I vaguely realise that Ben has been speaking to me. 'I'll keep you posted,' I say with forced jollity, tapping the side of my nose as he runs off into the playground. I think about the day ahead and just want to curl up right there on the pavement and go to sleep.

I hit a wall about lunchtime, and feel like I've been smacked in the face with a frying pan. Janice on reception notices me standing by the Standish Hall, gazing into the middle distance, and gooses me in my side, making me jump.

'What's up with you?' she demands.

I rub my face. 'Nothing. Didn't sleep well, that's all.'

Janice narrows her eyes and looks me up and down. 'Are you eating properly?'

I frown. 'Yes. I think so. Why?'

'My lamb bhuna is famous all over Manchester. Won't get a better one this side of Rusholme. You should let me make it for you one night.'

'I'm not mad keen on curry,' I say.

Janice looks at me as though I've just said I like to drown kittens of a Sunday afternoon. 'You haven't tried mine,' she says. 'Yet.' Janice puts a hand on my arm. 'You need to keep your strength up.'

'Do I? What for?'

Janice does her little laugh. 'You are funny, Nate. I like that.'

I'm still puzzling over Janice when I see Seema and Mr Meyer returning from lunch. Mr Meyer sees me and smiles vacantly. Seema scowls behind him. I wonder how far they've got on their rationalisation discussions? Whether me, Daisy and Harold are going to be out of a job soon? I suppose I should start looking for something new. I feel a vague sense of loss at the thought of it. I've always enjoyed my work here, but lately . . . it feels like it would be more of a disaster now to lose this position than it would have two or three weeks ago. And I don't really know why.

Except, of course I do. I start to drag myself up the stairs, hoping a change of scenery might take my mind off being so tired. Last night – or this morning, rather – behind those drapes in the Lever Wing, Daisy's hand nestled inside mine. I've spent most of the morning re-evaluating Daisy in my mind. She's like Bruce Springsteen. Well, not looks like him or anything; that would be a bit weird. But in the same way I was completely ambivalent about Springsteen for years, until about three years ago when I suddenly *got* him. It was like a switch had been flicked in my head and his genius was properly revealed to me. The same switch seems to have been hit regarding Daisy. I've spent the last few hours thinking about her smile, her hair, the smell of her, the way she creases her nose up when she's thinking hard about something, about how different she looked the other night when we were both on our disastrous dates. About the way she's so literal about things, which I suddenly find incredibly endearing.

And then I think about her confession. And I truly don't know what to think about anything any more.

A small group of pensioners is clustered around Barry in the Horridge Wing. I push Daisy to the back of my mind and go and speak to them, with a broad smile. A small, stooped man with big ears is pointing his stick at the dinosaur bones.

'Don't bloody believe in it,' he says.

'You stupid old fool!' shouts a woman with thick glasses and a thick woollen coat. 'It's right there in front of you!'

'I don't believe in it!' he insists, brandishing his cane. If he gets any wilder with that walking stick he's going to have the dinosaur in bits on the floor. 'When did you ever see any buggering horse that looked like that strolling around?'

'It's not a bloody horse, it's a dinosaur!' says the woman in disgust.

I'm about to step in and calm them all down when Dorothy arrives and starts her spiel about Baryonyx, where the bones were found, and when it was thought to have roamed the earth. This just seems to make the old boy even more furious, so I edge away from the group, confident Dorothy's got it in hand, and head towards the Lever Wing.

The teapot is back. I find myself simultaneously excited that there's been a development, and a little sick to my stomach because Daisy is going to be annoyed that, once again, the mystery thief has managed to return the stolen exhibit while I've been on duty. It's gone one, so I decide to take my break. I head upstairs to the Theodore room to get the book and take it back down to the den. Funny, that. Daisy reading the same book. Makes me feel like we had a connection all this time, even though neither of us knew it. I wonder what her favourite stories are from the Greek myths? I should ask her. I settle down in the den to have a read for half an hour, but after just a few minutes I can feel my eyes drooping and before long I'm fast asleep.

Curiously, when I wake up I'm no longer in the museum. I'm standing in a tunnel, with sand on the ground and stone walls and a low stone ceiling. The darkness is punctuated by flaming torches in sconces set into the rough stone. I feel my way forward, coming to a junction, the tunnel splitting off to the left and right.

I don't know which way to go, but in my hand is what looks like a huge ball of wool. I glance back the way I've come; the wool is stretched out behind me. I continue to unravel it as I go, choosing the left tunnel and walking on through the semi-darkness until I hit another junction. This goes on for some time – and at no point do I realise I'm dreaming – until eventually the tunnel opens into a wider space. At the centre of which . . .

. . . is my father. In his white shorts with The Black Bomber crudely embroidered on them, his fists encased in his gloves. He adopts a pose, his fists up, raising one eyebrow at me.

'You should have a bull's head,' I say to him.

He sneers at me. His voice is exactly like I remember it. 'This isn't one of your stupid books.' He nods at the ball of wool in my hand. 'Put that down. You won't be needing it.'

I remember then that Daisy gave it to me. She is standing at the entrance to the labyrinth, wrapped in a white robe, her hair piled up on top of her head. 'Please don't abandon me on Naxos when you've killed the monster,' she says, giving me the wool so I can reel it out behind me and find my way out of the maze.

'I won't,' I promise. We have both read the story of Theseus and the Minotaur in the book, and know that this is exactly what happens to Ariadne.

'If I lose the wool I'll not find my way back,' I say to my father. But I put it down on the sandy ground anyway.

Dad shakes his head, and spits on the sand with disgust. 'Haven't you got it yet? Take off that jacket. And that shirt.'

So this is it, then. He wants to fight. Wants to have the fight we never had, the one that the brain aneurysm robbed me of. So be it. I shake off my jacket and start to unbutton my shirt.

As I do, I see he's unlacing his gloves with his teeth, and pulling one off, sandwiched in his armpit, and then the other.

'Bare knuckle?' I say. 'Like the good old days? That famous Terry Garvey right hook?'

Dad laughs, cruelly, meanly. He throws first one glove, and then the other, in the sand at my feet as I take off my shirt. The torches dance in some sudden breeze, distorting his shadow, making it more gigantic and monstrous than it should be.

'Put them on,' he orders me.

'I don't have to do what you say any more.'

'Put them on.'

I feel compelled to, though I don't know why. I bend down and get the gloves, and slide my fists into them. He walks over to me and laces them up, not taking his eyes from mine. He nods his head backwards. 'Stand there. In the middle. Where I was.'

I do as he says. I stand in the middle of the dancing shadows in the room at the centre of the labyrinth while my dead father appraises me from the edge. There are tunnels leading off the room at all sides; I'm not even sure which one I came in through any more.

I put up my fists. 'Are we going to do this, then?'

Dad laughs. 'You're not here to fight me. You are me.'

And then he disappears, blinks out, leaving me alone, bare-chested with my gloves up. I pick up the ball of wool to retrace my steps to Daisy but it hangs loose, as though it's been cut with a knife. I have no idea which of the tunnels to take, no clue how to get out of the maze. I'm trapped here.

'Nate!'

I open my eyes sharply and my stomach tumbles as gravity whirls me around, dumping me on the floor of the den, the chair skittering out from under me. I look uncomprehendingly at Daisy, glaring down at me. Her hair is stringy and damp and her coat is soaked with rain.

'You fell asleep? In the security office?'

I glance at my watch. Oh my god. I've been out for hours. As I start to apologise and pick myself up, I remember something.

'Daisy! The teapot! It's back!'

She looks at me with a kind of blank, dead-eyed stare. 'It doesn't matter, Nate. None of that matters any more. Why don't you just go home?'

25

Daisy

I suppose we'd been lulled into what you call a false sense of security. The cancer had moved in to Mother and lived there, just like Rosie and I lived in the house with her. It was like a lodger, one who never went out anywhere, but just sort of lurked around. Yes, it made her ill, and, yes, it was the worst thing that had happened to us in the last few years, but we'd all sort of come to terms with it.

Except the cancer wasn't happy with just sitting there quietly in Mother's bones. It had decided it wanted to make its presence felt a bit more. Maybe it thought it wasn't getting enough attention. Perhaps it decided to have a tantrum, like a spoiled toddler or one of those ghosts that throws plates around a kitchen. A poltergeist.

We all knew that Mother had been getting worse since about six months ago, but she didn't seem to be getting any more worse, if that makes any sense. We thought – or at least, I thought – that perhaps this was as bad as it got. Yes, she spends most of her time in bed, but we had settled into a rhythm, Mother, Rosie and me, and we were coping.

But it wasn't as bad as it was going to get, apparently.

The cancer unit is a newish building separate from the main

hospital, and we've been going there every two months for updates from Dr Singh. The week before the appointment I have to take Mother to the local GP for blood to be taken, and when we see Dr Singh he's got the results of her tests in front of him. For the past three or four times we've been he's always smiled kindly and said, 'Steady as she goes!' in a sing-song voice.

Dr Singh isn't smiling today.

He talks a lot about blood cell counts and pain relief and uses words like 'aggressive'. I studiously take notes of everything he's saying in a spiral-bound notebook, glancing at Mother every few seconds. She listens to him impassively, and nods every time he pauses, as though encouraging him to continue. I'm so busy trying to get everything down on paper that Dr Singh is saying that I don't fully take it all in. So I'm a little shocked when Mother says, 'How long have I got, doctor?'

'Mother! Things aren't at that stage yet.' I look hopefully at Dr Singh. 'Tell her not to be so silly, doctor.'

He smiles, but not one of his Steady as she goes! smiles. He looks from Mother to me and back again and says, 'Well, it's difficult to put an exact figure on it. But with another round of chemotherapy and some new combinations of medication, there's no reason we can't expect to see you around for a while yet.'

I frown at Dr Singh. 'What's a while? Twenty years? Ten?'

'Daisy,' says Mother.

I ignore her. 'I mean, we are talking years, of course, aren't we? Tens of years?'

'Daisy,' says Mother more firmly. Dr Singh switches his gaze from me to her, and I look at her as well.

'I don't want to know,' she says. 'I've changed my mind. Pretend I didn't ask.'

'We always knew this was incurable, but manageable,' says Dr Singh. 'We are managing it as . . . well, as best that we can. But when it comes to estimates . . . I would say we want to be as hopeful as we can but . . . err on the more conservative side of things.'

Mother stands up. 'I told you both, I don't want to know.'

'I want to know!' I say.

'It's my life, Daisy,' says Mother wearily. 'And my death, too. I'll deal with it how I want to.'

I look angrily at Dr Singh. 'But I'm her carer! As is my sister Rosie! We've got a right to know these things, surely?'

Dr Singh pulls a face. He starts to talk about patient confidentiality and Mother sighs. 'Daisy, we've taken enough of the doctor's time. Can we just go home, please?'

In the cab on the way home, I feel Mother looking at me. It makes me cross for some reason, though I know it shouldn't. I should be more sympathetic.

'What?' I snap.

She raises her eyebrows and looks out of the window. I put my hand on hers, but that just serves to remind me of being with Nate, and makes me feel even worse.

'I don't want you to die,' I say, and I know it sounds soft and small and pathetic.

When Mother looks back at me, her eyes are shining with tears. 'Do you think I want to? But it comes to us all. It just might be coming to me sooner than any of us would like.'

'I'm not ready for you to go,' I say as the taxi driver negotiates a busy roundabout. 'I've not . . .'

'You've not paid for it,' says Mother. She looks at me with shrewd, narrowed eyes. 'Don't you think I know what this is about, Daisy? You moving back in? Making Rosie come home? You taking care of everything, looking after me, working nights?'

'It's because you're our mother and we love you—'

Mother cuts me off. 'It's because you're paying for what happened. To Rosie. You think this is your penance, don't you?'

I open my mouth to protest but then close it again. Mother's always had my number. Ever since I was tiny. I could never get away with lying to her. She could always see right through me.

'Remember you wanted to be a policewoman when you were little?' she says.

The pivoting of the conversation disarms me a little. I blink and say, 'Yes, well, I . . . well, there's no chance of that now, is there?'

'Nothing bad happened after . . . after the Rosie thing,' says Mother, glancing at the taxi driver. 'There would be nothing to stop you applying. Maybe after I'm gone. Nobody really knows about what happened.'

'I know what happened,' I say tightly. 'And that's what counts.'

'You need to start thinking about yourself, for once,' says Mother, as the taxi turns into our street. She stifles a yawn. 'Ooh, that visit has taken it right out of me.'

'Let's get you inside and comfortable,' I say. 'Nice cup of tea. Then we can think about what to eat later.'

Mother says she's going for a nap when we get inside, and I set to furiously cleaning the house in the absence of anything else to do to take my mind off things. I am angry at Dr Singh and angry at Mother and angry at the cancer. I am angry at Nate for being so lovely and angry at myself for telling him about Rosie, and surely driving him away. I am angry at the house for never staying tidy and angry at the milk for being so low. I text Rosie and ask her to buy milk on the way home and I take the recycling out to the wheelie bin. I am angry at Rosie for all the empty wine bottles in the bin, which are now joined by empty beer bottles from Ian, who is obviously spending half of his time here. I clean and I stay angry until Rosie walks through the door. She looks at me and slaps her forehead. 'Bugger. I forgot the milk.'

'For god's sake, Rosie!' I shout. 'You only had one thing to do!'

She looks at me and blinks. 'All right, don't get your knickers in a twist. I'll nip back down to the parade now and get some.'

'I'll go before I go to work,' I say. 'Sit down, Rosie. I need to talk to you about Mother.'

'Then I need a glass of wine,' says Rosie, going to the fridge. Of course she does. I wait until she's poured it and sat down at the kitchen table, and says to me, 'What's happened?'

'It was her appointment today.'

Rosie slaps her face again. 'Oh, god, yes. I completely forgot.'

I sit up straight. 'Yes, well, we're all going to have to be a bit more on the ball now.' I take out my notebook and start to read out everything Dr Singh said. Rosie listens quietly, steadily draining her glass, then goes for a refill while I tell her about the closing conversation we had.

We sit and look at each other for a moment, then Rosie sort of shakes her head and holds out her hands, palms up.

'Things are getting worse,' I say, as though Rosie is hard of understanding.

'Well, we knew they would,' she says softly. 'She was never going to get better from this.'

I know this. In fact, it's exactly what Mother said on the taxi ride home. But that doesn't mean it's all right. Rosie says, 'Tell me what Dr Singh said again.'

I tell her about the chemotherapy and the new pain relief

medication and she nods. 'Well, things are in hand as much as they can be, Daisy.'

I stare at her. How can she be so . . . uncaring about it all? I drop my voice to a whisper and say through gritted teeth. 'Rosie. Mother is dying.'

'I know,' says Rosie, copying my voice. 'So do you. So does she. This is not news.'

She is making me feel like I want to slap her in the face. This is not a good place for me to be in. I stand up and go to the sink and rinse out the cup I'd been using for tea. 'She's been asleep all afternoon.'

'You get off to work,' says Rosie. 'I'll go up and see if she's awake and wants any tea before Ian comes round.'

I turn round and gape at her. 'Ian is coming round? Didn't you hear what I said? We all need to be on the same page here.'

Rosie glares at me. 'Yes, Daisy. I'm not thick. But life has to go on. I came to terms with Mother's cancer a long time ago. So did she. If anyone needs to get on the same page as everyone else, it's you.'

Which is why, when I get to work and Nate falls backwards off the chair where he's been sleeping in the security office, then looks up to tell me that the teapot is back in the Lever Wing, I'm afraid I react in a way that, from the way his face falls, isn't what he is expecting.

'Are you all right, Daisy?' says Nate with a frown when he's unfolded himself from the tangle of limbs on the floor and stood up.

Then everything just feels too much. Mother, Rosie, the horrible boys at the bus stop, the threat of unemployment . . . it's like someone has stirred it all up in a bucket and said, 'There you go!' and dumped it over my head. I can feel a sob trapped in my throat and try as I might I can't stop it escaping, dragging tears with it.

And all I can think of is hiding behind the banners in the Lever Wing, my hand clutching on to Nate's in the darkness, clinging on to him as though he was a rock in a stormy sea. Before I know what I'm doing, my hand is going out almost of its own volition, and placing itself in his. He looks down, and then up at me. Then my sobs come thick and properly.

'Daisy,' says Nate, and the uncertainty in his voice is all I need to hear. I drop his hand like it's red-hot.

'Forget it,' I say numbly. 'I just had a bit of bad news. I'm not myself at the moment.'

'I'm sure everything will be all right . . .' says Nate, frowning at me. He hesitantly puts his hand back on mine. Oh, the feeling of it is like nothing I have ever known. Like I'm being protected, somehow.

But it's not me that needs protecting.

'It's not,' I say. I take my hand back again, and fold my arms across my chest so he can't touch me again. 'It's not all right. And I can't do this.'

I can't do this any more, Darren said to me. *Not after what you told me. You make me feel scared, Daisy.*

'Do I make you feel scared?' I say to Nate.

He looks at me curiously. And I see it in his eyes again. He is scared. After what I told him. Of course he's scared. He starts to make protestations but they're weak and pointless.

'You *should* be scared of me,' I say. I feel numb and cold and just sort of . . . elsewhere. I take off my coat and hang it up, ignoring Nate talking to me, as if he's not there. Then I walk out of the security office to do my first patrol. When I return half an hour later, Nate has gone.

When I go down to the reception just before six to get ready for locking up, Janice calls me over to the desk and leans conspiratorially across it. 'So,' she says, her voice low, 'our night out in a couple of weeks.'

I'd forgotten about that. 'Oh. Yes. I'm not really sure . . .' I say. If there's one thing I'm really not in the mood for, it's a party with people from work.

Janice ploughs on regardless. 'Something I wanted to talk to you about,' she murmurs. 'Nate.'

I can feel myself reddening. What does Janice know? Did Harold know we were behind the banners after all? Who's been talking? Nate? Oh god. He's told her about Rosie. I was stupid to trust him. It's probably all over the museum.

'I'm not sure I know what you mean, Janice,' I say frostily.

Her face twitches and it takes me a moment to realise she's winking at me. 'Come on, Daisy. Do you think he's dishy, or what?'

'Dishy?'

'He's very tall, isn't he? And quite handsome. Been divorced a good while now.'

'I'm not sure what this has to do with me,' I say desperately, looking around wildly for an excuse to leave.

'You work with him, Daisy,' says Janice. 'You must have noticed.'

'Noticed what?'

'The way he looks at—'

'He doesn't look at me at all!' I say shrilly.

'—me,' finishes Janice, and frowns. 'What?'

'What?' I say.

Janice squints at me. 'I said, you must have noticed the way he looks at me. Like a starving man at the window of an all-you-can-eat buffet. He's gagging for it, don't you think?'

A stream of people appear in the lobby, and I rush to open the doors to let them out. The last of the visitors. The clock hits six and Janice has her coat on within seconds, grabbing her usual clutch of carrier bags. I absently wonder if Janice could be the prime suspect for the thefts. She could easily smuggle something out in that collection of bags. I suddenly feel a little bad for shutting down Nate when he tried to tell me the teapot was back. He was only trying to help, and it was me that had got him involved in all of this in the first place. I'm thinking of his arms around me when I realise Janice is standing in front of me at the door, looking at me strangely.

'Daisy,' she says, 'when I said that you must have noticed the way Nate looks at me, you didn't think I was going to say . . .' She gives a little trilling laugh, and shakes her head, as though the thought is so ridiculous it needs to be shrugged out of her head. 'No. Of course not. What am I thinking? Good evening, Daisy.'

'Good evening,' I say, watching Janice totter up the street. I could imagine Nate and Janice together. They seem like the same sort of people. Ordinary people. Normal people. Not like me. I think of grabbing Nate's hand in the security office, of letting him hold me, and I burn with shame. Nate Garvey and Daisy Dukes?

No.

Of course not.

What am I thinking?

26

Daisy

The night of the Big Sleepover event has got me all of a fluther, as Mother would say. I'm so used to having the museum to myself after six o'clock that I feel on the back foot to have so many people not only staying on after work, but for so many members of the public to start trickling in from seven o'clock onwards. And to have the prospect of them staying all night, bedding down in the halls with sleeping bags and pillows and flasks of tea. Harold has been given the night off, as we're all going to be there until nine on the Saturday morning, when the weekend security firm will take over. In the meantime, there will be talks, tours, film showings projected on a big screen put up in front of the trade-union banners in the Lever Wing – they're doing all the *Jurassic Park* movies, apparently – and some candlelit ghost stories in the Theodore room for the adults and older children.

Sue and Bonny Sue have made a buffet to serve up in the canteen, and Dorothy's guides are all done up in fancy dress from Manchester's past . . . Victorians and Cavaliers, that sort of thing. Nobody mentioned getting changed to me, so I didn't bring any other clothes apart from the uniform I would normally wear, but after the museum has closed for the day

I spy Janice going into the ladies' toilets and emerging in a dress that's far too young and tight for her, tottering on high heels and trailing an almost acrid cloud of perfume. Janice's transformation puts me a little out of sorts, for reasons I can't quite put my finger on.

Seema seems very pleased with the turnout as the public starts to come in, handing their tickets to Dorothy and her guides on the door. I stand with her as she watches them arrive, the families and the couples and the small groups of adults who seem in good spirits and arrive buoyed on a smell of alcohol.

'This is very good, Daisy,' Seema confides in me. 'Very good for the museum's future. This sort of community engagement is the direction in which we need to go to ensure a steady flow of footfall. And, crucially, getting the family market as well. We're already thinking of hugely expanding our summer holidays offer.'

I get the feeling that Seema isn't really talking to me. She's just talking at whoever happens to be in her vicinity. She just wants it known that she is all about the ideas, and although the letterheads have Mr Meyer's name on them as museum manager, it's actually her who's the power behind the throne.

I do a patrol, but it's more of a wander, really. It feels strange having so many people in the museum. This is what it must be like for Nate all the time. No wonder he's never seen any of the stolen items being taken away or returned. All these people! My gut reaction is that it would drive me mad, but the more I walk through them as I pass from hall to hall, the more I seem to enjoy having so many people around.

I wasn't sure whether I should ask Seema if I could not do the Big Sleepover thing, given the turn of events with Mother. Rosie said I was being stupid. She said Mother was actually no more ill than she was a week ago . . . it's just that now we know about it. That kind of makes sense, I suppose.

Mother's condition hasn't really changed recently. It's just our knowledge of how sick she is that's been updated. Maybe if we didn't know, we wouldn't worry as much. As I climb the final staircase I wonder if it's better not to know, or to have all the information? I'm the sort of person who likes everything out in the open. I was thinking that when I was talking to Rosie and she was absent-mindedly rubbing her arm, where the scars are. I was talking to Rosie but I was thinking about Nate, and what Janice had said last night, and how it bothered me that she thought it the most ridiculous thing in the world that someone like Nate could have an attraction to someone like me. And then I think about how he held me after that disastrous date, and how he hugged me in the den yesterday, and the electric sparks that flew when our hands touched on the stake-out.

But then there's the thing that happened, the thing that's simultaneously out in the open but also the thing that nobody ever talks about, and it's like an invisible balloon, inflating between Nate and me, pushing us apart as he holds me in the street and hugs me in the den, forcing our hands to separate behind the banners in the Lever Wing. When the thing was hidden away I could, despite what Janice said, have a tiny, private moment in my head where I can imagine . . . well. It's like grainy old film footage, or over-exposed photographs, or rapidly changing scenes on a TV where someone's cycling through the channels with the clicker. Briefly glimpsed fantasies of Nate and me. Together. But now I've told him about what I did to Rosie, it intrudes on the scene, and the old film footage goes white in one corner and burns into nothingness, a sudden wind scatters the photographs away, the TV picture narrows to a single white line and goes blank.

'Stupid stupid stupid Daisy,' I mutter to myself.

'What's that, love?'

I blink and realise my feet have taken me to the cafe, where Sue and Bonny Sue are laying out plates of sandwiches and cakes under clingfilm, and setting up urns of hot water and fruit juice. Bonny Sue is looking at me expectantly.

'Nothing,' I say. 'Just talking to myself.'

'At least you get some sensible conversation!' guffaws Bonny Sue. 'Want a piece of lemon drizzle cake before those kids get their grubby paws all over it? You can take one for Nate.'

'Why would I take one for Nate?' I say, too quickly.

Bonny Sue frowns. 'Because you work together? I thought you could stash them in the den?'

'It's not called the den, it's called the security office,' I say quietly, suddenly aware that I've been calling it 'the den' in my head recently. That's Nate rubbing off on me. I blush slightly as I realise that Rosie would make a dirty joke out of that phrase.

Bonny Sue wraps me up two pieces of lemon drizzle cake and I take them back downstairs to the security office. They've started showing the first Jurassic Park movie on a big temporary screen in the darkened Lever Wing, children and their parents sitting on cushions in rows on the polished floor. I stand at the entrance to the hall and watch them for a moment. It must be nice to have a family you can do things with. I don't really remember us doing much when me and Rosie were little. Nothing like this, anyway.

I'm coming back out of the security office when I practically bump into Nate. He's wearing jeans and an untucked black shirt, and carries a sports jacket in his hand. He looks down at me and bites his lip. 'Were we supposed to wear our uniforms?'

'I don't think it matters. I didn't bring anything else to change into.'

'That's a shame,' says Nate. 'You looked nice in those . . . clothes. The other night.'

'My sister Rosie chose them for me,' I say, then internally groan. That makes me sound like I'm a child and can't dress myself. Which, I suppose, is half true. I've never been very good at knowing what makes me look good, or at least, not ridiculous. That's why I like jobs where you get a uniform. At least that's one less thing to worry about. You are what you are in a uniform, and there's nothing you can really do about it one way or the other.

'You look nice in those clothes,' I say, mainly for want of something to break the silence. I wonder if that was a little too familiar, though.

Nate looks down at himself and grins crookedly. 'This old thing?'

'It looks new,' I say, frowning and plucking a piece of fluff off his sleeve.

'It was a joke,' says Nate. He's trying to be kind to me. I can sense it. But there's a difference between being kind and trying to be kind. And then he turns round as we both hear the high-pitched laughter of Janice. My fingers are paused with the piece of lint sandwiched between them. I suddenly feel as though I'm guilty of something, but I'm not sure what it's supposed to be.

'What's going on here, then?' says Janice, her hands on the hips of her too-tight dress in mock outrage. 'Is this man bothering you, Daisy?'

I know it's meant to be a joke but I don't really understand why it's funny, though Janice's bird-like laugh tells me that it's supposed to be.

'Did you not bring your boy, Nate?' says Janice.

'Ben,' I say, and they both glance at me.

'He's watching *Jurassic Park*,' says Nate. 'Oh, that reminds me, Daisy, I brought your book back.'

Nate fishes in the inside pocket of the jacket in his hand and pulls out the Murakami I lent him. Janice laughs again, this time ever so slightly desperately, it seems to me, as though she's trying to draw Nate's attention away from me and back to her. She leans forward a little, exposing her cleavage a little more.

'Books! Never saw the point! If a book's good enough they'll make it into a film, and that only takes a couple of hours to get through.' She puts a hand on Nate's arm. 'Do you ever go to the cinema, Nate?'

He shrugs. 'Sometimes. Usually with Ben when I have him for the weekend.'

'We should go!' she says, as though the idea has just that second occurred to her and it's not something she's been thinking about for ages. Then, to make sure that Nate understands she doesn't mean to help out with his childcare arrangements, she adds, 'Just me and you! Midweek. Maybe get a drink first. Something to eat.'

Nate glances at me and looks doubtful. 'Um. I'm not sure . . .'

'That settles it!' cackles Janice. 'It's a date!'

Nate's frown deepens and he glances at me. 'Well, I don't really—'

'So you keep your paws off him, Daisy Dukes!' says Janice delightedly, lightly slapping the wrist of my hand that's still got the piece of fluff pinched between the fingers.

Then Dorothy appears at the bottom of the staircase, beckoning wildly. 'Where's the mop and bucket, Janice? Some child wet herself when the Tyrannosaurus came on in the film.'

As Janice bustles away with Dorothy, Nate shakes his head slowly and says, 'Wow. What was that all about?'

'I think that was Janice staking her claim,' I say. 'Like one of those praying mantises I saw on a wildlife programme once.'

Nate does a little comedy shudder, then seems to remember he's got the book in his hand. I take it from him and flip it open, saying, 'Have you finished it alrea— oh. This isn't mine.'

'No,' says Nate sheepishly. 'I got a new copy. I'm sorry, an accident happened to yours. Well, not an accident, really. Ben happened to it. It's still readable, and I'll finish it, but I couldn't return it to you in that state.'

'Oh,' I say. I feel unaccountably moved. I mean, I know I put that bookplate in saying they hadn't to be damaged, but I never thought that anyone would take any notice of it. To be honest, I've never really lent my books out to anyone before. It's quite nice to have someone to share them with. Even if they wreck them. 'That's very thoughtful of you.'

Nate follows me back into the den while I put the book in my bag. 'Do you know what we're supposed to do, exactly? I mean, are we doing actual security guarding? Or are we just here to make up the numbers?'

'There doesn't seem a lot for us to do,' I admit. 'I suppose we're on hand if—'

'Ooh,' says Nate. 'Lemon drizzle cake. Bonny Sue's handiwork, I presume? Shall I put the kettle on?'

When we've eaten the cake (very tasty) and drunk the tea (Nate doesn't put enough milk in) he looks at his watch and says, 'The movie is finishing up. Better go and find Ben.' He pauses, then says a little uncertainly, 'Do you want to come and meet him?'

I don't have a lot of experience with children, but logic dictates that a son of Nate must have been brought up decently. I'm not sure what I'll talk to him about. Perhaps it's just enough to say hello.

'Yes, of course.' I brush the crumbs into the bin and stack the plates by the little sink to wash and return to Bonny Sue.

'He's a good kid,' says Nate, leading me out of the den and to the stairs. 'I mean, it wasn't easy for him when Lucia and me divorced, but they're resilient, aren't they, children? They get used to the new normal fairly quickly.'

The credits of the movie are rolling and the families and children are getting up from their cushions. As we walk in, Dorothy waves at me and motions for me to turn on the lights at the switches by the door. Nate says, 'There's Ben. I'll go and grab him.'

I flick the switches and the lights stutter on, and I hear Nate cough behind me. I plaster on a big, friendly smile and turn around. All I have to do is say hello. The smile sticks on my face for a moment, then slowly falls.

Nate is standing there with his hands on the shoulders of a small boy. Ben's eyes widen as they meet mine. Nate says, 'This is my son, Ben. Ben, this is—'

'Crazy Daisy!' says Ben, gaping at me in astonishment.

It's him. Ben. Nate's son. He's the boy from the bus stop.

27

Nate

It takes me a moment to piece it all together. What Daisy said about being hassled by a gang of kids every afternoon on her way to work. Ben calling her Crazy Daisy. Him wanting to go out with his mates that last weekend, hanging around on the parade.

'What did you just say?' I hiss at him. I can feel the muscles tightening in my jaw. 'What have you been up to?'

Ben turns to me, his face slack, his eyes filling with tears. 'I didn't mean—'

I grab Ben by his upper arm. 'Ow,' he says.

'Nate,' I hear Daisy say, but her voice is drowned out by the roaring in my ears. I don't think I've ever been so furious in all my life.

'Come with me,' I demand, dragging him out of the room and not waiting for him to answer or comply. I can feel people staring at us, at me, but I don't care. I march him to the stairs and start down them, holding him tightly by the arm, keeping him upright as his feet struggle to keep him upright on the carpeted steps.

'Nate!' Daisy calls from behind me.

I ignore her and drag the protesting Ben across the lobby

and to the security office, slamming the door behind me and sitting him down roughly on the chair at the desk.

'What have you done?' I say, trying to keep the wobble of anger out of my voice. Ben is crying openly now.

I take a deep breath, then another, and walk up and down the den, shaking my head. I look at Ben and he meets my gaze with his big, watery eyes, then looks away.

'Daisy has been coming into work upset,' I say, as evenly as possible, 'because she has been getting abuse every day from a gang of thugs at the bus stop.' I take another deep breath. 'Look me in the eye, Ben Garvey, and tell me right now that it wasn't you.'

Ben says nothing, just looks at his hands and heaves a great sob, his shoulders shaking.

'Stop crying!' I shout, my voice reverberating around the tiny den. They can doubtless hear me all over the museum. I don't care. 'If you're a big enough man that you can stand around the streets harassing lone women then be a big enough man to admit it to me.'

There's a long silence. Ben says in a tiny voice, 'I'm sorry.'

'Not good enough!' I roar. Ben jumps, looking up at me with eyes filled not just with tears, but terror. Good. Give him a taste of his own medicine. 'I want to know *why*.'

'They said I had to,' he says raggedly. 'Or I couldn't be in the gang.'

I roll my eyes and slap my forehead. 'The gang. So it's the *gang* is it, now? The sort of gang that abuses women?'

'It was just meant to be a bit of fun.'

'Do you think it was fun for Daisy? She was in tears here the other day.'

Ben puts his head lower and his own crying intensifies. It just makes me even more angry. 'And what after you've finished terrifying someone on the streets? What then? Stealing from a shop? Ripping off a car? Pulling a knife on some other kid from a different gang? You think this is a *game*, Ben? Or maybe, is it the fast track to ruining your bloody life?'

'They're not like that,' says Ben. There's an edge that's crept into his voice; he's not as contrite as he was a second ago. 'They're my friends. They look out for me.' He looks up and his tears have dried, and there's something harder and flinty in his eyes. 'They're my family.'

'I look out for you,' I say quietly. 'And you've got family. Me and your mum.'

'Well, it's a shit family!' screams Ben, so sudden that it shocks me into taking a step back. 'All I can remember from when I was little is you and Mum shouting at each other and now all you do is whinge about each other behind your backs. And you think that if you buy me a stupid Xbox or take me on a stupid holiday or make me go to some stupid football match then everything is all right.' He glares at me. 'It's just stuff that doesn't matter.'

'You ungrateful little sod!' I shout. My heart is racing. I can hear myself breathing fast and hard, like a bull. 'Me and your mum break our backs to provide for you!'

'It's just stuff!' he shouts again. 'Nobody ever listens to me! Nobody takes any notice of me! Except the gang. They're more family to me than you've ever been.'

I can barely hear Ben for the blood pumping in my ears. He's glaring at me, but there's something else in his eyes, something like triumph. 'Go on!' he screams. 'I dare you!'

Then the door opens and I hear Daisy's voice, horrified, calling my name. And it's as though I twang back into my body, like I've been stretched further and further from it, and I realise with a growing sensation of sickness sitting in my gut like a brick that I've got my right hand up, ready to hit my son.

I can only imagine what it looks like, Daisy in her full security-guard uniform appearing to escort me and Ben to John's car, while Lucia rants and raves at me in the street outside the museum. If my job wasn't at risk before, I reckon it certainly is now. Ben insisted I call Lucia to come for him. She and John were just about to set off for a meal. He sits and glowers at the steering wheel, not looking at me.

'For god's sake, Nate,' says Lucia. 'You only had to do one simple thing. Have some time with your son. Is basic fatherhood completely beyond you?'

'You don't know what he's done,' I say, but my own voice sounds sullen and childish, even to me.

Lucia puts her face close to mine and hisses, 'He said you were going to hit him.'

'I would never . . .' I begin, but the memory of realising I was holding my hand in the air burns shame into my face.

'Your father's dead,' says Lucia, turning to get into the car. She brings the window down and shakes her head at me. 'You don't have to keep his legacy alive.'

I stand there for a long moment, watching the car drive away, realising that Daisy is still standing just behind me. More than anything, I don't want her to have seen what she did. But I'm terrified to think what might have happened if she hadn't come in when she did.

I turn to Daisy, but can't bring myself to meet her eyes. 'I suppose you hate me, now.'

When I eventually look at her, she's got her head on one side, as though considering me, and what I did. She says, 'Do you want to go on the roof?'

I try a lopsided smile. 'What, to throw myself off?'

'No,' says Daisy. 'To talk.'

'I never knew we had a roof,' I say, as I follow Daisy up a ladder from a tiny room at the back of the canteen. She pushes open a wooden hatch and climbs out. 'I mean, obviously we've got a roof, but . . . whoa.'

I follow Daisy out of the hatch and on to a flat, felt-covered space bordered on all sides by the pointed gables of the museum building. 'Do you come up here a lot?'

Daisy shrugs. 'No. Never, in fact. Apart from the first time I found it.' She frowns. 'Why would I?'

'Because it's beautiful,' I breathe. From here you can see right across Manchester, see the lights in the buildings, the arteries of the roads snaking between the architecture. The sky is clear with the most promising hint of spring warmth so far this year, the stars twinkling in their masses above us, the sounds of the city floating up, dislocated and distant yet somehow reassuring. There's life going on out there, wonderful, brilliant, beautiful life. For a moment it takes my breath away and allows me to forget everything.

But only for a moment. Somewhere among those brick canyons and bright lights is John's car, carrying Lucia and Ben away from me. Maybe forever. And I can climb as many ladders as I want, and for as long as I like, and I'll never get far enough away from what I almost did.

'You wouldn't have hit him,' says Daisy, as though reading my mind.

'I might, if you hadn't come in.'

'Have you hit him before?'

I shake my head. 'I always vowed I wouldn't. Not after . . .'

I look around because I feel like I need a sit down. There are some crates of bricks and tiles at one side, left here by the builders the last time they were doing renovations. Daisy walks over to them and empties two, placing the tiles in the other boxes, then upturns the crates so we can sit on them, with our backs against the raised gables.

'Red wine?' she says, and I blink, surprised, at the bottle in her hand. She blushes and says, 'I picked it up off the buffet table in the cafe. I didn't think Sue and Bonny Sue would mind. Given that it's an emergency.'

'Did you pinch glasses as well?' I say as Daisy unscrews the lid. She looks crestfallen. 'Oh, no. I didn't think of that.'

'Never mind.' I take the bottle from her and take a long swig straight from the neck. I wipe the top with my sleeve and hand it back to her, and, after giving me an uncertain smile, Daisy does the same, screwing up her face.

'Bit rough, but it does the job,' I say. I look up at the stars for a while, pondering the distances between us and them. You get to thinking like that, it makes you feel small and insignificant and that your problems are of no interest to anybody, anywhere, at all.

Then Daisy nudges me and hands me the bottle again. 'Tell me,' she says softly.

So I do. I tell her about Terry Garvey. I tell her everything.

I'm not religious and never went to church as a kid, so I don't really know what confession feels like, but I imagine it's a little like I'm feeling now. A little spent, a little empty, a little lighter. I almost feel like I could put my head back against the brick wall and go to sleep. If it wasn't getting so chilly. I notice Daisy suppress a little shiver, and without thinking I shrug off my jacket and place it around her shoulders. She gives me a look that I can't read, and I wonder if I've overstepped the mark. It just felt like a natural thing to do.

Daisy says nothing for a long time then she murmurs, 'You aren't your dad, Nate.'

'I know I'm not,' I say. 'In fact, I've lived all my life determined to be the exact opposite of him.' I pause, thinking
back a decade, when things were different. 'When Ben was
born, it felt like a chance to wipe the slate clean. To finally
lay his ghost to rest. I had a big list of things that I was not
going to do, that I was going to avoid, so I would never be
like my father. And top of that list was not hitting my son.
Not hitting anybody. I saw too much of that growing up.'

And yet, there I was, hand poised above Ben, ready to
give him a smack. My number one rule, about to be broken.

'He used to call me Tigger, when he was little. Ben,' I
say, suddenly remembering. 'I'd forgotten that. How awful.'

'From Winnie-the-Pooh?' says Daisy.

I nod, suddenly incredibly sad. 'He said I was always
bouncing around and making him laugh.' I look up at the
stars. 'I wonder when I stopped doing that? And why I didn't
notice?'

Daisy takes a mouthful of the wine then hands the bottle
to me to finish off. 'Sometimes it's not enough to know what
we shouldn't do. We have to know what we should do as
well. And that's often a lot more difficult.'

'I thought me and Ben . . . could be friends,' I say. 'I thought
if I tried to find some pleasure in what he enjoyed, and he
did what I like doing, then we'd always have a connection.
Always be friends.' I look at Daisy. 'He didn't need a friend.
He needed a father. Guidance and boundaries and love and
support. I'll never let anybody say I don't love my son but
. . . maybe the other stuff . . . when he didn't get it from
me, he got it from others.'

'This gang,' says Daisy. She pulls my jacket tighter around
her. 'In a way this is all my fault. If I hadn't told you what
happened with those boys you'd never have got angry with
Ben.'

I shake my head firmly. 'No. I needed to know. So I can stop it going any further. There's nothing on you with this.' I pause, remembering what Ben said. 'You're the victim here. I can't believe he was responsible for those things. Those names they called you.'

Daisy says nothing, but stares out at the lights of Manchester beyond the museum. I say, 'Do you think we should go back down? I bet you're cold, and we've finished that wine.'

She doesn't make any move to go, just stares out at the night. Eventually she says, 'Well, at least you know why the call me Crazy Daisy. We tried to keep the thing quiet, obviously, but it's almost impossible that stuff won't get out. They don't even know why they say it, somebody heard somebody's mum say something once, who heard it from someone else, who got half a story from another person, who's neighbour's daughter was in the same class as Rosie, who might have said something in confidence to somebody once. That's how these things happen, isn't it? Chinese whispers.' She looks at her feet, and shivers. 'Are you even allowed to say that any more?'

'You're not crazy,' I say softly. 'It happened a long time ago.'

She looks at me, as though searching my eyes for something. Then she raises her eyebrows slightly. 'Oh. It's gone.'

'What?' I say, puzzled.

'You had a look, before. When I told you. A look I recognised. One that said you were . . . scared? Disgusted? Mistrustful?' She looks away. 'It's gone. That's all. I don't even know why I mentioned it.

'Daisy,' I say and she looks back at me. Her eyes on mine. There's something between us, spooling from her gaze to mine. So strong I can't look away.

I don't want to look away.

I feel a lurch in my chest, as though a gossamer thread

connects me to Daisy, and something or somebody has just pulled it taut.

I don't know if it's the wine or the cold air or what, but suddenly I feel like I know her. Properly know her. Like I've always known her.

And then my phone rings.

I blink, as though I've been jolted awake, and take out my phone. Stupid 0800 number. Spam. Of all the moments to ruin. I'm about to slip the phone back into my pocket when Daisy says, 'What was that tune?'

'My ringtone?' I say. '"At Last" by Etta James. She was my mother's favourite. Used to play her all the time.'

Daisy has a peculiar look on her face. 'Can you play it again? All of it?'

I fumble around on my phone's Spotify app until I find it, and set it going. The strings of the intro seem to swoop and glide and fill the night. We listen to it in silence until it finishes.

'That's beautiful,' says Daisy. 'But so short.'

'Three minutes. Exactly as long as it needs to be. All the time it takes to fall in love.' I press play again and stand up. I feel reckless and mad and something feels like it's going to burst out of my chest. I hold out my hand. 'Dance with me?'

I expect her to say, *what, here?* or *I can't dance*, or *don't be ridiculous, Nate*, but instead Daisy stands up, never taking her eyes off mine. She puts her small hand in my paw and allows me to draw her to me, moulding her against my body. She puts her head against my chest as though she's listening to my heart. We move together, barely swaying, but in perfect time. Etta is singing about the skies above being blue, and that's exactly what it feels like. As though the night sky above is there just for us in all its unknowable glory. By the time she's on to the line about the spell being cast, I feel just about bold enough to take Daisy by the shoulders and move her away from me, our eyes locked together.

'Can I kiss you?' someone says, and it rather surprises me to realise that I said it.

She doesn't say anything. Doesn't take her eyes off me. I remember the electric touch of her hand on the stake-out night and feel ripples of that crawling all over my body. Daisy's lips part. I put my hand on the side of her face and she leans into it, her eyes flickering.

Somebody sighs. It might be me. It might be her.

I lean forward. To kiss her.

'Cooo-eee!'

The spell that Etta cast is broken. I snatch my hand away and Daisy shuffles away from me and I stand up straight.

'Now what on earth are you two up to?' says Janice, cackling loudly as she emerges on to the roof. 'Daisy Dukes, didn't I tell you to keep your hands off Nate Garvey?'

I exchange a quick glance with Daisy and we both begin to speak at the same time.

'Daisy felt a bit sick—'

'I needed to show Nate a security issue up here—'

Janice folds her arms and taps her foot. 'Well, well, well, you'd better get your stories right, is all I can say. So if your *security issue* is resolved, and Daisy is feeling *better,* you might want to come down and deal with a fight that's broken out between two dads over who's made the best plasticine dinosaur. To be quite honest, it's their kids who were supposed to be making them anyway . . .'

28

Nate

It's like Daisy said. Everything is the same, but different. I can't un-know what I know about her. And I can't shake the memory of that kiss we nearly had. So very nearly. And that felt so right that it hurts me not to have done it.

And there's Ben, as well. When I go to take him to school on Monday, expecting the silent treatment from Lucia, I'm surprised to find her apologetic. She's got the full story out of Ben over the weekend and has torn a strip off him. His Xbox and games and pretty much everything is in black bin bags in the kitchen.

'I've told him he can have them back if and when I ever wake up and not feel furious at him,' she says while Ben hangs his head over his Weetabix. 'He'll be lucky if I haven't taken them to the dump by next weekend.'

Before she goes to work, Lucia takes me to one side and says quietly, 'What do you think we should do about this? This gang? It's not like when we were kids, Nate. They might just be little more than children but you know the trouble they get into. Knives. I've seen enough stab victims come into the hospital to last me a lifetime. I don't want our son to be the next one.'

Ben is grounded, of course, until he's twenty-one, says Lucia. But she's right. It needs nipping in the bud now, because despite what she says we can't stop Ben going out at all, forever. 'I'll sort it,' I say.

'How?'

'I don't know yet. But I'll sort it.'

Lucia nods. 'I keep thinking about that poor woman.'

'Daisy.'

'She was the one you work with? In the security uniform when we came to pick Ben up?'

'Yes.'

Lucia has that look on her face. The one that says she knows something and I'm about a million steps behind her. Except this time I'm not that far behind her.

'She likes you. Daisy. I could tell.'

'How could you tell?'

Lucia shrugs. 'Women can tell. Do you like her?'

Ben appears at the door from the kitchen. 'I suppose corn-rows are out, then?'

Lucia glares at him until he runs away, then gives me the warmest smile she has done in years. 'I don't remember getting the memo that said you weren't allowed to be happy, Nate.' She kisses me on the cheek. 'I've got to get to work. Think about it. And don't give that kid an inch until he can prove he's sorry for what he did.'

That Monday I'm nervous about seeing Daisy again for the first time since the Big Sleepover event. After Janice interrupted us, Daisy went straight home after making it right with Seema, citing a headache. Which I'm not surprised about, after all that red wine. I was going to slink off as well until Janice collared me and dragged me up to the cafe, which had become an impromptu drinking lounge for those adults not sequestered in the halls with their children, huddled in sleeping bags and listening to ghost stories told by torchlight.

'What were you talking about up there on the roof?' Janice said reprovingly, pouring some warm wine into a plastic cup. 'And I heard there was some drama with your kid.'

I shrugged non-committally and sipped at the wine. To be honest, I'd had enough to drink and my mind wouldn't stop turning over and over the way Daisy's face looked when I almost kissed her. The pull I felt to her. The way my heart felt like it was opening up, waking up, loosening itself out of the dry prison it had suddenly found itself in.

I somehow ended up getting roped into telling a ghost story, and then it was time for lights out and by means fair or foul I found myself in a sleeping bag in the Horridge Wing right next to Janice, who had changed in the toilets into a pair of tiny shorts and a vest.

'I hope that big dinosaur doesn't give me nightmares,' said Janice. 'You'll protect me, won't you, Nate?'

When the excited babbling of the children had quieted and the halls were echoing with the regular breathing and gentle snores of the visitors, I lay there on my back in the sleeping bag, staring into the darkness. I felt Janice reach across and lay her arm on me, resting on my lower stomach. I lay silently for a moment, while she waited to see what I'd do, then I feigned a big snore and rolled over, shrugging her off and turning my back to her. I lay like that until the first slivers of dawn's light filtered into the museum, thinking about Daisy.

The Monday handover is just like it's always been. Daisy is businesslike and brusque and acts like we haven't seen each other at all since the last time we were in work. She asks me several questions about all of the non-events of the day, and doesn't even say goodbye when I leave. I wait for her to mention the

almost-kiss, but she doesn't. I go home via Derek's Dominoes
. . . sorry, Big Macs, and read the juice-warped pages of the
Murakami book, stopping every chapter to turn back to the
bookplate at the front. *This is the property of Daisy Dukes.* I trace
the handwritten dates with my finger, when she gave it to
me and when it was due to be returned. I am overdue. I have
given her a new thing, but is it enough?

Janice begins to haunt me around the museum. She creeps up
on me as I'm reading the Greek myths book in the Theodore
room one lunchtime and says, 'Boo! Don't you find it spooky
in here? I would with that skull.'

'I'm on my break, Janice,' I say. 'Is there a problem?'

'No,' she says. 'I wanted to ask your opinion. Did you like
that dress I wore at the Big Sleepover thing?'

I'm struggling to remember it but I don't want to appear
impolite, so I say, 'Yes, it was very nice. Why?'

'I was wondering if I should wear it again for the do. Or
get something new. What do you think?'

I frown and shake my head. 'Do?'

Janice slaps me on the arm and laughs. 'You are silly. Week
on Saturday. The spring do. That everybody's going to. Even
your funny little friend Daisy.'

I blink. Oh, yes. That do. 'Daisy's going?'

Janice frowns. 'Yes. Why? Anyway, what do you think
about this?'

She takes out her phone and shows me a page on a clothes
shopping website. There's a model about twenty years younger
than Janice wearing an orange dress that doesn't leave much
to the imagination around either the bust area or the thighs.
I shrug and hazard a guess. 'Very nice?'

Janice laughs loudly and slaps my arm again, this time
leaving her hand there, gently squeezing my bicep. 'Ooh,
Nate Garvey, you are very naughty!'

'Am I?' If I always felt a million steps behind Lucia, I feel a million miles away from Janice.

Janice gives me a narrow-eyed look over her glasses. 'You know very well you are. I think you're right. I'll get this one. It's a bit racy but . . . I trust your judgement, Nate. You only live once, eh?'

One night I dream about my father again. He's not in the Minotaur's labyrinth this time, though. He's just looming over me, brandishing his fists, and laughing. 'The further you run from me, son, the closer you get to me. Do you get it? The further you run, the closer you get. Now why not give your old Dad a hug?'

I mull over the dream all day, until Daisy comes on the shift. 'Nothing missing,' I say when we do the handover.

She looks at me blankly. 'What?'

'Nothing missing. No more thefts for a few days. Why do you think that is?'

Daisy ponders. 'I don't know. Why? Does it matter?'

I can't just go on doing this weird dance as though nothing's happened. It's driving me mad. I say, 'Daisy, you do remember the stake-out? And hiding behind the banners? And what happened on the roof?'

'If that's everything,' she says quickly, 'you should probably clock off.'

Before I go I tell her about my dream. 'What do you think it means?'

She shrugs. 'Exactly what you said on the roof. That you're trying too hard not to be your father.'

At least she's finally acknowledging that the roof did actually happen. I was beginning to doubt myself. 'But why would he want me to hug him?'

Daisy closes her eyes and shakes her head. 'I've no idea what your subconscious is trying to tell you, Nate. Maybe that running away from him isn't the answer. Maybe that you have to make peace with your memory of him.' She pauses, considering. 'Was there never any good in him at all?'

'If there was, it's overshadowed by one big, bad thing.'

Daisy smiles tightly. 'Yes, big, bad things tend to do that. Good evening, Nate.'

I kick myself all the way to the bus. Why didn't I engage my brain before speaking? Now she definitely thinks I only see her one big, bad thing as defining her. Just like Terry Garvey's fists defined him. How can I make peace with that? That would mean letting my father in, and even just a little bit would infect the rest, take me over.

Or would it? By the time my bus gets me home, I've had an idea.

They aren't hard to find. There are five of them, loitering around the closed shops on the parade, outside the butchers. They're all older than Ben, some of them with erratic sprouts of growth on their chins. They all give me a glare as I walk up to them.

'You know Ben Garvey?' I say.

They all shrug. One of them, the oldest and tallest, a black kid with a thick gold chain around his neck, holds my gaze. 'He in trouble?'

'What's he done?' says an Asian lad. 'Cross the road without waiting for the green man?'

They all snicker, falling silent as I fix them all with my glare. Gold Chain says, 'You his old man?'

'Why you bothering with a kid his age?' I say.

Gold Chain shrugs. 'Coz of your old man. The Black Bomber, my uncle says. Terry Garvey. Mean right hook.'

I frown at him. 'That doesn't make any odds. I'll ask you again; why you bothering with Ben?'

'Thought it might give us a bit of cred–i–bil–ity,' says Gold Chain, stretching out the word. 'Junior Black Bomber on our squad.' He sniffs and looks away. 'Shame he's such a pussy.'

And here it is.

Here is the point where I can choose to be my father, or choose not to be.

I could reach out and grab Gold Chain by the front of his black T–shirt and push him hard back against the wall of the shop. I could put my face close to his and snarl at him, tell him that if I ever see him so much as talking to Ben again I will fucking end him.

That is what Terry Garvey would have done.

I am not Terry Garvey.

So I say, 'What did your uncle tell you about the Black Bomber?'

Gold Chain's trying to style out some cool, but I can tell he's afraid. I can smell the fear on him. And that's because I am not angry. Or rather, I am; I am furious. But I am not allowing that to cloud my senses or my judgement. I am in control. I am honing my fury. Forging it into a weapon. A weapon I can choose to deploy, or not. Just like Dad could do in the ring, but was unable to do at home.

'He said he was the best,' says Gold Chain casually.

'He was the best,' I say. 'And he taught me everything he knew. So let me say this, and let me say it just once. You do not harass women in the street. You do not even look at women in the street. And if I hear you have been bothering my son, any of you, I will be back. Do you understand?'

Gold Chain nods, all pretence of toughness melting away from him. I see him for what he is. Little more than a kid. But one that needs teaching a lesson.

I let him go. I could have roughed him up. I could have hit him. I felt like fucking killing him for what he's done to Ben. I say thoughtfully, 'You know what? Nobody needs any excuse to talk trash about black kids. Why don't you do something useful, for a change?'

I turn away and don't look back. I didn't hit him. I didn't kill him. I chose not to. I chose not to be my father. And as I walk away, it feels for all the world like I'm finding my way out of a labyrinth, at long last.

On Saturday I go to the grave. I take flowers. Not just for Mum, this time, but for him as well. It feels like something I need to do. To draw a line under things.

'I still hate what you did,' I say to the headstone. 'But I don't think I hate who you were. Not any more.'

I remember what Daisy said to me. I think of the good times. It surprises me to find that there were any at all, let alone so many of them. They'd been hiding in the shadows of Terry Garvey's right hook. But they were there.

'You were right,' I say. 'The further I ran from you, the closer I got. I spent so much time trying not to be you, that I forgot to be me. And, like it or not, there's a lot of you in me, Dad. So I did it. I gave you a hug. I embraced you. I played the tough guy. But I knew when to stop. And I've proved that doing that doesn't mean I am you.' I arrange the flowers in the pot and stand up. 'You could have been better, Dad. It was possible. I've seen that now. You didn't have to be like you were. And I don't have to run away from you any more. Nothing is inevitable.'

I walk away from the grave. I don't really feel like I need to come so often any more, maybe not every other Saturday. Maybe once a month is enough, maybe even less often. Because I wasn't coming for Mother, as much as I told myself I was.

I was coming to make sure Terry Garvey was still in his box, that he hadn't clawed his way out of the dry earth to come for me, to try to make me what he was. He can't do that. Not any more.

Everything is the same. But different. Just like Daisy said.

29

Daisy

Rosie holds the top up against me, considers it with her head cocked to one side, then pulls a face and sticks it back on the rack. She casts around like a police dog sniffing for a hidden villain, her eyes narrowed. 'A-ha!' she exclaims and heads off towards another carousel of clothes. I follow her wearily.

'Rosie, I've already got four tops here,' I say, holding up the clothes hooked to my finger.

'You can take five items into the dressing room,' she says, looking critically at a khaki green shirt, then at me, then back at the shirt. 'Try this.'

We have already been out what seems like hours and I am worried about Mother. We are allowed infrequent visits by a carer for what they call 'respite', usually about once every month or six weeks. Rosie has booked one to allow us to go into Manchester city centre this fine Saturday afternoon, ostensibly to buy me something to wear for the work do next weekend.

'I'm not even sure I want to go.'

'Of course you do,' says Rosie, herding me towards the dressing rooms. We have to wait in a long line of women who seem eminently more comfortable than I am in this shop with its distressed wood and metal decor and its relentlessly banging dance music. 'I take it Nate will be there?'

I shrug as non-committally as I can manage. 'It's a staff do. Nate is staff. So, probably.' I can feel Rosie's stare on me and I turn to her, annoyed. 'What?'

'I'm just wondering what you're waiting for, Daisy,' she says. 'Life won't stand still and wait for you. You have to keep up with it.'

'Did you get that out of a fortune cookie?' I mutter as the queue shuffles forward. To change the subject I look at the ticket on one of the tops Rosie has picked out for me, and my eyes widen. 'The price of this!'

'You can afford it. You never go anywhere, Daisy. You never buy anything. You must have pots of money stashed away.'

Well, maybe not for much longer, if we end up getting the boot from our jobs. I haven't told Rosie about all that, yet. I don't want her to worry about what would happen to our arrangement looking after Mother. Not that Rosie is really the worrying type. She'd just shrug her shoulders and start trying to find me another job. But I want to be sure about what's happening before I involve the family.

Rose is not for being put off though, as the queue moves again. 'So, what do we know about him? He's divorced, one kid, lives on his own. He's what, thirty-seven? Thirty-eight?'

'Something like that.'

'And he's good-looking, right?'

'I suppose.'

'Would you?'

'Would I what?' I say, frowning.

Rosie slaps the palm of her hand against her forehead. 'Jesus, Daisy.' Before she can elaborate, it's our turn and Rosie comes with me into the dressing-room cubicle, hanging up the tops on the hooks. 'Get 'em off, sis.'

I quickly take off my T-shirt and as I start to put on the first item, a sort of silky shirt with military styling. Rosie shrieks. 'Oh my god, Daisy, when did you last buy a new bra? When did you last get a bra fitted?'

I look down at my chest. 'I can't remember.'

'That is positively grey. And your tits look like two melons in a hammock. Marks and Sparks next, I think. Take that top off, I don't like it.'

I start to climb into the next shirt and say quietly, 'I told him. About what happened. When we were kids.'

Rosie stares at me, frozen in the act of putting the silky shirt back on its hanger. 'You did what?'

'Told Nate. When we did that stake-out.'

Rosie closes her eyes and breathes deeply. 'And why would you do that?' she says calmly, though her voice has an edge.

I wait until she opens her eyes to scrutinise the second shirt. 'No,' she says. 'Try the orange one.'

'Because I thought it was better to get it out of the way. After what happened with Darren. I don't want to go through all that again. Don't want to get so far down the road.'

Rosie takes over the buttoning of the shirt and takes a step back in the narrow confines of the cubicle to take a long look. 'Yes. I like that.' She shifts her gaze to me. 'Down the road? You were living with Darren. Everybody thought you might get married. You honestly think it could be like that with Nate?'

'I didn't mean that,' I say, flustered, taking off the orange top. 'I meant—'

'You meant you've thought about it though,' says Rosie, handing me the last top. 'Put this on.'

'I thought we were getting the orange one.'

'We haven't seen this one, yet. That's the thing, Daisy. You have to try a few before you find the right one. You don't just buy the first one that seems to fit and then when it turns out to be not right for you just give up and don't go out to buy another top.' Rosie rubs her chin. 'Yes. This one. See? We had to try on four to find the right one.'

I take off the shirt and hand it to her, and put my T-shirt back on. 'Is that a *metaphor*, Rosie?'

She looks at the label in the last shirt. 'No, it's J by Jasper Conran. Now, a skirt next, I think.'

After what feels like a week of shopping I have a whole new outfit for the works night out, including shoes, a handbag, a new bra that does actually make a world of difference in terms of comfort, and even knickers, which actually have less material in them than the handkerchiefs in my pocket, never mind the pants I usually wear. Before we go back Rosie insists we go for a drink. 'You have to when you've been shopping,' she says. 'I think it's the law.'

We find a cafe with outside tables bathed in spring sunlight, just off St Peter's Square. I want a pot of tea for one but Rosie looks at me reprovingly and orders a large glass of white wine for each of us. A tram clatters past and then Rosie says, 'I think it was a mistake to tell Nate what happened. There was no need. It was such a long time ago and—'

'I had to tell him,' I cut in. 'I told you. It's better to get these things out in the open from the off. I've learned that lesson.'

The waiter brings our drinks and when he's gone Rosie says, 'And how did he take it?'

I shrug, remembering that look in his eye. 'Exactly as you'd expect. It's fine. It's for the best.' I take a sip of the cool, crisp wine.

I don't want to tell Rosie about the dancing and the nearly-kiss on the roof. I'm not even sure myself it happened. Or didn't happen. Nearly happened. I've never felt like I did in that moment when Nate almost kissed me. Like my skin was on fire and a tornado was blowing in my mind. Like I needed a wee really badly, but it wasn't a wee I wanted. I never had that with Darren. Maybe it was the wine.

After Janice interrupted us and we went back down to the museum to sort out the battling dads (the plasticine dinosaur-making competition was declared a draw by Nate, which seemed to mollify both of them. Mollify. Good word) neither of us mentioned what had happened. We barely saw each other for the rest of the event. I think that means he regretted what nearly happened. Maybe I was wrong about not seeing the look in his eye. Maybe he is just good at hiding things. Maybe the thing that happened is just too much for him.

I say to Rosie, 'I just have to accept that I ruined my own life a long time ago. I don't deserve to be happy.'

Rosie looks like she's on the verge of saying something, but instead takes a drink of her own wine. She lights a cigarette and blows the smoke into the air. Eventually she says, 'Speaking of being happy . . . there's something I want to talk to you about.' Rosie stares into her wine glass, a little sadly, I think. 'Well, you know I've been seeing a lot of Ian . . .'

It's true. Ian has been round every night, staying over more often than not, and they always go out at weekends, to pubs and restaurants and the cinema. It's not that long since they met but Ian seems to have become a fixture in Rosie's life.

'I really like him, Daisy. I mean really like him. He makes me laugh. He makes me feel special. He makes me—'

I put my hand up, remembering the cat noises Rosie makes from her room when Ian stays over. 'That's enough. I get it.'

'He's the one, Daisy. I'm sure of it.'

I'm not sure what to say to this. 'I'm happy for you,' I offer in the end. Then frown. 'But you don't look happy.'

'He's been offered another job,' says Rosie. She looks at me. 'In Spain. With a big construction company. His friend works for them, and he's got Ian a job in the plumbing department. It's great money and he gets settled status. And it's a beautiful part of the world.'

I put my hand on hers across the table. 'I'm so sorry, Rosie. Just when—'

'He's asked me to go with him,' she blurts out.

I crinkle my brow. 'What, for a holiday?'

'No. For good. To live with him.'

'In Spain?'

'In Spain.'

I take my hand away from hers. 'And you've told him you can't?'

Rosie looks me dead in the eye. 'I've told him I want to.'

'Mother's ill, Rosie. She's dying.'

'I know, Daisy.'

'So that means you can't go,' I say. I wish we were talking about anything else. Clothes. Wine. Telly. Nate, even.

Rosie takes her time in answering. 'No, it doesn't. Not really. It means I have to choose whether I go or whether I stay. And what that would mean for everyone else.'

'No,' I say, more fiercely than I intend. 'You can't go, and that's that.' I glare at her. 'I might have news, too. Job news. I might be losing mine.'

Rosie's face falls. 'Oh, god, Daisy, why? What's happened?'

'There's nothing definite, yet.' I look down at my hands. I feel sulky and miserable. I can feel the black dog padding about, weaving between the tables of the cafe. 'They might get rid of all of the security guards. We're still waiting to hear something formally.'

'Bloody hell.' Rosie rubs her then signals for the waiter. 'I need another. Same again?'

'No,' I say. 'We should get back to Mother.'

Rosie picks her phone off the table to check the time. 'We've got ages yet. We should talk this through between us before we go to Mum with any options.'

I can feel the anger rising. 'There are no options! She's sick and getting worse. We both need to be around her. I told you what the doctor said.'

Rosie orders another large glass of wine. 'It could be a year. Two. More. I can't wait that long, Daisy. I can't miss my chance.'

'You're just selfish, Rosie. You've always been the same.' I stand up and grab my bags. 'You always just think about yourself, about what's right for Rosie.'

Rosie looks away. The waiter comes and delivers the next glass, which she starts on immediately. I give her a withering look. 'I'll see you at home. In whatever state you drag yourself back in.'

The carer is a lovely woman called Kath who bustles around constantly. I don't think she ever stands still. It's about the third or fourth time we've had her in for the respite days, and she seems to get on well with Mother. When I get back Kath is washing the pots from Mother's lunch. She gives me a broad smile as I drop my bags by the kitchen table.

'Bit of retail therapy, love? Fantastic. I tell my Colin that there's nothing like a good shop but men aren't wired like that, are they? He wants a pair of jeans he goes into the first shop that sells jeans and buys the first pair of jeans that fit him. Where's the fun in that?'

Kath scoots around me and pops the butter back in the fridge. 'Just made her a bit of toast. She said she was peckish. Gave her a lovely bit of pie for her lunch. Then she had a nap. She is grand, your mother.'

It's then that I notice on the worktop next to the microwave the two empty bottles. Whisky. I pick one up and sniff the neck, recoiling at the stale alcohol stench. 'What are these?'

'Had a party, have you, love?' says Kath, putting on her thin coat. 'Found one behind the sofa and one at the bottom of your mother's wardrobe. Nothing like a party, is there? I tell my Colin all the time, we should have more parties. He's more for a cup of tea and a night in front of the History Channel. Loves his History Channel, Colin. Don't know why I married him, really. But after so long you think, well, what's the point in even thinking of—'

'Kath,' I cut in. 'You found these in the house?'

'Behind the sofa in the living room and at the bottom of your mother's wardrobe,' she repeats.

I stare at the empty bottles with rising anger. How could she? How could Rosie do this? Knocking back whisky and hiding the bottles? And in Mother's room, to cap it all?

Rosie really has gone too far this time.

30

Daisy

Rosie is about an hour behind me, and when she comes into the kitchen I have left the two empty whisky bottles prominently displayed on the table. I am standing with my back to the sink, sipping a cup of tea. Rosie looks at me, then at the bottles, then goes back to hang up her coat. When she comes back into the kitchen I say, 'Well?'

'I feel like I'm getting told off by the headteacher,' she says. She goes straight to the fridge and gets out a half-empty bottle of wine. It occurs to me that Rosie would probably say it is half-full.

'Don't you think you've had enough?' I say.

Rosie's face goes stone-hard. She glares at me. 'No, actually, Daisy, I don't think I've had enough. I will decide when I've had enough. Not you.'

I nod to the whisky bottles. 'When did you put that lot away? I mean, I thought the wine was bad enough. I'd started to see whisky bottles in the recycling bin, but thought they were just . . . well, I don't know what I thought.' I try to put on a kind voice. 'You've got a problem, Rosie.'

'Yes,' she says. 'I have got a fucking problem. I've got a mountain of problems. But being alcoholic isn't one of them, if that's what you're thinking.'

'There's no need to swear,' I say.

Rosie opens her mouth to speak and then changes her mind. She actually bites her lip, as if it's the only possible way she can stop herself saying whatever she so obviously wants to say.

'And hiding them! Did you not think I'd find them, eventually? Who do you think does the cleaning around here? It's not Mother and it's certainly not you. Did you think the fairies came in while you were at work?'

Rosie takes a deep breath and stares pointedly past me, through the window. I'm hitting my stride here. I can't stop speaking. 'What do you think Mother would say? What were you planning to do? Go into her bedroom and say, *oh, by the way, I'm an alcoholic and I'm moving to Spain, see you around*?'

'Right, you sanctimonious cow, come with me,' says Rosie. She stands up and grabs one of the bottles, and with her other hand seizes my wrist. 'I've just about had e-fucking-nough of this.'

'Where do you think you're going?' I say, trying to pull my hand away, but Rosie redoubles her grip and hauls me across the kitchen and to the hall and up the stairs. She storms into Mother's bedroom without knocking.

Mother looks up. 'Oh, hello love. Was your shopping trip nice?'

To my horror, Rosie throws the empty whisky bottle on the bed, where it bounces and settles right next to Mother. Mother looks down at it, her eyes wide. Then she begins to cry.

'Happy now?' I say fiercely, dragging my hand away from Rosie. 'Look what you've done to her. Why don't you tell her the rest of it, eh? Give her the full monty?'

'I'm sorry,' says Mother, sobbing violently.

'You've nothing to be sorry for,' I say sharply to her, then stop. Rosie is staring at me with a look that is half triumphant, half bereft. Mother is cradling the whisky bottle like it's a newborn baby. I look from one to the other and say slowly, 'What is going on here?'

'The bottles aren't mine,' says Rosie. 'They're Mother's.'

Two hours later Mother is dozing and Rosie and I are in the living room, with the Saturday night TV volume down. It's been a rather fraught afternoon, all told.

I am hugging a cup of tea and Rosie is pouring herself a glass of wine. I look at her reproachfully, and she glares back at me. 'If you're going to say do you think you should be doing that? then don't, all right, Daisy?'

I shrug. I am looking through my phone at websites for local alcohol support services. I say, 'I think we should start with this NHS one. It says we should try the GP first.'

'Mum won't go to the doctor,' says Rosie. 'The main reason being, she doesn't think she has a problem.'

'You agree she's got a problem, though? Drinking whisky? Hiding the bottles all over the house?' Something suddenly occurs to me. 'That's why she's always sucking Extra Strong Mints! And like an idiot I keep buying them for her.'

'You got off lightly,' mutters Rosie. 'Who do you think shells out for the whisky?'

My mouth drops open. It hadn't actually occurred to me up to this point where Mother was getting her drink from. 'So you not only knew about it,' I say slowly, 'you've actually been helping her do it?'

Rosie sighs heavily. 'I didn't have a lot of choice. I only found out myself when she got ill. With the cancer. And couldn't go out to buy it. She begged me not to say anything to you. She knew it would only worry you.'

'So it was going on before the cancer?'

Rosie nods, glancing at me and then looking away. 'How long?' I press.

Rosie doesn't answer immediately, then says quietly, 'According to her, it started to get serious after . . . after what happened.' I don't know if she knows she's doing it, but she flexes the muscles in her right forearm and the scars there undulate slightly. The scars where I stabbed my sister.

I let out a deep breath and lean back on the sofa. 'Great. So, something else that I'm responsible for.'

'Daisy . . .' says Rosie, putting a hand on my arm.

'What?'

She screws up her face, as though wrestling with something. Eventually she says, 'You can't keep blaming yourself. Not for something that happened all those years ago.'

I stand up. 'I'm going to check on Mother then go to bed and read.' At the door I stop and turn to Rosie. 'You're right, it did happen a long time ago. But it keeps happening, doesn't it? It's like an earthquake. We keep getting aftershocks. It's never going to end.'

Mother, of course, point-blank refuses to go to the doctor. We get her downstairs for a family conference around the kitchen table. Her weepy contriteness of Saturday has gone by Sunday lunchtime.

'I won't do it,' she says firmly.

'I told you,' Rosie says to me.

I glare at her. She's not helping. I say to Mother, 'There are treatments. They can help you reduce your alcohol consumption.'

'I don't want to reduce my alcohol consumption,' says Mother calmly. 'I'm quite happy with it.' She looks pointedly at Rosie. 'I mean, I wouldn't say no to something a little more expensive, rather than that mouthwash you bring me. But beggars can't be choosers, I suppose.'

'Mother,' I say, trying to keep my voice as calm as I can, 'it will kill you.'

'Daisy,' says Mother back, adopting the same reasonable tone, 'the cancer will kill me first. At least let me die happy.'

We establish that Mother is drinking about five shots of whisky a day. I check the alcohol content on the empty bottle and do some calculations on my phone. 'Oh my god. You're on five units a day. The recommendation for a woman is fourteen a week.'

Rosie laughs scornfully. I point angrily at my phone. 'It says here! On the NHS!' I narrow my eyes. 'Maybe you should go to the doctor as well.'

Rosie flips me her middle finger. Mother puts a hand on my arm. 'Daisy. Love. We all do things we know we shouldn't.'

I frown. 'I don't.'

'Yes, well, okay,' says Mother. 'Most of us do things that we know we shouldn't. It's what they call a . . .' She looks to Rosie.

'Calculated risk,' says Rosie.

Mother nods. 'That. I know I shouldn't be drinking so much. But I've tried to stop. It made me even more ill. I don't get smashed, love. I just have a glass every few hours. It just keeps me on an even keel. I don't think my body could live without it now.'

'That's why it's an addiction,' I say patiently. 'And they can cure addiction. With drugs and counselling and time—'

'Time's one thing I don't have, Daisy,' says Mother softly.

I can sense that Rosie has something to say. I look at her and she says, 'There . . . might be another solution.' She gets up and goes to the living room, and when she comes back she's got that brochure for Elysian Fields, the hospice and care home.

I start to protest but Rosie says, 'Just hear me out. Both of you.' She flicks through the brochure and folds it over to show us both one of the pages. 'They've got this specialist dependency unit, for residents who might have certain . . .

issues. Just think, if Mother was here she could be getting the care and help to—'

'No,' I say firmly. 'Haven't we already been through this?' I look at Mother. 'Tell her. Tell her you won't do it.'

Mother takes the brochure and reads the page at which Rosie has opened it. She looks at her. 'Have you any idea how much this place costs, Rosie?'

'No,' she admits. 'I haven't looked into that side of things.'

'I have,' says Mother. 'When I went to have a look at this place you want to shut me up in, I went in and asked them. They said that if you go in as a care home, it's thousands. A month, that is. Made my eyes water.' She flicks through the brochure. 'The hospice side of it, though, that's free. They do it as a charity, see, raising money. And they get funding from the NHS. It's marvellous, really. But if you were to put me in there now, I'd have to be in the residential home until the end-of-life care kicked in.'

I glance at Rosie and she's looking at me. She says, 'You could sell the house to pay for it.'

My eyes widen with horror. 'But this is our home! What would we do?'

Rosie looks away. Well, we know what Rosie would do. Bugger off to Spain with Ian.

Mother says thoughtfully, 'I always thought when my time came it would be here. At home. With my girls around me.' I hear Rosie take a sharp breath. 'That's what I always wanted. When I found out I was ill.'

Nobody says anything for a long while. Then Mother says, 'I could do with a drink.'

'I'll put the kettle on,' I say, scraping back my chair.

Mother gives me a tight smile. 'I was thinking something stronger, love. There's a bottle in the airing cupboard if you wouldn't mind.'

I cook us a chicken for tea on Sunday, with roast potatoes and stuffing. Mother has taken to her bed again after her whisky, and eats it there, watching *Countryfile*. Rosie and me eat ours at the kitchen table.

'Is Ian not coming around?' I say. 'There's plenty of chicken.'

'He has to sort out loads of paperwork for the Spain job,' she says, a little sullenly in my opinion. 'And he's looking at property. To rent, at first, but he's hoping to buy down the line.'

'So he's definitely going to take it, then?' I say. 'Even if you don't go?'

She gives me a filthy look and pushes the leftovers of her dinner around her plate. 'I've told him he has to. It's a fantastic opportunity for him. Life doesn't stand still, Rosie. I've already told you that.'

I pick up the plates and scrape the remains of the roast into the bin. 'Well, it's all settled, anyway. You can do what you want. I'm not letting Mother sell the house. And I'm going to stay here and look after her. I'll make it work, somehow, even if you go. Even if I lose my job.' I turn to Rosie. 'I owe it to her. After what happened. After what I did to you. I have to pay for that, Rosie, and this is how I do it.'

31

Nate

The Saturday night of the do is supposed to be my weekend with Ben, so I tell him and Lucia on Friday morning that I'm not going to bother going out.

'Sod that,' says Lucia. 'You can have him tonight until Saturday teatime and he can come back here to sleep. You all right with that, Ben?'

Ben shrugs, and nods. Since the incident at Big Sleepover things have been a lot better. I don't know if he's had any contact with the gang, but I'm guessing not. He looks more relaxed and content, and Lucia and I had a long talk about trying to put up some kind of united front with him, as much as possible. 'You might not be my husband any more, but you'll always be Ben's dad,' she says. 'Let's try to work together a bit better. For his sake.'

'Can I bring my Xbox over tonight?' says Ben.

'Fortnite tournament?' I hazard.

He nods. I give him a grin. 'Maybe you can show your old duffer of a dad what it's all about.'

Before Lucia goes to work she digs out several carrier bags from the living room. 'I went shopping for some clothes.'

'Oh,' I say, nonplussed. I don't know why she's telling me this.

'For you,' she clarifies. 'For the do. You've always been shit at choosing your own clothes. You're not going out in those chinos and that checked shirt again.'

I peer into the bags. There appears to be a pair of black jeans, a grey roll-neck thin woollen sweater, and even some new boxer shorts and socks. Lucia says, 'I want you to look your best for Daisy.'

I open my mouth to protest, but then I realise something. I want to look my best for Daisy as well. I've thought of little else over the past week, even if it's been business as usual at work. We've still only seen each other for the handover, but her absence in most of my day actually makes me think of her more. I have been biding my time. Waiting for the works outing. So we can talk properly, for the first time since the Big Sleepover. So instead of protesting I say to Lucia, 'Thank you. That's really thoughtful.' I look into the bags again. 'What if they don't fit?'

'Do you know what size you take?' says Lucia, raising an eyebrow.

I think about it, and shrug. 'No, not really.'

'So it's a good job that I still do. You can leave them here and get them when you pick Ben up after work.'

There's a definite bounce in my step as I walk into the museum. There are blue skies and blossom on the trees and the promise of warmth on the breeze. And I have new underpants.

'Morning, Harold!' I announce as I walk into the den. He's sitting there with his coat on, a couple of worn plastic carrier bags between his feet.

'About bloody time,' says Harold. He peers at me suspiciously. 'What have you got to be so cheerful about?'

I shrug and put the kettle on. 'It's spring, Harold, when a young man's fancy turns to thoughts of love.'

He rolls his eyes. 'Rather you than me with that one. What we used to call a man-eater.'

I do a double take, spilling the coffee granules off the spoon all over the desk. 'Daisy?'

Harold laughs. 'That bloody Janice. Off reception. Everybody knows she's set her cap at you. She's like a giddy schoolgirl.' He stands up. 'Like I said, good luck. You'll need it.'

'I'll see you at the do tomorrow?' I say, trying not to think about what he's just said. Janice. Oh my god.

'Not for me,' says Harold. 'I'm well past nights out. Quiet Saturday in with our lass, as usual.'

It must be my good mood that makes me a little reckless, because I say, 'Why do you work this godawful shift, Harold? At your age? Doesn't your wife mind?'

Harold suddenly glares at me. 'None of your bloody business,' he mutters. I bend down to get Harold's bags for him, just at the same time that he does. We both grab a handle and one of the bags falls over, spilling its contents on the floor.

'Bloody idiot,' says Harold. I squat to help him shove the stuff back in. Then I pause. And look up at Harold.

'I've got to go,' he says quickly, grabbing his bags and bustling out of the den without another word.

I can feel excitement bubbling up inside me as I head out of the den to do a quick turn around all of the halls. I can't wait for Daisy to come on shift tonight. I've barely got across the lobby when Janice calls me from reception. 'Nate! Hello!'

My heart sinks but I turn to her and put a big smile on. 'Hello, Janice. Is it urgent . . .? Because there's something I need to check up on.'

'Just wanted to make sure you've got all the details for tomorrow night,' she says. I've never really known what *coquettishly* means, though I've read it in a lot of books, until I see how Janice smiles at me.

'All good,' I say. 'Looking forward to it.'

'I *bet* you are,' says Janice. 'Tut tut, Mr Garvey.'

I smile politely and make my escape, unable to shake that image Daisy put in my head when she called Janice a praying mantis.

My good mood continues all day. I can't remember the last time I was so buoyant for so long. In fact, it lasts until precisely four-fifty in the afternoon, when Daisy comes in customarily ten minutes early for her shift.

'Daisy,' I say, before she's taken her coat off. 'There are two things. First, about the do tomorrow night—'

'I'm not going,' she says bluntly.

I feel like I've missed my footing. I was going to ask her if she wanted me to pick her up in a taxi, suggest that we arrive at the do together, possibly even grab a drink on our own somewhere first. I feel my smile melt away. 'What?'

Daisy looks at me as though I'm stupid. 'Everything I told you. About my sister.'

I shrug. 'It was a long time ago. It doesn't matter. Besides . . .' Neither of us have broached the subject of the kiss we nearly had. I'm not quite sure how to talk about it myself. I feel like a tongue-tied schoolboy whenever I think about it.

There's a flicker of something in Daisy's eyes, a slight crinkling of her brow, but she busies herself tidying up my cup from the desk. 'It does matter,' she says quietly. 'It keeps mattering. I'm not going tomorrow. There's too much happening at home.'

I can feel the good humour rushing out of me like air from a punctured tyre. Daisy puts my cup in the sink and, without looking at me, says, 'I don't know what you thought might happen, Nate, but it isn't going to. It can't. It wouldn't work. It never does.'

When she does turn around – is there a hint of tears in her

eyes? – she says, 'What was the other thing? You said there were two things.'

'It doesn't matter,' I say. And it doesn't. Not any more.

I don't tell Lucia and Ben about Daisy. I keep my smile on when I go to pick up Ben, Lucia gives me the bags of clothes, and she gives me a peck on the cheek and tells me to have a good time. I don't protest when John offers to drive us round to my place. When Ben gets out and goes to the boot to get his stuff, John says, 'Lucia told me what you did. With those ruffians.' He gives me an appreciative wink. 'Nice work, Nate. You're a good dad.'

I have been looking up recipes online so I can make Ben some proper tea rather than just getting a takeaway from Derek. The curry goat isn't a total success, but it's edible enough, and Ben has fun making it with me. Then I watch him play his video game for a fairly incomprehensible but admittedly diverting couple of hours, me shrieking and jumping up and down as other players sneak up on him and try to kill him with a variety of increasingly ridiculous weapons.

While he's playing I go to get something from under my bed, that's been gathering dust for a lot of years. I never thought I'd get it out. But now seems the time.

Ben turns away from the TV to watch me banging a hook in the wall of the living room behind the sofa and hanging the framed photograph there. I get a duster and some Mr Sheen and wipe down the glass.

'Grandad,' says Ben. 'The Black Bomber.'

It's the photo that was up on the easel at his funeral. Mum kept it, and I didn't have the heart to throw it out, even though I wanted to. I never thought I'd actually get it out from its hiding place, though.

'Why are you putting it up?' says Ben. 'You don't have any pictures of Grandad up.'

'No,' I say. I sit on the sofa and pat the cushion for him to join me. 'But I thought it was time. And it's time we talked about him.'

Ben obediently snuggles under my arm while I think about what I want to say. 'Your grandad . . . he did bad things, Ben. And for a long time I tried very hard not to be the same sort of person he was. But though I didn't use my fists in the way he did, maybe I failed just as much as he did at being a father.'

'You're a good dad,' says Ben, and I have to stifle a sudden sob. 'I did bad things too. With the gang. To Daisy.'

I nod. 'And that's sort of the point of all this. Terry Garvey used to hit people for a living, and he didn't know how to stop hitting people when he wasn't in the ring, and things were going bad for him. And me . . . well, like you said, me and your mum failed you as well. Led you to going to that gang for the support you thought you needed. And then you did those things.'

Ben moves slightly away from me and looks at me with his big eyes. 'I said I was sorry. Are you going to tell me off again?'

'No.' I pull Ben closer in to me. 'Just because people do bad things, it doesn't make them bad people. Do you understand that? We never know what a person has been through, or what has brought them to the point where they do bad things.' I turn my head to look at the photo of my father. 'Which is why I've put the picture up. To remind me that in everybody there's some good. There's good in everyone, Ben. They just need the right chance to show it.'

After some hot milk and a bit of telly, Ben's eyes start to droop and I tell him it's bedtime. 'Will you read me a story?' he says sleepily. He hasn't asked me that for ages.

'What do you want?' I say as I tuck him up in the bed.

He smiles. 'You know who you reminded me of when you were bouncing about while I was on Fortnite?' I shake my head. 'Do you not remember what I used to call you when I was little?'

My heart suddenly feels like breaking. *When I was little.* He's only ten now. But so grown-up, in so many ways, as well.

'Tigger,' I say, reaching for the battered old book of Pooh stories on the shelf. Ben had been entranced by the cartoons when he was tiny, and before Lucia and I divorced, I'd just started to get him into the A. A. Milne stories. 'Which story?'

'The sad one,' says Ben.

The sad one. The very last chapter of the Pooh stories. Where Christopher Robin takes Pooh up to Galleon's Lap, an enchanted place that overlooks the whole of the Hundred Acre Wood. And Christopher Robin tells Pooh that their adventures are at an end, because he has to go off to school, and there is no place for honey-loving bears or excitable tigers or motherly kangaroos at school. Childish things must be set aside.

It's the most heartbreaking thing I have ever read, and even now it brings forth the tears. It used to make me cry because Ben was getting older and I knew we'd lose the magic of those early years where everything was an adventure. It made me cry when Lucia and I were getting divorced, and I feared I would never see Ben properly again. And now? Now it makes me cry for a loss of something I almost had, but didn't. Daisy.

Even though Ben is snoring lightly I continue to read until I've finished the story. As I put the book back on the shelf, Ben stirs, still mostly asleep, and reaches out a hand to me.

'You know the most wonderful thing about Tiggers?' he mumbles.

'No,' I whisper. 'What's the most wonderful thing about Tiggers?'

'You're the only one,' says Ben, then rolls over and snuggles down under his duvet, and is asleep.

I switch off his bedside light but sit there for a while on the edge of his bed, utterly destroyed.

Despite myself, despite everything, on Saturday evening when Lucia and John have picked up Ben I put on the new clothes my ex-wife bought for me and book a taxi to take me into Manchester city centre. Before it arrives I look at myself in the mirror on my bedroom door. Lucia has done good. I look . . . presentable. I wish Daisy were coming, but she's not. We're just co-workers again. We'll see each other for a few minutes a day, as I hand over to her, and that will be it. Just like before. Well, for as long as it all lasts. Until they make us redundant, if that's what they're going to do.

Like my mood, the sky has darkened over the course of Saturday and the first drops of rain start to patter down as I get out of the cab in the Northern Quarter. We're meeting in a pub and when I rush in from the suddenly violent storm that's gathered above us, everyone is already there. I move between them, being the Nate they know, smiling and joking and dancing from person to person, making everybody laugh. While I feel empty inside.

Janice, of course, makes a beeline for me. 'Well?' she says, giving me a twirl. I give her a smile.

'Nate!' she says, slapping my arm. 'This is the outfit I showed you! That you said I should buy! I followed your advice! What do you think?'

What I think is that I really shouldn't have come out tonight. But I say something I hope is nice, and I have a drink, then another. We are going on for a curry, but not until later. I drink some more, and begin to loosen up. They're a nice bunch of people, really, who work at the museum. Be a shame if it all comes to an end.

At some point in the evening I feel Janice tugging my sleeve and pulling me outside. It's still raining heavily, and we shelter under a wide umbrella over a table outside the pub. 'What are we doing here?' I say, looking around. It's gone dark while we've been inside the pub. 'Is it time for the curry? Only I was thinking I might give that a miss, to be honest.'

'I've got something in my eye,' says Janice. 'It's really hurting me.'

'Oh.' I'm a little confused. 'Do you need one of the first-aiders? I think Dorothy is one.'

She takes off her glasses and pulls the bottom of her left eyelid down a little. 'Can you just take a look? Can you see anything?'

I squint at her eye, then shake my head. 'Nothing.'

'Look closer, Nate, it's killing me.'

I bend in further, peering into her eye. 'Janice, I can't—'

Then she clasps a hand at either side of my head, pulls me forward, and clamps her lips on mine, kissing me hotly and forcing her tongue into my mouth.

And from the corner of my eye I see Daisy Dukes, standing in the rain, watching us with a look on her face that I find impossible to read.

32

Daisy

I nip to the shops on the parade on Saturday afternoon for a few bits including, to my incredible distaste, a bottle of whisky for Mother. Rosie has insisted. She says it would be worse if Mother just stopped drinking than carrying on, which doesn't make any sense to me. Surely if something's hurting you, you stop doing it. Like me entertaining any prospect of anything happening between Nate and me. I feel like over the past few weeks I've been fed some kind of slow-acting drug that made me start to like him so gradually I didn't notice what was happening. But, in the long run, it would have just turned out bad. So I stopped it, before it could hurt me.

When I come out of the off-licence I see those boys. That gang. Nate's son Ben isn't with them, though, which I'm glad about. One of them sees me and nudges the others. Here we go. But the biggest one, the leader of the pack, shakes his head. And they all look away. Well. Every cloud has a silver lining, as Mother says.

I run a few more errands and then make my way back to the house. Rosie is pouring herself her first glass of wine of the day, as far as I know, then she goes into the yard to light a cigarette. She squints at the sky. 'Looks like rain for your do tonight.'

I grunt non-committally as I put the shopping away. Rosie says, 'I took Mum a cup of tea up. She was asking questions about the care home.'

'Well, there's no point, is there?'

'She asked to see the brochure again.'

I slam a tin of beans on the worktop a little more forcefully than I intend to. 'We've already talked about this, Rosie. It's not going to happen. I'm going to look after Mother.'

Rosie shrugs and goes into the living room to watch some TV. One of her shows about people going to have a new life in a sunny country. I feel a bit of a pang of guilt about her and Ian. I mean, it's not forever, is it? She could visit him. And go out there for good after Mother . . . I push the thought away.

I have a cup of tea and look through the care home brochure again at the table. I'm sure Rosie has left it out on purpose. I mean, it does look like a nice place. But Mother doesn't want to go and I don't want her to go, so that's that.

'Do you mind if I have a bath first?' says Rosie, popping her head around the door. 'Ian's coming over tonight. Thought you wouldn't mind as you're going out.'

I don't put Rosie right, just let her go and have her bath. She's playing music on her phone. It sounds good. Upbeat. Happy. I have a sudden memory of our father, playing CDs in the living room. Until Mother told him to turn them down, or off, and it ended in an argument. I wonder if his new wife and children let him play his music? I wonder if he's even still alive? I never felt the urge to find out. Mother always said that he had his chance, and he abandoned his family, so we should just leave him to his choices. Your choices determine your life, she always said, and his life didn't have any space for us in it.

While Rosie is in the bathroom I go into my bedroom and lie on the bed, reading for a while. The clothes I bought last weekend are hanging up on the outside of my wardrobe. I keep glancing at them, then put down my book and stuff the clothes inside the wardrobe. Out of sight, out of mind.

I hear Rosie go downstairs and I pop my head around Mother's door, but she's having a nap. I'll sort out her tea later. I go back and read for a little longer, losing myself in the book until at some point my eyelids droop and I nod off.

And dream. I dream of a different life. A better life. A life with Nate. Perhaps it's only in my dream-life that I can admit to myself that . . . well. That I could, if things were different, perhaps love him. Love him like I never loved Darren. Love him like I never thought love could exist, except in books.

I dream of the feel of his hand on mine behind the drapes. I dream of the kiss we almost had on the roof. I dream of the fizzing, popping feeling I had in my head, in my whole body. I dream of the magnetic pull I felt between our lips as his head moved towards me. I dream of a life that could be, if things were altogether different.

I dream we have a cottage somewhere. In the countryside. Except it's not a cottage, not any more, it's a big, rambling, tumbledown house. Quite, quite beautiful. It reminds me of Bleak House, from the Charles Dickens novel.

'Hashtag NotBleakHouse,' says Nate in my dream. I laugh at his stupid joke. It makes me feel good. To laugh. I do it so rarely.

I don't know what we do for jobs in this dream life. We obviously don't work at the museum. No more Daisy does nights and Nate does days. We are together all the time, and the sun streams in through the windows, and we have breakfast across from each other at a big table in the kitchen. And then Nate comes around to my side of the table, puts his arms around me from behind, and kisses the top of my head.

And I am fizzing and popping again, like when we used to get space dust in little paper packets from the shop and put it on our tongues and the noise seemed deafening and you'd stick your tongue out to your friends and ask, in a stupid, tongue-stuck-out way, whether they could hear the amazing fizzing and popping that was so deafening in your head.

They never could. Because it was only for you. Just like this dream is only for me. Just like nobody would ever understand how so little contact – a smile, a joke, a holding of hands, an almost-kiss – could mean so, so much to me. Rosie would never understand, with her phone apps and her loud sex with Ian. Rosie would never get this, never in a million years. And in my dream, as Nate kisses my head and enfolds me with his arms, I feel safe and protected and cared for.

Dreams can be cruel.

Because things aren't different, and can never be. Mother is dying. Mother is alcoholic. Rosie wants to leave for Spain. And I am haunted by the thing that happened. The thing that I should stop calling the thing that happened because it's out there, now. I've told Nate. I've unstoppered the bottle, let loose the genie. Revealed my dirty little secret.

The thing that happened. Furthermore known as the day I stabbed my sister. The day I revealed my true colours. The day I showed that I am evil, or mad, or untrustworthy, or any of these things. Not normal. Never normal.

Crazy Daisy.

And in my dream Nate melts away from me, his hand fades from my grasp, the polarity of the magnetic pull that brings our lips together is reversed and we feel the invisible push of it, keeping us apart.

This is why dreams are cruel. They show you what might be, and then they snatch it away from you with the truth.

I wake sharply, and am surprised to find I have tears on my cheeks, until I remember my dream. Stupid Daisy. Showing a crack in your armour. Allowing hope inside. Only to be dashed on the rocks. Stupid, stupid Daisy. I glance at my phone and see that I have only been asleep for twenty minutes. I read once that you only enter deep, dream-sleep after nineteen minutes, and if you want a nap you should set your alarm for that amount of time and you'll wake refreshed. That means that within one minute my stupid Daisy subconsciousness presented me with the life I could have had, and then snatched it away from me. Probably not even one minute. Enough time for electrical connections to fire in my brain. Seconds. Milliseconds.

I wipe the tears from my face with my sleeve and pick up my book again. At least with books, you can trust that the author is going to do the right thing. Books aren't cruel like dreams can be.

It's almost dark when I next look up at the sound of a creaking floorboard outside on the landing. My door pushes open and Rosie stares at me, eyes wide.

'Daisy! What are you doing? I just came up to ask if you want Ian to run you into town but you're not even ready! You've not even had a bath!'

'I'm not going,' I say.

'What? What do you mean, you're not going? What about Nate?'

'What about Nate?' I say, annoyed. 'Why are you so obsessed with him?'

Rosie sits down on the edge of my bed, even though I hadn't invited her to. 'Because you like him, I can tell. And this is your chance to see him out of work. Relax. Get to know him better.'

'I don't need to get to know him better,' I say, returning to my book. Rosie takes it out of my hands and lays it down on the bed.

'Daisy. Get ready. Now.'

'No. Give me that book.'

Rosie rolls her eyes and takes a deep breath. 'This is because of what you told him, isn't it? You think it's going to be like Darren all over again.'

'I can't escape what I did,' I say quietly. 'I'll never escape it.'

Rosie's face hardens. 'Right. Come with me. I have just about had enough of this.'

She takes my wrist again and drags me up off the bed, pulling me out of the room. I pull my arm out of her grip but follow her into Mother's room. She turns on the big light.

'Rosie!' I say, aghast, as Mother stirs and squints at us. 'What are you doing?'

'Tell her,' says Rosie. 'Tell her now.'

Mother's face goes from sleepiness to confusion to something that looks like . . . dismay? I frown at Rosie. 'Tell me what?'

'I cannot do this for one day longer,' says Rosie to Mother. 'None of us can. Either you tell her now or I will.'

'Tell me what?' I demand. 'What are you talking about?'

Rosie drags up the sleeve of her top and thrusts her scars at me. 'This. This is what I'm talking about.' She turns to glare at Mother. 'Well?'

Mother sighs raggedly and looks at Rosie, then at me. She closes her eyes for a second then says, 'You didn't stab your sister, Daisy.' She opens her eyes and looks sadly at me. 'It was me.'

33

Daisy

The story is the same as the film that runs in my head. Up to a point. And then it changes. It's what you might call the director's cut.

I slowly wash the carving knife, rubbing the blade with the scouring pad. I am thinking of that snatched image of Father throwing me up in the air, the blue sky whirling around me, his arms outstretched to catch me again.

This bit is the same.

'It's your fault,' says Mother, slowly. Her voice is low and not sounding like her at all. 'We were happy until we had kids.'

This bit is the same too.

I am spinning in the air again, laughing half in terror, half in elation. Father is holding out his hands to catch me, to keep me safe.

This is not in Mother's version, but it is in mine. And when she is telling me what happened, the memory remains.

I lift the knife from the water and watch the bubbles drain from the blade.

'It's all your fault!' Mother screams suddenly. Rosie goes quiet and looks at her, eyes filled with fear.

What happens next I can't quite remember properly. I seem to think that Mother made a grab for the knife, but I don't know if that was to stop me doing what I did, or after I'd done it. Everything is just black from that moment.

What happened was that Mother did grab the knife from me, but not to protect Rosie or myself. She did it because she was in an uncontrollable fury, screaming, shouting, ranting. She did it because she was drunk. Rosie takes up the story when Mother can't continue.

Mother grabs the knife and Rosie is crying and I am crying and Mother is telling us both to shut up, shut up, shut up, then she lifts the knife high and brings it down hard and screams, 'Shut! Up!'

And the knife quivers and shakes, its point embedded in the worktop, its blade straight through Rosie's forearm.

I collapse on the floor in a dead faint. Rosie is almost mute with terror and agony. Mother runs to call for an ambulance. And while it comes she whispers to Rosie. But not words designed to comfort and calm. Words to deceive.

'I can remember it vividly,' says Rosie coldly. 'You said to me, "If they find out I did this they'll take you away from me. Both of you. They'll put you in a children's home. They'll never let you see me again. We have to say that it was an accident. We have to say that Daisy did it.".'

I look from Rosie to Mother, sniffling in her bed. 'Is this true?' I say, unable to get my voice louder than a whisper.

Mother nods wretchedly at me. 'It all worked out, in the end. I did it to keep us together, love.'

Rosie is facing me, grabbing my hands, her eyes filled with tears. 'I'm so sorry, Daisy. I'm so sorry. I didn't know what was happening myself at the time. I was so little and so hurt and so frightened. I got to believing it was you myself. And then when we got older . . . I just never knew how to tell you. And Mother begged me not to. Said there was nothing to gain by dragging it all up.'

'All my life,' I say quietly. 'All my life I believed I did the bad thing.' My stare snaps towards Mother. 'Worked out, in the end? Are you sure about that? Because I'm fairly sure this lie has absolutely ruined my life.'

I feel light-headed, like I'm going to faint. This has been the defining point of my life. The thing that made me who I am today. Everything since I was nine years old has been informed by the fact that I stabbed my sister in a rage that I couldn't even remember properly. Remember at all.

And there was a reason for that. Because it didn't happen.

It didn't happen.

For all these years I've been like Prometheus from the Greek myths book, chained to the rock by Zeus for stealing fire and giving it to the mortals, an eagle coming to him every day to rip out his liver. Every day I've torn out my own liver, punished myself for stabbing Rosie.

And it didn't happen.

I feel empty and sick and elated and devastated all at the same time. All that life wasted. I am sad and furious and sickened. And yet . . . all my life to come. Without the shadow of this hanging over me. As though I have been cleansed. As though I have been purged.

And with that thought I run from the room, and just make it to the bathroom, and bend over the toilet, heaving out the food and tea I've eaten today, retching and gagging until there's nothing left inside of me.

And with it goes the thing that happened. The thing that didn't happen. And when I stop throwing up, and wipe the drool from my mouth, I feel . . . different.

I go back into the bedroom where Mother and Rosie are

sitting, wide-eyed, waiting for me. They can tell. They can tell that I'm different now. That things have changed.

Mother is saying *sorry, sorry, sorry* over and over. I put my head in my hands. 'I thought I was crazy. I thought I was dangerous.' I look at Rosie. 'How could you? How could you be . . . complicit in this? For all these years?'

Now Rosie is crying openly. 'I'm sorry,' she says snottily. 'I was only a child. Younger than you. I just did what I was told.' She looks daggers at Mother. 'I just did what she told me to. And then as the years passed . . . it became too late to say anything. I think I half believed it had happened that way myself.'

'I could never let anyone love me. I drove Darren away.' I close my eyes. 'Nate. I pushed Nate away from me.'

I hear Rosie gasp. 'Nate. You can go. Now. To see him.'

I shake my head. 'No. We have to talk about all this.'

'Bollocks,' says Rosie, wiping the tears from her eyes. She pushes me out of the room, looking over her shoulder at Mother. 'We will talk about this. We have to. But you're going to get something good out of this, Daisy. You have to. Or you'll never forgive yourself.'

Rosie propels me into the bathroom. 'Shower. Now. Then get dressed. And do your make-up.'

'There isn't time, Rosie,' I protest. My mind is whirling. I can't be doing this. I need to talk this through, with Mother, with Rosie. But at the centre of the tornado there is one thought: Nate.

'There is,' insists Rosie. 'If you get your arse into gear.' She touches my face. 'Please, Daisy. I need to make twenty-five years of lies up to you and I need to start now. And you'll thank me for this, one day, I promise you.'

I'm not convinced I'm going to do anything until I stand in the shower and the needles of hot water pound my skin.

And it feels like I'm washing something away. Something I've carried with me all my life. Something that was a lie. I can feel my shoulders relaxing, a weight dissipating in my stomach, a fog lifting in my brain.

It wasn't me. I didn't do it. I didn't hurt Rosie.

My stomach lurches and I lean forward and throw up again, and I keep throwing up until there's nothing left. But I don't feel bad. I don't feel empty. I feel as though I'm just making room. For the truth. For myself.

Half an hour later I'm standing in the living room, shyly asking Rosie what she thinks.

'Gorgeous,' she says, fiddling with the back of the tight skirt. 'And you'll be even more fab once I get all these bloody price tags off. You really don't go clothes shopping very often, do you, Daisy?'

Rosie is staying in with Mother and, I presume, having a serious conversation with her. Ian is driving me into town. 'This is like a movie, innit?' he says, grinning, as I strap into the seat. 'Like the end of *Bridget Jones* or something. We need a good song for this.'

Ian scrolls through his phone while Rosie manically waves at him to go, then a song bursts out of the speakers. '"Something Good" by Utah Saints,' he says. 'Top banana. Let's go, Bridget.' Then he slams the car into gear and burns away from the kerb, and for a moment I think that yes, something good really is going to happen, at last.

It's pouring down by the time Ian drops me on the road near the pub where they're all meeting. I thank him and then, impetuously, which isn't like me at all, give him a quick kiss on the cheek.

'Don't do anything I wouldn't do!' he says cheerfully.

I put up my umbrella and hide under it from the pelting rain, heading towards the pub. There are tables outside with big parasols over them. As I get closer I see a figure, and my heart catches in my throat. It's Nate.

And then I see who he's with. I don't understand what I'm looking at, not at first. Then I do. A sudden gust of wind takes the umbrella out of my hands, and I let it go. The rain batters down, soaking me to the skin. And I just stand there and watch.

Nate. And Janice. Kissing.

Then Nate glances up and sees me. Our eyes meet. I can't read the expression on his face. It could be anything. I can feel my new shirt plastering itself to my body, my skirt sagging with the weight of rainwater.

Nate straightens up and gives me a sort of half-wave. 'Daisy!'

Stupid, stupid Daisy. As if something good could really happen to Daisy Dukes. The universe gives you the tiniest chink of light, the smallest ray of hope, and then it makes it rain, and darkens the night even further.

I turn around, and I run.

34

Daisy

I can't run in the stupid shoes that Rosie made me buy so I kick one off, and then the other, and leave them there in the street. I run barefoot. I don't know where I'm running to. I'm just running. Away. From everybody. Nate and Janice. Mother. Rosie. Ian. Work. The cancer. Everybody and everything. The rain is coming down and the cars are beeping their horns as I dash across roads. A tram swishes past me and I run. I run past the Arndale Centre, and the Royal Exchange Theatre, and St Ann's Church. I run. I can hear Nate shouting for me to stop but I keep running, until I come to the River Irwell, sluggishly flowing in front of me. But that won't stop me from running. I head for the Trinity Bridge, the central pillar and the white spider-web cables illuminated by the orange strip lights that run along the footbridge. Beyond it the curving Lowry Hotel is lit up, behind every light a room, in every room a life. A life that has to be better than mine. I pause on the bridge, envying those lives.

'Daisy! Daisy, wait! Please stop!'

And I do stop, because my feet are cut and ragged and suddenly I don't have the energy to run any more. I walk to the middle of the bridge and look up at every illuminated raindrop that falls on me, each one a drop of sunshine from someone else's dream.

I turn towards Nate; he's leaning on the balustrade, holding his ribs. He puts up a hand while he tries to catch his breath, shaking his head. He's as drenched as I am. We stand there on the bridge for a long moment, just watching each other.

'It's not what you think,' he begins.

'No,' I say. 'Things are never what you think.'

'Just hear me out,' says Nate, taking a deep breath.

'Actually,' I say, 'I'd like you to hear me out. Nobody ever hears me out. Nobody ever listens to me.'

'I listen to you, Daisy,' says Nate, so softly I barely hear him above the pounding rain. 'What do you want to say?'

I stare at him. I don't know what I want to say. Not any more. There's too much happened today. I could just lie down here on this bridge, in this rain, and go to sleep.

Eventually, I say, 'I found something out today. About what I told you.'

Nate takes a step closer to me. 'About your sister?'

I nod. I smile, but I'm crying at the same time. 'It wasn't me. I didn't do it. All these years, I thought I had. But I hadn't. It was my mother.'

'Jesus.' Nate takes another step towards me.

'Since I was nine years old I believed that I did that. And it's coloured every single thing in my life.' I look out at the river. 'Just think, everything could have been totally different if I'd known. I might have let myself live a little. I might have let myself love.'

Nate opens his mouth but doesn't say anything. I look at him. 'I'd never told anyone about what I thought had happened, Nate. Not since Darren. Not until I met you. It was a bitter-sweet moment. It felt good and right to talk to you. But even as I was doing it I knew that it would make you hate me.'

'It didn't.'

'Maybe. But it would have done, eventually. It would have always been there, between us. And at some point you'd have said to me that you couldn't stop thinking about it, that I made you frightened.'

'I wouldn't have,' says Nate. He takes another step.

I give him a sad smile. 'Do you know what? I believed that, too. For a while. For the first time in my life, I'd met someone who I thought it might not matter to, if I could allow myself to take the risk. I thought I'd met someone I could perhaps allow myself to trust. That's why, when I found out, I came straight here. I don't know what I was going to say. I don't know what I thought might happen. But it doesn't really matter, does it? Because what happened was you and Janice.'

Nate shakes his head violently. 'No. Daisy, no. That was Janice . . . she said she had something in her eye. When I bent to look . . .'

I laugh. 'Right. That old chestnut, as Mother would say.'

'It's true!' says Nate.

I shake my head. 'Janice has been all over you for weeks.' I sigh. 'She likes you. You should go out with her. She's a nice, normal woman.'

'I don't want normal,' says Nate softly, almost too softly to hear. 'I've tried normal. It didn't work. I want something else.'

Something strange flutters in my chest. I don't have a name for it because I've never experienced it before. I wonder if it might be hope. But I swallow, and push it away from me. I don't do hope. I don't know how to. Hope is not something that you can put on a schedule or a handover report. It refuses to be quantified or made sense of or examined. I read some poems by Emily Dickinson, once. They were mainly about death, but she had one called 'Hope Is the Thing With

Feathers', and she was exactly right. Hope is like a bird, wild and free, and something you glimpse far away. Hope escapes if you try to grasp it. It does not bear close scrutiny. And if you do, somehow, catch hold of hope, and put it in a cage, for your own pleasure, then it will wither and die. Best not to entertain hope at all.

'It doesn't matter anyway,' I say. 'Not any more.'

'But why not?' says Nate fiercely. The rain is washing over him, like someone has dumped an entire ocean on us from above. 'It's all changed, hasn't it? The thing you were scared of, it can't happen now, can it? Because there's nothing to push me away from you.'

'But it's too late,' I say quietly, not knowing if he can hear me over the torrential downpour, and not really caring. 'I'm already broken.'

And with a sinking heart I know it's true. It doesn't matter whether I stabbed Rosie or not. I might as well have. Because from that moment on, my life was changed. That was the pivot around which everything turned. That was the basic clay from which Daisy Dukes was formed. Every decision I ever made, every single thing I ever did, every word I spoke, it was all informed by that one moment. I am who I am because I believed I did that thing, and even though I know now that I didn't do it, I can't unmake myself, can't wipe away twenty-five years of living. And I wouldn't want to. I'm Daisy Dukes, and this is who I am.

'Can I say something, now?' says Nate. His shirt is plastered to his chest, his jeans are sodden.

He takes a step and I hear his shoes squelch even above the noise of the rain bouncing off the bridge.

'We're all broken, Daisy. In one way or another. Show me somebody who life hasn't broken in some way. Life kicks lumps off us from the moment we're born, unless we're very lucky, or very rich. And most of the time, not even that can help. You're broken, Daisy. So am I. So, probably, is Janice, and Seema, and Dorothy. Your sister. Your mother, definitely, I'm sure.

'What broke me? My father taking out his failure on me and my mum. My fear that I would become him. Lucia divorcing me. Ben . . .' Nate closes his eyes and wipes the rain from his face. 'Ben hanging with that gang and doing those horrible things, to you. But what we all do, Daisy, is fix ourselves. Sometimes it isn't easy, and sometimes we don't do a very good job, but we patch ourselves up and we limp on, because what's the alternative?'

'So we're all broken.' I shrug. 'And we fix ourselves as best we can.'

Nate nods. 'But what if we can only fix ourselves so much? What if we need another pair of eyes on us? What if . . . what if two broken people can fix each other up a lot better than they can do on their own?'

There it is again. The thing with feathers. 'What are you saying?' I say.

Nate speaks, but his words are drowned out by the droning horn of a Metrolink tram passing by at the bottom of the bridge.

'What?' I say.

He pinches his nose and takes a deep breath.

'I didn't hear you,' I say.

'Daisy,' says Nate. 'I think I love you.'

Nate takes a step towards me again. This time I step forward as well, until I'm close enough for him to wrap his long arms around me, bend down, and kiss me.

We somewhat miraculously find my shoes after retracing our steps, where I kicked them off. As I put them back on Nate says, 'I like your new clothes.'

'My sister chose them. I like yours as well.'

'My ex-wife bought them.' He looks across the road. 'I don't suppose either of us fancies joining the work do, really, do we?'

I smile. 'We're like a pair of drowned rats.'

Nate leans forward and kisses the top of my soaking head. 'I've got an idea. Why don't we go to the den? We could dry our clothes off a bit on the heater and have a cup of tea. And there's something I need to show you.'

'You know how to show a lady a good time,' I say.

Nate breaks out into a wide grin. 'Daisy Dukes, was that a joke? We really are entering into unexplored territory here.'

'Yes, we are,' I say, and lean into Nate, allowing him to put his arm around my shoulder as we walk to the museum. Definitely unexplored territory, and no mistake.

'Well?' says Nate. 'What do you think?'

I think we look ridiculous. We had let ourselves into the museum, very quietly because it was the weekend and the security was being handled by the outside firm. There was no sign of them, or that they'd even been there recently. I doubted that they did more than a cursory sweep once a day.

Leaving puddles across the floor we'd gone into the den and Nate said, 'I'll wait outside while you get changed.' He went to get two pink and grey button-up housecoats from where the cleaners stashed them. I took off my clothes, down to my new bra and knickers, which were sodden as well, and put the wet things over the radiator. Nate knocked and opened the door a crack, putting his arm round with one of the housecoats clutched in his hand.

What happened next was very unlike me. I seemed to have jettisoned all good sense along with everything else. But for the first time in my life, doing something spontaneous felt good.

I grabbed his arm and pulled him into the den. Nate stared at me, eyes wide, as I stood there in my underwear. 'Aren't you going to get out of those wet clothes?' I said. 'And then kiss me again?'

What happened next was a world away from what used to happen with Darren. I'm not going to give you the details, obviously. But let's just say that the handover will never be the same again. It can't be. Because all the time I've known Nate that's all we had. The handover. Meeting briefly for five minutes or so, giving the baton of the working day one to the other. Both of us broken, like everyone else, and so very nearly not discovering that the answer to making us both a little less broken was right in front of us all this time. And I wonder what would have happened if we'd never taken a closer look at each other, and I wonder how many other people are standing so close to the person who might be able to fix them up, even just a little bit, and never realising it?

So here I am, standing with Nate, both of us wearing the cleaners' housecoats and nothing else, holding hands in the Malone Room and peering into a glass cabinet. Which is not a sentence I ever thought I'd say in my entire life.

'I think you're right,' I say. 'There's definitely something missing.'

'It's a toy,' says Nate. 'A stuffed dog sort of thing. Clockwork, I think. Bit moth-eaten.'

The display is of old toys and games, spinning tops and catapults and that sort of thing. But there are no labels on anything. 'How do you know?'

'Because,' says Nate, 'I think I've solved the mystery.'

35

Daisy

'Don't you think it's too late?' I say as Nate bundles us into a taxi. I can't imagine what we look like in our creased and still-damp clothes.

He looks at his phone. 'It's half nine. If he's not up we'll come back tomorrow. But I have a feeling he will be.'

The taxi takes us to Urmston, a house that sticks out like a sore thumb on a street of huge properties with high fences and access-controlled gates. Nate lets out a low whistle. 'Who'd have thought it? Millionaire's Row.'

'But look at the house,' I say. It's as big as the others, but shabby to the point of dereliction. The garden is open to the street and a tangled mess of overgrown grass and weeds. There's a light on in one of the wide bay windows, grubby white curtains pulled across it.

'Bet the neighbours love this place,' says Nate. 'Be worth an absolute mint if you did it up. As it is, looks like the poor relation.'

We walk up the cracked garden path and Nate knocks on the door, the black paint peeling off to show the warped wood beneath. He smiles at me and gives my hand a squeeze. I'm not really sure what we're going to do, and I'm secretly hoping that there's nobody in. But then we hear bolts being slid back and the turn of a key in the lock, and the door opens a crack. One eye in shadow looks at Nate, and then at me, then the door opens wider.

'You two,' says Harold. 'You look like you've been dragged through a hedge backwards.' He sighs heavily. 'I was expecting this. I suppose you'd better both come in.'

Harold is wearing a thick checked dressing gown over a shirt and some grey trousers, his feet in shabby slippers. He leads us into a dark hallway, with a wide staircase heading up to the floors above, and takes us into a kitchen. Half of the cabinet doors are hanging off and there's a big Aga at one end. Harold puts the kettle on and nods for us to sit at the kitchen table.

'Nice area,' says Nate. 'Didn't know you lived here.'

'All my life,' sniffs Harold, throwing three teabags into three cracked mugs. 'Was my parents' house; I got it when they died and me and Winnie moved in when we got married. Well before all these bloody yuppies moved in with their . . . what you call it . . . gentrification. Silly bloody prices they're paying for houses on this street.'

Harold dumps the tea in front of us and sits down, looking between us both. 'So, what is this, then? Hart to bloody Hart?'

Nate and I frown and exchange glances. Harold sighs. 'Used to be on the telly. Married couple fighting crime.'

'Have you committed any crimes, Harold?' I say carefully.

He gives me a withering look. 'Well, you wouldn't be bloody here at this hour on a Saturday night if you hadn't thought I had, would you? I knew somebody would come round, or say something. Especially after he saw my bag yesterday.' Harold nods his head to Nate.

'What I don't understand, Harold, is why you've been taking

things? And why only for a few days at a time?' I say. 'Were you trying to sell them but couldn't get anyone interested?'

Harold looks mortally affronted. 'I'm not a thief, young lady!'

'Well, you have been stealing things,' says Nate gently.

'I've been borrowing things,' says Harold with a sniff. 'There is a difference.'

'Without permission,' I say. 'And why take them at all? You can look at the exhibits to your heart's content. You're working all night on your own.'

Harold takes a long drink of his tea, looking from me to Nate and back again. 'Well, I suppose the game's up now, isn't it? I've been busted. You might as well know the whole story.'

Harold stands up and goes out of the kitchen, popping his head round the door a second later. 'Don't worry, I'm not doing a runner. I'm not going on the lam. I just need to see if everything's all right.'

'What do you think's going on?' I whisper to Nate.

Nate shrugs. 'I suppose we're going to find out now.' He takes a drink and looks at me over the rim of his mug. 'I think the next question will be, what do we do about it?'

Then Harold comes back into the kitchen and beckons us up. 'Come on,' he says. 'I think you'd better meet Winnie.'

Harold leads us into a cosy living room with a real coal fire. The TV isn't on but the radio is burbling quietly away in the corner. On a chair by the fire, and underneath a tall lamp with a dull yellow bulb, sits who I assume is Winnie. She's wrapped up in a duvet and is bird-thin, with a shock of white hair. Her face is grey and lined but her eyes dance as she watches what's on the little coffee table in front of her.

'The dog,' says Nate. 'From the museum.' The toy takes an uncertain whirring step forward, then sits down on its backside and waves a paw. Winnie laughs delightedly.

Harold sits down in the chair opposite her and leans forward. 'Winnie, love. We've got visitors.'

As soon as she takes her eyes off the toy dog, the light in her eyes seems to dull. She looks at me, then at Nate, then back to me, and frowns. 'Do I know them?'

'No,' says Harold gently. 'They work with me.'

'At the factory?'

Harold smiles tightly. 'At the museum. I haven't worked at the factory for twenty years, love.'

She looks suddenly upset. Harold is immediately up on his feet, putting a calming hand on her shoulder. 'It's all right, love. It's easy to forget. I'm going to go and make your cocoa and talk to my friends in the kitchen.'

Winnie seems to rally, and looks at me curiously as Harold winds up the toy dog. 'Are you sure I don't know you? What's your name?'

'Daisy Dukes,' I say. 'I'm fairly sure we've never met.'

'Well, you've a look of someone I know,' she says, then Harold sets the dog off clanking and whirring across the table, and Winnie claps her hands again delightedly.

'The Alzheimer's came on about two years ago,' says Harold, pouring us all another cup of tea and making Winnie a mug of cocoa. 'She was always very particular about how she looked, Winnie was. I think that was the most shocking thing, really. She wouldn't have a wash or get dressed if I didn't remind her.' He picks up the cocoa to take to her. 'She's eight years younger than me, you know. Only sixty-five. She looks ten years older, sometimes. Bloody horrible illness.'

When Harold comes back he stares into the tan depths of his tea. 'If I'm lucky, she's calm. But she thinks it's twenty, thirty, forty years ago. A lot of the time she doesn't even know who I am.' Harold stifles a sob and wipes the back of his hand across his nose. 'Forty-five years we've been married. The other day she screamed at me because she thought I was a burglar.'

'I still don't understand why you've been taking things from the museum, though,' says Nate.

'I think I do,' I say, remembering the delight in Winnie's eyes when Harold set the toy going. 'Did Winnie have a clockwork dog like that when she was little?'

Harold sighs. 'Aye. Just like it.'

'And the weaving shuttle . . . she used to work in a mill?'

Harold nods. 'She used to play with one of those Mickey Mouse gas masks, as well. Had been her cousin's in the war. And she wore a hat like that on the model in the seventies. Very stylish, was Winnie.'

'They're memories for her, aren't they, Harold?' I say softly. 'They let Winnie . . . anchor herself to times when she was happy.'

Harold heaves a sigh. 'It keeps her calm. Been doing it for months. Gives her a bit of respite from whatever's going on in her head most of the time. And gives me a break.'

Nate leans forward across the table. 'Is that why you carry on working that godawful shift? So you can borrow stuff?'

'Well, partly,' says Harold with a shrug. 'That's just a bonus. Really it's for the money. It's not cheap keeping this leaky old house going. Our pensions don't go very far.'

'But you must have some help,' says Nate. 'Who looks after Winnie while you're working?'

Harold glances at both of us. 'Nobody. I got some pills from the doctor. Said they're for me, that I have trouble sleeping. I give her a couple with her cocoa every night and it puts her straight out until I knock off in the morning.'

My eyes widen. 'Harold! You can't drug her! And what if something happened? A fire or something?'

Harold balls his fist and bangs it against his forehead. 'I know! I know! But I don't know what else to do.' There are tears in his eyes. 'I suppose you're going to dob me in, aren't you? I'll get sacked. I can't afford to lose my job. I got these loans a while ago. To help out. From the internet.'

I take Harold's hand in mine across the table. 'We're not going to tell anyone. But this has to stop. You have to get Winnie some proper care. And we'll sort these loan people out. It's time you both had a rest, Harold.'

He seems to relax, but there's sadness in his eyes. 'That would be nice. But how? And where?'

'I might have an idea,' I say. 'But I need to think about it.'

Before we leave we say goodbye to Winnie. She points at me. 'I know who you put me in mind of. Barbara Rice.'

I blink at her. 'That was my mother's name. Before she married.'

'That's right,' says Winnie. 'Married that Dukes fella. We were thick as thieves, me and Barbara, before I got married and moved here.' Her face suddenly falls and she looks around. 'Where's Harry?'

'I'm here, love,' says Harold.

Winnie looks at him in horror. 'You're not Harry! You're an old man! Where's my husband?'

'You'd better go,' says Harold quietly. 'She won't calm down while you're here.'

'One thing,' says Nate as Harold takes us to the door. 'Very quickly. We looked at the CCTV footage. Before it bust, which I presume was you pulling that cable out of the wall. Why were you never on it taking the stuff?'

Harold shrugs. 'I deleted the file every day and just put an old one in with a new date. I might be old but I'm not stupid. Me and Winnie did a computer course at the community centre, before the Alzheimer's got her. But that got to be a bind and I knew somebody would cotton on eventually, so I just ripped the bloody wiring out.'

He looks over his shoulder as Winnie shouts, 'Harold? Where are you?'

Then he looks at me and Nate. 'And thank you. I don't know what you've got planned, or if it'll help, but it's nice to talk to someone for a change.'

Outside Nate calls for a taxi. He says, 'Do you have a plan?'

'I think so,' I say. 'But I need to talk to my mother, first.'

'Will I see you tomorrow?'

I smile at Nate. 'I've a lot to sort out. Monday. For the handover. And then we'll take things from there.'

He nods. 'Well, we solved the mystery, then. But it doesn't look like it'll help to save our jobs, if it comes to that.'

'No,' I say. I entwine my fingers around Nate's. 'But perhaps there are more important things in life than that.'

36

Nate

There seem to be quite a few versions of the story of Orpheus and Eurydice, but the one I like best is the one in the book in the Theodore room. Orpheus is the son of Apollo, and nobody can resist the music he plays on his lyre. He falls in love with a beautiful mortal called Eurydice, who loves him back with equal vigour. But their story is to end in tragedy.

Eurydice and Orpheus are to be married, but one day, while she is dancing with nymphs, she is bitten by a snake, and dies. The heartbroken Orpheus petitions the gods to allow him to visit the underworld, and with his beautiful music he entrances Hades, the lord of the netherworld, who agrees that Orpheus can take Eurydice back to the world of the living, on one condition: if he turns around to look at her before they have passed back to the mortal realm, the deal is off.

Obviously, this being the Greek myths, Orpheus can't help but look back to check Eurydice is following, right as they are about to emerge. He falls at the final hurdle. She is whisked back to the underworld, and they are parted forever.

I close the book and put it back on the shelf. I feel as though it's the last time I'll read it. It's like it represents the time that Daisy and I were apart, but so very nearly together, connected by the book but always parted by it.

In a way, we've both been trapped in our own personal underworlds. And we've both emerged, like Orpheus and Eurydice never quite managed.

That's because they did it wrong.

If you walk side by side, then there is no leader. No follower. And it's impossible to look back. That's what Daisy and I intend to do. Face everything together. And look forward, not back.

We have persuaded Harold to call in sick on Monday morning, while we try to sort things out. The thought of poor Winnie left on her own every night, drugged up to the eyeballs, while Harold worked the graveyard shift . . . it makes me tear up. I always just had Harold down as a slightly cantankerous old bloke. Far too often we forget that behind every pair of eyes we make a second's contact with on the street or at work or in a pub, there's a whole life.

Going to work feels strange. Everything is the same as it was before, but nothing can ever be the same again. We still work the same shifts. We still have only a few snatched minutes to see each other when we do the handover at the end of my work and the start of Daisy's. I still need to be up to take Ben to school every morning, Daisy needs to be at home to look after her mother. Things will change, but slowly, gradually. Then again, we have time. We have patience. And there's the weekend to look forward to.

On Wednesday there is a staff meeting again, which means I have to stay on after work and at least get to spend more time with Daisy. This is not an exciting new initiative, though. This is the sort of meeting that can never be anything but bad news.

Seema stands in front of a PowerPoint presentation with the word RATIONALISATION in what to my mind is a highly unsuitable font for the news that is about to follow it. Daisy squeezes my hand as Seema gives us all the droning guff before she gets to the meat of it.

'So, you will be aware that since we lost our weekend guard some months ago, we have employed the services of an external company to handle security on Saturdays and Sundays.' Seema avoids looking at either Daisy or me. 'We have been in talks with this company and we have agreed to let them bid to extend their contract to cover the whole week.'

There's a rumble of conversation and everyone else turns to look at Daisy and me. Janice pulls a sad face. It's funny, I thought she'd be furious at me after I pulled away from her kiss and ran after Daisy on Saturday night, but she was apparently so drunk she can't even remember what happened, or doesn't really care.

Seema puts up a hand. 'There's nothing definite yet. We're a long way from making any permanent changes. There will be full and proper consultation if it comes to that. But in the meantime, we have agreed that the company will have a four-week trial. Which means that Nate, Daisy and Harold will be put on a fully paid furlough for a month, from Monday.'

Daisy and I already know this, having had meetings with Seema and Mr Meyer earlier. Harold has been told by telephone. Perhaps a month or even a week ago this might have been terrible news. A disaster. But things have changed. Everyone turns round to give us sympathetic looks.

'But we love Nate and Daisy!' says Bonny Sue. 'You can't get rid of them!'

'Do you?' says Daisy, frowning.

Bonny Sue gives her a reproving look. 'Of course we do! What are you on about?'

278

'And they do make a lovely couple,' says Janice, winking at me. I feel Daisy drop my hand as though it's red-hot, her eyes widening. Janice laughs. 'You two. What are you like? I think we all knew before you did.'

On Thursday evening John takes me to Harold's. We find him and Winnie in the living room, poring over a brochure that Daisy has taken to him. Place called Elysian Fields. According to Daisy, he was very resistant to the idea at first, refused to 'lock Winnie away'. Until Daisy pointed him to the assisted living section. Winnie could get proper care in the dementia unit, and live with Harold in a little apartment on site. Harold was coming round until he found out how much it cost. Which is why John and I were there.

I have to admit, John's growing on me a bit. And he's good for Lucia. I can see he makes her happy. And Ben likes him, which doesn't make me feel nearly as threatened as I thought it would. As we get out of John's car outside Harold's house he lets loose a low whistle.

'This is prime real estate, Nate,' he says. He looks up and down the street. 'Million quid houses, at the very least.' He starts taking a few photos of the house on his phone. 'I mean, this is a wreck. Probably better to rip it down and start again. But the location . . .'

'We're not here to rip him off, John,' I caution. 'We make him a fair deal, right?'

John puts a hand over his heart. 'Scout's honour, Nate.'

Harold makes us all a cup of tea and I dig into the carrier bag I've brought with me. 'I found this at home. I think it was my mother's. Thought you might like it.'

Winnie's eyes widen as I hand over the Dansette record player. It was stuffed in the back of one of the cupboards, with a pile of seven-inch singles. All from the late sixties and early seventies, real mixed bag. I kept the Etta James single, though. 'At Last'.

'I've got one just like it, haven't I, Harry?'

'Used to have, love,' says Harold gently. 'Long time ago. Ee, look at that. David Bowie. You went a bomb on Bowie, do you remember?'

Winnie chuckles. 'He's lovely!' Her face falls for a moment. 'Oh, he died, didn't he? Poor fella.'

'So,' says Harold, as Winnie sorts through the records, 'I've had a look through that brochure that young Daisy brought. She says she'll take us to see it at the weekend, if we want.' He looks around the room. 'I don't know. Lived here all my life. Thought it might pass down the family. Except me and Winnie never had kids. Don't know why. We just never could. So we loved each other a bit more instead.'

See what I mean? Cantankerous old Harold. Only saw him for five minutes every morning. And now he's threatening to make me burst into tears. I lean forward and say, 'It's just bricks and mortar, Harold. It's just a place. The home you make is wherever you and Winnie are. You go into this place, you'll be together. You don't need to work just to fight a losing battle keeping this place standing. You don't need to leave her any more.'

Harold looks at Winnie, love in his eyes. 'It's the cost, though, isn't it? Blew my mind when Daisy did the sums.'

'But you can sell this place,' I press. 'It'll more than cover it.'

Harold shakes his head again. 'I don't know. I don't know. All these memories. All these years.' He looks at John. 'What do you think it's worth?'

John writes a figure on a notepad and pushes it across the coffee table to Harold.

'Right,' says Harold after a moment's pause. 'Where do I bloody sign?'

On Friday I leave work for what might be the last time. Do what might be the last handover with Daisy. I perch on the desk as she takes off her coat and hangs it on the hook. 'Anything to report?' she says.

'Yes,' I say. 'I'm madly in love with you.'

She nods, poker-faced, and puts the kettle on. 'I'll add that to the files. Thank you. Was there anything else?'

'Just thought that you might want to give me a kiss, as it's our last handover.' I'm feeling giddy and reckless and I don't care.

Daisy walks to the door, pushes it closed, and turns the key in the lock. She turns and gives me a smile. 'Oh, I think we can do better than that.'

So it's unsurprising that I have a bit of a bounce to my step when I go to pick Ben up for the weekend. Lucia gives me a narrow-eyed look. 'It's true,' she says wonderingly.

'What's true?'

'Ben said you'd got your Tigger on again. He was right.' She smiles. 'Do you remember when he used to call you that?'

I nod. A little sadly, a little happily. 'Yes. Lucia. I'm sorry things didn't work out between us.'

She shrugs and turns away, but not before I see the wetness in her eyes. 'It happens,' she says. 'It's life. But we got something precious out of it. Ben. And nobody else but us two could have made him. Nobody else in the world. We'll always have that.'

I'm glad she's turned away because I can feel tears pricking my own eyes. God knows what's wrong with me lately. I'm emotional at everything. I think it's all those years that I trained myself not to cry in front of my dad, no matter what he did. Because tears were a sign of weakness, and if Terry

Garvey scented weakness, he was on it like a lion. But he's gone, now, for good. At least, that side of him has.

'Lucia,' I say, 'I'm glad that you're happy. With John. He's a nice guy. I really like him.'

She turns at last, giving me a smile. 'I do, too. I think I love him, in fact. I was worried about telling you.' She cocks her head on one side. 'What about you? And Daisy?'

'It's early days . . .' I say.

'Nate,' says Lucia, giving me a hard stare. 'Don't you dare faff around and throw away this opportunity. You're good together. You're a good fit. She's lovely. Don't dilly-dally about and do nothing for so long that you let her slip through your fingers.'

'It's all so difficult,' I say. 'Everything's up in the air. Her mother, and our jobs, and—'

'Stop making excuses!' says Lucia firmly. 'Take this opportunity to change, Nate. For the better. Carpe diem and all that. I really don't know what you're waiting for.'

I shake my head and hold out my hands. 'It's just me, Lucia. This is what I do. Faff and dilly-dally. It's what I've always done. It's probably why we got divorced.'

Lucia puts a hand on my face, like she used to do. 'Nate,' she says kindly, 'I was always a bit hard on you. I'm sorry for that. I probably said some things I shouldn't have, over the years. You were a good husband. And a good dad. And you'll always be a good dad to Ben. We both let him get involved with that gang, both let him down. You're the one who sorted it out. You're a good man, Nathaniel Garvey.' She pauses, and a smile plays on her lips. 'But you are as thick as pig-shit, sometimes. Daisy's waiting for you. You need to act now.'

I shake my head exasperatedly. 'I mean, what do you expect me to do? Ask her to move in with me or something?'

Lucia raises her eyes to heaven and clasps her hands in front of her. 'Hallelujah,' she says. 'I think he's finally got it.'

37

Daisy

And just like that, everything is different.

I think everyone expected me to be angry with Mother, and with Rosie for keeping the secret so long. On the Sunday we meet around the kitchen table to talk. But I am not angry. I cannot see the point in being angry.

'I'm sorry,' says Mother. 'Really, Daisy, I'm sorry. And I'm sorry for making you lie, Rosie. I've been a terrible mother.'

'You did a terrible thing,' I agree, 'but that doesn't mean you're a terrible person. And you're not a terrible mother. We're all here, aren't we? In relatively one piece? You brought us up on your own.' I smile at Rosie. 'I think you did a pretty good job, all things considered.'

Rosie gives me a smile, but with a curious look. 'But you said . . . said it had ruined your life.'

'My life is what I'm doing now,' I say. 'Everything that happened, good or bad, brought me to this point. If things had been different, perhaps I'd have had a better life. But would I be right here, right now?'

I think a lot about what Nate said to me on the Trinity Bridge, the rain lashing down around us. Everybody's broken, in some way. Sometimes big ways, sometimes small ways. And we all fix ourselves, to some degree. And having someone else can help that process.

But I don't need fixing. And the past doesn't need fixing. It can't be fixed; it is what it is. All we can do is try to make the future a little less broken.

'I think you should go into Elysian Fields,' I say to Mother.

Rosie looks at me. Mother looks at her hands. I say, 'I mean, we're not going to force you. Not if it's not what you want.'

'What about the house? I'll have to sell it. It was always going to be for you girls . . .'

'It doesn't matter,' I say. 'We don't want it. Rosie wants to go to live in Spain with Ian. I think she should. She could visit every couple of months.'

'Every month,' says Rosie hopefully. She looks at me. 'What about you?'

I shrug. 'Something will turn up.'

Mother considers. 'It's funny, you meeting Winnie Gayle like that. Fancy her being married to that Harold you work with. We were ever such good friends when we were younger. And you think they'll move into Elysian Fields as well?'

'I'm going to take the brochure to them later,' I say. 'Look, Mother, just think about it. You don't need to decide anything now.'

'I've already decided,' says Mother. 'I think it would be a good idea. I think I'd enjoy it. And I think I'd be happy knowing that you girls were happy at last. If I can do that for you, then I can be content. Finally be content.'

When Mother has gone back upstairs for a nap, Rosie takes me to one side. 'Why the sudden change of heart?'

I think about this for a moment. 'I don't think my heart has changed,' I say. 'I think I've just set it free, at last.'

Rosie unexpectedly gives me a big hug. We've never been huggers. At least not since the thing that didn't happen.

'I'm sorry,' she whispers into my hair. 'I just never knew how to tell you about everything. I tried to bottle it all up.'

'I thought that was why you were drinking,' I say. 'Because you were scared of me. And you didn't know how to tell me.'

Rosie pulls away and holds me at arm's length by my shoulders. 'Daisy,' she says, 'I don't think I've got a drink problem, you know. I wish you'd stop with this.'

'You drink a lot,' I say quietly.

'We'll just have to agree to disagree, sis. People are different, you know.'

Sis. She's never called me sis. I like it. But it suddenly makes me cry. 'I worry about losing you,' I say.

Rosie smiles at me. 'You're not going to lose me.'

'But you're going to Spain. I am losing you. And I feel like I've only just found you.'

'That's just miles,' says Rosie, her tears falling freely now. 'Distance. Geography. Me and you, we're connected here. Forever.' And she takes my hand and puts it over her heart and then does the same with her hand on mine. Her sleeve rides up and I see her scars. We both do. She smiles. 'Not despite those scars. Because of them. And what they did to both of us for so long. I love you, Daisy.'

'OK.' I nod, smiling through my tears. 'And I love you too. Sis.'

So Mother moved into Elysian Fields, and so did Harold and Winnie. Rosie went to Spain with Ian. And I moved in with Nate. Everything changed, in the course of a couple of weeks. And, of course, Nate and I were given a month's paid furlough while the Manchester Museum of Social History decided whether it still wanted us or not.

'Four weeks off, paid,' says Nate as we clear our things out of the den on the last day.

'Maybe forever off,' I say.

'What are we going to do with ourselves?' he says.

I take the Mykonos postcard down from where he pinned it all that time ago, and smile. 'I think I might have an idea.'

The dusty path winds gently upwards through dry grasses and the wizened, bent trunks of olive trees, the glittering tapestry of the Aegean spread out below us and the cicadas chirping all around. Nate puts an arm around my bare shoulders and points out to the sea, just beyond a beautiful cottage surrounded by its own orchard of oranges, lemons and pomegranates, and a tiny private beach sloping away from it. In the garden three chickens stride around a flopped-out dog hiding from the midday sun in the shadows of the trees.

'That's where the guy in the taverna said there's a sunken temple, about two hundred metres off-shore,' says Nate. 'You can go diving to it. I bet it's amazing.'

A beautiful woman in a kaftan and a broad-brimmed sun hat emerges from the cottage, and takes a glass of wine to a table where a laptop is already open. As she starts to tap at the keys I think there must be no better life in all the world than the one this woman has.

'Just imagine,' I say, 'Poseidon's garden adjoining yours.'

'We might be in the land of legend, but we are not living in the Greek myths,' says Nate, steering me away from staring at the woman and back on to the path. 'We're not at the whims of the capricious gods. We're masters of our own destiny. And we're going this way.'

At the top of the climb is a large stone building with a cobbled courtyard at the front. Framed against the cloudless blue sky it appears carved from gold. A battered scooter is parked against the gate, but there's not a soul about, apart from one figure in the courtyard, hiding from the blazing sun beneath an olive tree.

'Boo!' shouts Ben. 'What kept you?'

It was my idea that we should try to get a holiday in Greece, and that we should ask Lucia if she would allow Ben to come with us, as it was the Easter break. I think Nate was nervous, after everything that happened with Ben, but we've been getting on fine. More than fine. He's a good kid. Intelligent, too.

It's funny, but I would have never thought of a holiday in Greece, even as I dreamed of the place every day reading the book of myths. I had made my world too small. It was just me, Mother, Rosie and work. And everything in my tiny world was a handover. Passing the baton from one person to another. Each person doing their bit, then leaving it to the next. But it was easier than I thought to make my world a little bigger. All it took was letting one more person into my life. And that opened up everything, like I open my books, and let all those other stories spring out. Nate, of course, and Ben. Lucia and John. Harold and Winnie. Rosie and Ian. Mother. All connected, not just isolated figures any more.

'I can't believe we've come on holiday and you're actually going into a museum,' says Ben with a laugh.

'We'll go to the beach this afternoon, I promise,' says Nate. 'I just wanted to see it. The guy in the taverna said—'

'Busman's holiday,' I say. 'That's what Mother would say. Are you coming in, Ben?'

'I might just sit here and read my book,' he says. Nate bought him a book of Greek myths at the airport and he's devouring them. 'This story with the cyclops is wicked.'

'Well, we won't be long,' says Nate. 'Stay in the shade and drink plenty of water. And don't wander off.'

It's cool in the museum and we're the only ones there. We wander between the glass cabinets, looking at pieces of pottery and ancient arrowheads, pieces of statuary and fragments of clothing. The past. Pieces of the broken past. In a museum, where they belong. I give Nate's hand a sudden squeeze, and my heart seems to fill.

'Do you think we'll ever go back to our jobs?' says Nate quietly.

'I'm not sure I want to,' I say. 'We'd never see each other. Perhaps it's time for something new.'

'What could we do, though?' says Nate. 'What could we do together? Now I've found you, I don't want to only see you for a few hours a day.'

There's a sudden commotion at the back of the museum and a door opens. A shabby-looking man in a police uniform comes out, being remonstrated with in rapid-fire Greek by a woman in a trouser suit and wearing glasses. He angrily waves her away and storms out, and I hear the sound of the scooter that was parked outside sputtering into life.

The woman sees us and shakes her fists, saying in English, 'Idiot. Idiot police.'

'Is there something wrong?' says Nate, and she beckons us over.

'I am the manager of the museum,' she says. 'I called the police because there has been a crime. The idiot says he can do nothing. Come and see.'

She leads us through the door and into what appears to be a storeroom. There are four statues on plinths, all of gods and goddesses. And every one is missing its head.

'Who would do this?' rages the woman. 'And how? The door was locked. There are no windows. They were fine last night.' She takes off her glasses and pinches the bridge of her nose between her fingers. 'I am sorry for shouting. It was that idiot who refuses to help. But I just cannot understand it. Please, do continue to enjoy the museum. Nobody can help this.'

When I turn to Nate, he is already looking at me, a half-smile playing on his lips. That's the thing with making your world bigger. It just keeps on getting bigger and bigger all the time. The possibilities become endless. And something occurs to me. Since everything happened, since . . . since Nate happened, I haven't seen or felt the black dog once. Maybe my world is getting so big that it's lost my trail.

'My name is Daisy Dukes,' I say. 'And this is Nate Garvey. Maybe we could help, actually.'

The manager looks at us quizzically. 'How?'

Nate smiles at her, and then at me. 'Let's just say that we have a little experience of solving mysteries in museums . . .'

Acknowledgements

Hey, I wrote another book. That's my name there, right on the cover. I sat down at my laptop and wrote all these words about all these people. Yep, I definitely wrote this book.

However, I didn't *make* this book. Not on my own. You can find a list of everyone who was involved in it on the credits pages at the back, and I'm grateful to each and every one of them for doing their jobs so brilliantly to get *The Handover* in front of your eyes.

There are some people who need special mention, though. I've been privileged during my publishing career to work with some very special editors. It's a job title that, for me, never quite conveys the depth of work that they do. 'Editing' suggests something that's done after the fact of writing, a series of checks and balances and clarifications and questions. My editing at Trapeze has always been so much more than that.

If you're very lucky, you get to work with an editor who is almost as invested in the story as you are. They champion it in house, they push for its success, they cheerlead it often before a word has even been written. But more than that, the best editors get under the skin of your story even as you're writing it. They get to know your characters alongside you, even as they're taking shape in the margins of your words. Very good editors are one step ahead of you on the story, they guide you, suggest ideas, tell you when something is not working and, equally, cheer you on when something is fabulous.

And I've been incredibly fortunate not to work with just one editor like that on *The Handover*, but two.

The book started life with Katie Ellis-Brown, who stepped in when the editor on my three previous Trapeze novels was on maternity leave. It's fair to say that this book would not be what it is without Katie's drive, enthusiasm and support, and I owe her a great debt. Katie went on to pastures new about the same time that Sam Eades returned from maternity leave, and the book was completed under her editorship. Working with two editors at the top of their game on one book has been a wonderful experience.

I started writing *The Handover* before any of us were aware of the dreaded C-word. I finished the first draft in the middle of our first lockdown. What a long, strange trip the last year has been. But we don't need to talk about that; we've all lived through it. For that very reason, I chose not to make reference to the pandemic in this story. All novels are, by their definition, set in worlds fictional and apart from ours, no matter how similar they look. The act of writing, of creating a person who doesn't exist, of chronicling an incident, no matter how small, that never happened, in effect creates a parallel universe. The world of *The Handover* is very much like ours, except maybe Coronavirus didn't happen, or it hasn't happened yet, or it happened but nobody talks about it. All that matters is our story, and the people in it.

Which is pretty much the same in real life. All that matters is the story we're living, and the people who share it with us. So thank you to my family, my friends, those people on social media who might or might not be real but who seem very nice, and my agent, John Jarrold.

It's my name on the cover of this book, but all those people, to one degree or another, have helped bring it out into the world.

David M. Barnett
Somewhere in the North

Credits

Orion Fiction would like to thank everyone at Orion who worked on the publication of *The Handover*.

Agent
John Jarrold

Editor
Sam Eades

Copy-editor
Donna Hillyer

Proofreader
Kim Bishop

Editorial Management
Clarissa Sutherland
Charlie Panayiotou
Jane Hughes
Alice Davis
Claire Boyle

Audio
Paul Stark
Amber Bates

Contracts
Anne Goddard
Paul Bulos
Jake Alderson

Design
Rachael Lancaster
Joanna Ridley
Nick May
Clare Sivell
Helen Ewing

Finance
Jennifer Muchan

Jasdip Nandra
Rabale Mustafa
Levancia Clarendon
Tom Costello
Ibukun Ademefun

Marketing
Tanjiah Islam

Production
Claire Keep
Fiona McIntosh

Publicity
Alex Layt

Sales
Jennifer Wilson
Victoria Laws
Esther Waters
Lucy Brem
Frances Doyle
Ben Goddard
Georgina Cutler
Jack Hallam
Ellie Kyrke-Smith
Inês Figuiera
Barbara Ronan
Andrew Hally
Dominic Smith
Deborah Deyong
Lauren Buck

Maggy Park
Linda McGregor
Sinead White
Jemimah James
Rachael Jones
Jack Dennison
Nigel Andrews
Ian Williamson
Julia Benson
Declan Kyle
Robert Mackenzie
Imogen Clarke
Megan Smith
Charlotte Clay
Rebecca Cobbold

Operations
Jo Jacobs
Sharon Willis
Lisa Pryde

Rights
Susan Howe
Richard King
Krystyna Kujawinska
Jessica Purdue
Louise Henderson